THE FRONTIERS OF THE SEA

THE FRONTIERS OF THE SEA

PETER USTINOV

UNABRIDGED

PAN BOOKS LTD · LONDON

First published in Great Britain 1966
by William Heinemann Ltd.
This edition published 1969 by Pan Books Ltd.,
33 Tothill Street, London, S.W.1

330 02384 5

The author wishes to thank *The Atlantic*
in whose pages many of these stories
first appeared

Printed in Great Britain by
Cox & Wyman Ltd., London, Reading and Fakenham

CONTENTS

The Frontiers of the Sea

Old men sit on walls and watch the sea; young men do it too, but dutifully. Among the nets and green glass baubles they do it, and seem to read the sky like a newspaper. At all points of the compass they sit on walls, as though the sea were a vast arena full of spectacle and pageantry and meaning, which, for them, it is. The smell of tar and rancid water, thick as blood to the nostril, hovers round the edges of the arena, and the old men no longer notice it. They have travelled beyond the trifling bits of observation a landlubber may pick proudly up on holiday; they have travelled beyond prose and poetry into that ultimate simplicity which separates them from life as surely as luck and seamanship have always separated them from death. They spend their days in a wordless limbo of comprehension. They think of nothing and understand.

Planted like trees, or rather like masts, on the best seats, they stare with the lustrous patience of old dogs at the vast hunting ground. They are part of the seascape, and it often appears that, ashes to ashes, dust to dust, they are slowly returning into nature without surprise or fear of death. The shells on the beach look like the abandoned toenails of these old men, and they are more beautiful there than on the foot, among all the other vestiges of decay, the broken wings, the sand-logged crabs, the silver fish with the surprised eyes, the woman's lonely shoe, the rusty toy. Cleansed and sterilized by salt and iodine in the great hospital of the sea, decay and corruption are as evocative on the shore as broken columns and noseless gods are inland, and they are older still. There are no compromises. No need is there to subtract the television aerials which are silhouetted against the peachy sky behind the Colosseum; no need to half close the eyes in order to eliminate the Autostrada which sweeps by the crumbling temples and frozen palisades. The sea is as it was, and if an airliner whistles and sobs above it for a while, it brushes it away as a horse wearily dispenses with a fly. Landed man has not yet found a way to take possession of the sea, to tame it and bend it to the glacial mechanical will, while the seaman knows better than to try.

With great indulgence, without comment, the old men watch the holidaymakers: the varicose columns of white flesh which stand in the shallows like chunks of veined marble under their canopies of gathered skirts; the opulent stomachs rising softly to the crater of the navel; the tiny children (the only sensible ones in the old men's unexpressed opinions) yelling their heads off with rage and fright as their laughing parents (the idiots) try to force them to learn to swim; the brown ladies, aglisten with pungent unguents, praying to the sun with that intense application which their forebears used to reserve for God, and with only an exorbitantly expensive handkerchief between them and scandal.

There go the cabin cruisers, the owners wearing rakish caps with anchors on them and braid on the peaks, and not a knot or a hazy knowledge of celestial navigation among the lot of them. And there the playboys and playgirls screech by on parallel planks of wood, standing first on one leg, then on the other, then sinking between the ridges of high water.

This was all midsummer madness, a malady of heat. The people from beyond the hills have skulls like eggshells, and the first ray of sun and the first whiff of sea air send them off in this lunatic flirtation with shallow water. The old men look through all this with the air of great lovers who have suffered a lifelong passion for a demanding mistress. They have delved to the depths of sorrow and vaulted to the pinnacles of delight, in silence and in solitude and for life. They vaguely notice these flatulent little outbursts, this unworthy bottom-pinching seduction of their element. They hardly hear the saxophones and hissing percussion as the tiny tumult barks away from the bars all night. They wait patiently for the autumn.

In the village of San Jorge de Bayona, one such old man was Vicente Mendendez Balestreros, and for a man with such a sonorous name, it was perhaps surprising that he could neither read nor write. In truth, he didn't have to, since he had only received letters from the government, and such letters were not worthy of an answer. He didn't talk very much, but his thoughts, while rare, were mysterious and abstract. He had no wife, since he had little enough without having to share it. Money never worried him, but he was jealous of the silent cathedral of his mind.

The summer was over, thanks be to God, creator of all seasons. The bars were either locked or else humbled by presence of the locals. The little boutiques, with names like Conchita and Eros, were shut, their minute windows empty. The two modern residential hotels, El Fandango and the Hacienda Goya, had their slatted blinds down, and there were no bikinis to hang on the balconies. The nights were noiseless once again, apart from the deep breathing of the sea.

Vicente, with no wife to scold him, and no great appetite, sat on the wall longer than the other old men. Whenever they left him, they never said goodnight, so envious were they of his liberty. Somehow in old age he had preserved his youth, while they had voluminous ladies waiting for them in their two-room cottages, venerable hags with hair on their chins like the hairs that leak out of overripe sofas, and with breasts that hang like a donkey's burden. They also had holy lithographs all over the place. Religion comes into the house with the women. The priest even dresses like a woman to propagate it.

Vicente was Catholic, but he didn't believe in God, unless belief in the sea can be conceived as a form of belief in God. He would mutter and make signs and kneel and kiss like all the others because he had been brought up that way, but when it came to belief, he could only subject himself to the guidance of reason, tempered always by the bitter paradoxes of experience. Priests he regarded not as men with a divine vocation, but rather as men skilfully avoiding work. The organ gave him earache, and the better it was played, the more intense was his pain. At the same time, he had no patience with members of other religions, unless they happened to be sailors, in which case they had better things to do than to bother with dogma.

One evening – it was well after ten, the moon was full, with black clouds scudding in ordered masses across the sky – Vicente was still on his wall, and all alone. Suddenly he shivered, and the toes of his bare feet curled up as though at bay. A cool wind sighed from an unexpected quarter, and a noise like a distant cavalry charge began to grow fitfully from the horizon. A sheet on a clothesline flapped like a sail when a ship changes direction. He rose. His face creased up as his hazel eyes looked into the distance, where the last colours of the day were by now only suggested by a trace of green, a touch of mauve, a tortoiseshell patch of black and orange.

He hobbled to the nearest cottage and banged on the door. One of the monumental women opened up and asked what he wanted. At this hour of the night, at almost any hour, there was a barrier between each man and the outer world. Vicente didn't say what he wanted. He merely pointed at the horizon with his chin. Eventually the man appeared. It was Paco Miranda Ramirez.

'What can you see there?' he asked.

Since Vicente couldn't be bothered to say, Paco walked out in his underwear, brushing away the stridencies of his wife, and had a good look at the horizon himself.

'It's too dark to see,' Paco said.

Vicente shook his head briefly in disagreement.

'What do you see?'

'Come indoors,' cried the wife.

'Silence, woman,' counter-cried the husband, who was always courageous in front of another man.

'A boat?' he asked Vicente.

Vicente nodded.

'In trouble?'

Vicente made a gesture, a languorous sweeping movement of his arm and a bridling of his head to suggest the enormity of the trouble.

Paco paddled off barefoot and woke some of the other men with talk of shipwreck. The reason the men responded with such alacrity to the call was that almost twenty years back they had towed a Belgian yacht to safety and been compensated by half its purchase price, which is a rule of the sea. This prize money had brought great happiness to the village, and one man, a certain Diego Liñares Montoya, had even been able to fulfil his life's ambition and die of cirrhosis of the liver as a consequence of this heaven-sent bounty. At that time too it had been Vicente, then a newcomer to the wall, who had peered into the inky night and sensed distress. His senses were respected throughout the local countryside, as the others knew, not without bitterness, that he had had the courage to remain a bachelor, and that in reward his eye and ear and especially his telepathy had remained unimpaired and pure.

'I bet he's made a mistake this time,' grumbled José Machado Jaen, as he helped push the heavy rowing boat into the water.

'And when you get your ten thousand pesetas, I'll be there to watch you eat your words,' said Paco.

The women stood in a wailing phalanx at the edge of the beach, their handkerchiefs to their mouths, avid for tragedy, praying. Vicente was like Ulysses at the stern, tiller in hand, guiding the boat as it entered the zone of sudden wind. The women saw their man disappear, reappear, disappear, reappear, and finally disappear into the darkness. Only the rhythm of the oars could be vaguely heard for a moment, and then it was swallowed by the gathering storm.

The seas became mountainous, but the men hardly noticed. It was only when Vicente held up his hand and they stopped rowing that they became conscious of the folly of it all. It was raining now, and the waves broke over them, covering their feet and even their calves with galloping streams of hysterical water. There was nothing in sight.

'We'll all drown, and it'll be a magnificent funeral,' shouted José Machado Jaen.

'The old man knows what he's doing,' cried Paco.

Vicente's expression never changed as he looked around him, his gnarled face wet with spray. He pointed, and they turned the boat briefly sideways to the waves, almost capsizing. There was no sign of mast or hull, no sound but the joyful anger of the sea. The men looked anxiously at Vicente, and he suddenly grew tense. They followed his gaze, and a dark object appeared momentarily, only to sink again in a deep trench of water. Try as they might, they seemed unable to approach it. High seas destroy all sense of distance. The dark object drifted away at one moment, the next it was upon them, sucked up against the side of the boat. It was a man.

These Spanish fishermen had cultivated feet as adroit as those of monkeys, and now they suspended themselves at dangerous angles over the side of their craft, and although they were often submerged by the elemental panic, they held on to the poor fellow, and eventually succeeded in dragging him aboard. Nobody could blame Vicente for the fact that there was no prize this time. His senses were as keen as ever, and he appeared to be doing the work of God, which, even if less lucrative than the best works of man, salved the conscience in advance against the next mortal sin. The crew felt humble and virtuous as they rowed strongly back to their village. They could be sure that they had taken part in a miracle.

The rescued man was half dead when they carried him ashore. He had a pair of rough white canvas trousers on, but his torso was bare, and dramatically thin. He was dark, but one could tell he was a stranger. His grey eyebrows met over the bridge of his aquiline nose, and his full lips expressed that sensuous disgust which people from the Eastern Mediterranean often share with their camels.

A feeling of biblical wonder had now so gripped them that it spread to the women, and couples vied with each other to offer hospitality to this half-dead man, and they almost came to blows in their struggle for visas to heaven. Eventually it was decided that the honour of giving up his sofa to this dripping shred of humanity should fall to one Antonio Martinez Mariscal, who was the oldest of the rescuers, and who would therefore presumably have need of this good mark in the profit column of the soul's account earlier than the others. The nearest doctor was in the small town of Maera de las Victorias some eighteen kilometres inland. Paco Miranda Ramirez set off on a rusty bicycle without lights to fetch him. Deprived of one good deed, he eagerly volunteered for another, more difficult and more exhausting. Eusebio Sanchez Marin decided to go on foot to the neighbouring village of Santa Maria de la Immaculada Concepcion to fetch the priest, so that all this virtue could be registered with the proper Authority. The others saw the volunteers off with the jealousy of Holy Week flagellants who find there aren't enough scourges to go round.

It was almost four in the morning and a feather of light lay gently on the horizon by the time Dr Valdes arrived in his rickety car, Paco Miranda Ramirez standing on the running board and holding his bicycle on the roof. One feeble headlight of the doctor's car kept winking suggestively like an aged roué at a stage door. As dogs and masters grow to resemble each other, so had the doctor and his car.

'Let's have a look at this miracle,' he wheezed as he entered Antonio's house. Vicente pointed at the stranger with his chin. The women made way, and the doctor saw a frightened little man in a shirt several sizes too large for him lying on Antonio's bed, as though he had been the subject of some Rembrandtian lesson in anatomy. Certainly his expression of fear was in large measure due to the circle of impressive women who had sat round him all night, muttering, telling their beads, and searching his face for a sign. All in all, it had been more nerve-racking than any shipwreck.

'He's not Spanish,' suggested Paco's wife darkly, meaning that access to the True Cross might be denied him. The other wives were not willing to go so far, and thought that perhaps he was a Basque, or a Portuguese from some remote province, or perhaps a South American. The doctor asked him how he felt. He grinned in a meaningless way, since he realized from the tone of voice that he was being addressed, but didn't seem interested or capable of answering.

'If you ask me,' said the doctor, 'he's as Spanish as everyone else here, but of a backward mentality – or else he has been the victim of a traumatic shock which has affected his powers of speech.'

'Is he Spanish, Vicente?' asked Paco.

Vicente shook his head negatively.

'What the devil does he know about it?' cried the doctor angrily. 'Can't even read or write, and suddenly he's an authority on whether a man is Spanish or not!'

Vicente shrugged his shoulders like a child who pretends he doesn't mind being punished.

By the time Father Ignacio arrived, Paco's wife was able to tell him that the miracle involved one of God's idiots, who had been saved from a roaring sea by those of solid mind. This, she suggested, had a comfortable ring of Christian charity to it, with a soupçon of celestial embellishment for good measure.

Father Ignacio, a man narrow both in body and in mind, knew intimately that no-man's-land of sceptical expectation in which many country priests put out their thoughts to pasture. He lived in the knowledge that miracles had occurred in other places and at other times, and yet he had the saddening but certain conviction that nothing extraordinary would ever happen to him. If it did, he certainly wouldn't know how to react.

The little man spoke suddenly, saying something like 'Shkipra'.

'Shkipra, Shkipra,' he repeated insistently when they asked him to elucidate.

The ladies made quite a few wild guesses at the meaning of this elusive word, eventually settling for madness as its most probable source. Dr Valdes racked his brain for any malady of that name, but he had taken his exams very long ago, and he required of his patients that they fall ill with a few well-defined complaints. Shkipra was not one of them.

Father Ignacio sharpened abruptly, and said, quite out of the blue, 'Senatus Populusque Romanus.'

The ladies looked at him inquiringly.

'What did the Reverend Father say?' asked Paco's wife.

'SPQR.'

'Shkipra,' agreed the little man excitedly, pointing to his own chest.

'The man is, no doubt, a Roman,' declared Father Ignacio, glaring through his metal-rimmed glasses. 'That is what he has been trying to tell us.'

'A Roman,' spluttered Dr Valdes, 'how d'you make that out?'

'Senatus Populusque Romanus,' replied Father Ignacio, 'the Senate and the People of Rome ... I remember seeing it on every dustbin in the eternal city.'

'And Rome is the seat of Mother Church,' reminded Paco's

wife with a sallow look of sanctity, 'the home of all miracles.'

'What the devil d'you mean!' Dr Valdes protested. He had
served in the Legion of Death and survived. 'Spain produces
more miracles than any other country in the world, and
without foreign assistance. The weeping Virgin of Fuenteleal,
the Fountain of San Leandro, which spouts blood, the
nodding Christ of the Thorns.'

Father Ignacio held up an indulgent yet peremptory hand.

'It is unseemly to enter into worldly arguments about the
extent of our and other people's miracles, especially since our
richness in these divine phenomena should make us tolerant
towards those less endowed. It remains that this simple
Roman peasant owes his life to the fact that some celestial
force visited our good friend Vicente and directed his eye to a
specific point in the heaving waters. It is enough that we and
this poor peasant share the true faith. The story is a perfect
one; its moral is as symmetrical and as lovely as a flower.
Deo gratias.'

'Amen,' murmured the ladies.

The door burst open, and Sergeant Cuenca Loyola of the
Guardia Civil stood there, his sinister patent-leather hat
reflecting the unsteady light of the candles. Behind him stood
Baez, his assistant.

'What's going on here?' growled Sergeant Cuenca Loyola.

'A miracle,' crowed the ladies.

'A miracle? I'm surprised. Surprised with the lot of you,
and disgusted. Father Ignacio, Dr Valdes, Paco, Vicente.
Don't you people know that I should have been the first to
have been informed of a new arrival? I could arrest you all
for attempting to smuggle a person into Spain.'

'If I hadn't been summoned, he'd have been a corpse by
now,' snarled Dr Valdes.

'I should have been called at the same time!' Sergeant
Cuenca Loyola was willing to make that concession. 'Now, to
work.' Baez took out a notebook and pencil.

'I'd like to know what the devil you think you're going to
write down on that pad,' Dr Valdes cackled.

'What we put down on our pad is official business, and I
want no reflection or comment on it whatsoever,' declared the
sergeant.

'I served with the Legion of Death,' protested Dr Valdes, 'and I know and respect the regulations, but even General Millan-Astray himself, genius that he was, may his soul repose in peace, couldn't have made sense of the silence of this fellow.'

'We'll make him talk,' said the sergeant, who believed that even the ignorant were in the habit of deliberately attempting to conceal their ignorance. 'Now, your name!'

The stranger smiled, and nodded.

Dr Valdes began spluttering with asthmatic laughter.

'He agrees with you, Sergeant!'

'Silence. I asked you for your name!'

'Shkipra.'

'Now we're getting somewhere,' remarked the sergeant with satisfaction.

'How do you spell it?' asked Baez.

'Shkipra.'

'He's illiterate,' declared the sergeant. 'Baez, write it phonetically. Now, in which province were you born?'

'Shkipra.'

'Date?'

'Shkipra.'

The sergeant exploded. 'And I suppose your father's name, your profession, the unit in which you performed your military service, they're all Shkipra!'

'Shkipra.'

Later in the morning, a handsome car pulled up outside the police station of San Jorge de Bayona, and three officers stepped out. They had been summoned urgently by Sergeant Cuenca Loyola. As they entered the chalk-white room, silent but for the baleful buzzing of imprisoned flies, the sergeant sprang to his feet, and indicated to Shkipra to do likewise. Poor Shkipra had begun to find the inability to communicate oppressive, and he just sat in pained silence, staring at the floor as though fascinated by something going on there.

'Never mind, never mind,' said Major Gallego y Gallego good-naturedly, sitting on a wooden form and beckoning to his colleagues to do likewise. 'Now Sergeant, what is the trouble?'

The sergeant glanced up. His style was going to be inhibited by the sudden appearance of the entire village at the tiny barred window, to say nothing of Vicente, who stood leaning on the frame of the open door, sullenly minding his own business in a place he had no business to mind.

'Clear away there, clear away from the window! Out! Out!' cried the sergeant.

'Easy,' said the major. 'Let us retain our composure, please. Now, Sergeant, let's have your report.'

Acutely aware of his loss of face, and cursing those administrative necessities which at times forced a man to have recourse to higher authorities, the sergeant cleared his throat.

'Well, sir, as I understand it, this person landed on Spanish soil in an unauthorized manner between twenty-three hours and twenty-four hours last night.'

The major smiled.

'Did he report to the police?' asked Captain Zuñiga.

'Did he have anything to declare?' asked Lieutenant Quiroga, local chief of customs.

The major asked for quiet with a gesture of his hand.

'What do you mean by an unauthorized manner?' he inquired.

The sergeant hesitated.

'A manner not in accordance with the usual manner of entering the country,' he said.

'If an angel from heaven suddenly landed on your roof, would you describe that as an unauthorized manner of entering the country?'

'No, sir.'

'Why not?'

The sergeant looked nervously at the priest, who, being outside the closed window with the rest of the village, could hear none of this.

'Well, yes, sir, I would regard it as unauthorized, unless I had previous instructions to that effect.'

'From whom?'

'From you, sir.'

The sergeant wiped his brow with a rag.

'Why from me?'

'From you or from Father Ignacio.'

'Very good.' The major chuckled. 'Now suppose you tell me exactly how this invading army crossed the Spanish frontier.'

'This invading army—?'

'This man.'

'He was brought in by the men of the village – on a boat.'

'On a boat? In other words, he was drowning in Spanish territorial waters?'

The sergeant heartily detested the major's tone without being able to understand it.

'He was drowning, yes – or at least swimming, sir.'

'It's one way of avoiding the expense of the more conventional means of transportation, although it can be wearying if you have a lot of baggage.' The major turned to Quiroga of the customs. 'I think we can be fairly sure, Quiroga, that he had very little to declare – how was he dressed on arrival, Sergeant?'

'In trousers, sir.'

'Trousers, that's all?'

'Just trousers, sir.'

'If he had anything to declare, Quiroga, it's probably what any member of the male sex might decently be concealing.' He laughed at his own levity, and then, with a touch of mock concern, he asked, 'The priest can't hear through that window, I hope?'

'No, sir.'

'Good, good. Now, Sergeant, what did this man have to say for himself when he had sufficiently recovered to talk?'

'Nothing, sir. He has consistently refused to say anything.'

'Refused? Has it occurred to you that he might be incapable of saying anything?'

'He has said one word, sir.'

'One word, Sergeant? Then he has not said nothing, as you have stated.'

The sergeant wiped his brow again.

'What is that word, Sergeant?'

'Shkipra.'

'And what does that signify?'

'I don't know, sir.'

The major sighed.

'To what question did he reply – what is the word again?'

'Shkipra, sir. To all questions, sir.' The sergeant held up his two-page questionaire. 'I have no idea in which column to place the reply, sir.'

The major turned to the stranger.

'What is your name?' he asked.

'Shkipra.'

'And how do you enjoy Spain?'

'Shkipra.'

'I see what you mean.'

The major drew a packet of Bisonte from his pocket and offered the man one.

'Cigarette!' said the man delightedly, accepting it.

'He says at least two words, Sergeant,' the major said menacingly: ' "Shkipra" and "cigarette".'

'Cigarette,' agreed the man.

'Now I tell you what we'll do. *Olá,* you!' called the major to Vicente, in the doorway. 'Run over to the school-house and bring an atlas of the world.'

'He's no use,' growled the sergeant; 'he can't read or write.'

'Did you understand me?'

Vicente didn't deign to reply, but left slowly.

The awe of the villagers was considerable when they saw Vicente return a few minutes later holding a globe high over his head like a beacon.

'That's not exactly what I meant,' said the major, 'but it'll do,' and he turned to the stranger. 'Shkipra?' he said.

The stranger knitted his brow with effort, and had difficulty with the curious shape of the map, but he worked his way around it. Suddenly he stopped gyrating the atlas and pointed at a small area with his finger, shouting excitedly, 'Shkipra, Shkipra!'

The major put his glasses on and examined the indicated area.

'Albania,' he announced.

'Albania,' echoed round the room.

'Impossible,' said Zuñiga.

'Tirana?' asked the major.

'Tirana,' replied the stranger, 'Dürres, Elbasan, Shkoder.'

'It is Albania,' declared the major, folding his glasses.

'But that's a Communist country,' said Quiroga.

'It's also very far away for a lonely swimmer,' reflected the major.

'What do we do now?'

After a pause, the major said, 'This is a matter for Madrid.'

'Meanwhile, I'd best lock him up,' the sergeant volunteered.

The major studied his man.

'Oh, I hardly think that's necessary, Sergeant; find him a few little things to do. I don't think he's much of a threat to our security.'

Before the sergeant could remonstrate, Vicente had made a clicking noise which attracted their attention. Looking at the stranger, Vicente invited him to come along with him. Without consulting anyone, or asking permission, the stranger rose and left with Vicente.

'Who is that?' asked the major in admiration. He had rarely seen such a display of authority as that exercised by Vicente.

'A poor ignoramus,' replied the sergeant with ill-disguised hatred; 'it was he who rescued El Albanes.'

'Then it is only just that they should become friends,' said the major. 'Come, we must make out our report to Madrid.'

And with a parting piece of charity, which proved he wasn't such a terrible man after all, he told the sergeant that there would be no need to fill up his questionnaire. The sergeant, however, was in no mood to see this gesture as anything but an insult, since in his opinion a sergeant with an unfilled questionnaire is only half a sergeant.

Every day, and sometimes far into the night, there were two figures on the seawall. They never spoke, since there was nothing to say and no common language to say anything in. Their eyes were unblinkingly fixed on the huge winter canvas, with its shrieking gulls and its vast uncertainties. Sometimes they would roll a cigarette or two; at other times they would tie and untie knots idly in stray bits of discarded fishing net. Occasionally some abstraction would make them both sit up and take notice or even smile. The nearest they ever came to any conventional communication was when one of them would stare quizzically at a cloud, and the other would nod slowly or shrug half a shoulder. The villagers were loath to intrude into the great silence, which became like a fount of peace, an influence on all who were open to it and who knew its history. Every now and then Paco's wife or one of the other ample señoras would arrive with some goody which had been left over or else specifically cooked for the two old men. And every morning the fishermen would ask Vicente's advice on the weather conditions, and he would reply with an affirmative or negative gesture. The Albanian, who understood the nature of the questions without any difficulty, would always reply silently in exactly the same way as Vicente, but with movements more suave and less austere than those of his friend, movements which had their roots in a more mellifluous choreography.

Noisy children would become quiet for a while when they passed the seawall on their way to and from school, and scrofulous dogs with degrading habits, who encircled people in vast untrustworthy patterns, shot with yellow looks and dishonest trepidation, would go straight up to the two old men, their sparse tails wagging and their eyes alert. The Albanian liked to pretend to throw stones. The dogs would turn in a single leap, waiting for the sound of the falling stone, and when it failed to register, they turned again slowly, with the patient look of one who is being teased. Every now and then a stone would whistle through the air, and smash itself giddily on other stones while the dogs flew howling after it, stopping perplexed in an ocean of pebbles, unable to identify the one that had been thrown, now as motionless as all the rest. Then some innocent villager would pass that way, and once again the dogs would hang their heads, bare their unhealthy fangs, and seem to tiptoe in apparently aimless but hate-filled circles round the intruder.

One day, Major Gallego y Gallego turned up again in his blue car, and they took El Albanes away. Vicente leaned against the car, and the major had to ask him to leave. He refused. They accelerated away, and Vicente stumbled into the road behind them. He walked a kilometre in the direction the car had taken, and then stopped in the naked Spanish landscape. Far from the sea, he was lost. Roads led nowhere. Here all was dust and dryness. Trees seemed to be dying, the bushes were grey with lack of moisture. Even the hot cackle of the cicadas sounded to Vicente like the noise of fleshless beings, the grinding of bones, the semaphore of death. Defeated, he turned back towards the sea and the confines of his understanding. His face was suffused with sorrow, an emotion more terrible than pain because of its longevity.

When he returned, he lay down on the beach and slept. At dawn, he woke, but did not rise. The villagers were upset to find him there; even more upset not to see him on the wall. Paco's wife cooked him some food, which he refused to eat. Their concern turned to anger on his behalf.

'Why couldn't they leave El Albanes here?' cried the wife of José Machado Jaen. 'What harm had he done?'

The men were less emotional, since they were tolerant about questionnaires and forms and applications and military service and war, and even if they didn't fully understand them, they recognized them as the barriers beyond which a woman's influence cannot penetrate. The zones of masculine folly are well guarded.

It was only when it became clear that Vicente had decided to die that the men joined in the chorus of complaint.

Father Ignacio came down to the beach, tripping on his cassock, to try and convince Vicente that suicide was a sin, but all his suggestions of hellfire and brimstone seemed like a relief from the useless wounds of this world.

Dr Valdes paid the beach a visit, at the behest of Paco Miranda Ramirez, who bicycled all the way to Maera de las Victorias again.

'If you don't eat,' Dr Valdes wheezed, 'I'll take you away, and in the hospital at Maera, a wizened and terrifying nun will practise what's known as intravenous feeding on you. D'you know what that is, Don Vicente? They make a hole in your arm the size of a finger, and pump beef tea in there until it begins to come out of your eyes. I knew a woman who, every time she cried, had beef tea rolling down her cheeks, so that everyone knew her shame, and instead of sympathizing with her tragedies, people used to say, "Aha, she has been to the good sisters in the hospital in Maera and had intravenous feeding, the wicked soul!"'

It was of no avail. Every time Dr Valdes wanted to feel Vicente's pulse, or look at his face, he rolled over on his stomach. Eventually the doctor left, discouraged, asking who was going to pay his fee.

As a last resort, the villagers urged Sergeant Cuenca Loyola to come down to the beach. It was hardly to be expected that he would succeed where the others had failed, but he made a brave attempt at gentleness all the same.

'Look here, hombre,' he said, trying to kneel in such a way that his uniform would not be soiled, 'there's nothing to get so upset about. El Albanes wants to go home to Albanera, or wherever it is those people live – Shkipra. How would *you* like to be in a country in which you don't know the language?'

Vicente looked at him feebly, nevertheless suggesting by his expression that it would be marvellous.

'Get some food inside you. Don't be a fool. I can't order you to eat, I can only ask you, which I do, you see. You've done a fine job with El Albanes, don't ruin it all. I've written a report, and you're in it. It's gone to Madrid. Your name is at this very moment on a desk in Madrid.'

The business of saving Vicente had become so perplexing that there was never a moment during the day when there wasn't someone hovering about, even local journalists, and the first person up in the morning would report to all the others that he was still alive.

'What can we do?' asked Major Gallego y Gallego, who had been consulted, and who was attracted, as ever, by the quirks of human nature and the inexhaustible stupidity of men. 'It has never been possible to prevent a man from dying when he wants to die. I'm not even sure that such an attempt isn't an invasion of personal liberty, whatever Mother Church may say. But what a reason for dying! It seems ridiculous to any lucid and educated man – and yet, if we think for a moment, isn't there something ennobling in the purity and simplicity of such a desire in this case? It is like the adolescent love of two schoolchildren, or, even more, like the unquestioning and silent devotion of a dog. A dog? It sounds like a pejorative comparison, and yet, much as I love my wife and children, the only being in the world I can always trust is my dog, precisely because he is silent. Words complicate and betray. I wouldn't know how to live without them, but blessed are those that can.'

'Yes, but isn't there something we can tell him?' asked Father Ignacio, who blushed at any vaguely Voltairian sentiment, and who was eager not to be involved in an argument with the major, more from a fear of contamination than anything else.

'I feel sure that if we could say that El Albanes has safely reached his homeland, or something of the sort, that he has been happily reunited with his family, it would influence our poor friend.'

'We can say that, but it would be a lie,' said the major.

'We mustn't lie, of course we mustn't,' retorted Father Ignacio. 'But isn't there any happy aspect of the truth we can render even happier?'

'Not yet. He was taken to Madrid. There are only two Albanian refugees in Spain, and they are both classified as unreliable by the police, so we still are totally in the dark as to how he swam into our territorial waters. There is, of course, no diplomatic representation, and we have had to rely upon the Swiss, as usual, to find a way of returning him to where he came from. Unfortunately, there was a delay, since the Americans got to hear of this, and wished to interview him, believing that Albanian or even Chinese submarines might be operating in waters frequented by an American fleet. An admiral, a vice-admiral, and three rear-admirals grilled him for three hours.'

'What did he reveal?' asked Zuñiga.

The major smiled.

'Shkipra,' he said.

One morning, when all hope had been given up, and the case of the man on the beach was beginning to excite the entire Spanish Press and even the international news agencies, and when the police had taken the decision to drag Vicente forcibly to hospital, the old man asked Paco's wife for bread in a feeble voice. He ate a little and drank a little consommé, and after a while struggled step by step to the wall, where he sat down, took a deep breath, and looked at the sea with contentment.

People like Dr Valdes believed it was a pity he hadn't died, just to teach him a lesson. Father Ignacio felt the proximity of new miracles, and caused the bells of the church to be rung as a sign of thanksgiving. The sergeant regretted that Vicente hadn't been dragged to the hospital, 'where lunatics belong'. Only Paco and the fishermen felt there was more reason than desperation in Vicente's sudden return to the wall.

'He wouldn't have gone there just because he was afraid to die,' Paco insisted, looking at the enigmatic little figure now once again where he belonged.

And, in fact, the truth was that to Vicente there was no mystery in an Albanian floating near the coast of Spain. It wouldn't have surprised him if the man had turned out to be a pygmy, or a head-hunter from Borneo. The sea is the sea, a place without frontiers and without surprises. Its rules are older and more binding than the law. A man overboard is saved whatever his race or creed, or at least his rescue is attempted, and, if necessary, nothing short of heroism will satisfy tradition. A battleship may pay a friendly visit to an open city, but whoever heard of a division effecting a friendly occupation of a town?

The land is where the trouble starts. The roads that lead nowhere, the dust and the sand and the starving trees, and the people, all crushed together in a heaving marmalade, and the churches and the barracks and the rippling tides of gossip, rumour, information.

Vicente did not think all these thoughts. He didn't have to in order to know how to behave according to his lights, which were bright and clear. His intuition was infallible, and his reflections so profound they would have defied expression even by a poet.

If he now decided to return to the wall, it was because a part of him – was it the toes, or the eyes, or the inner ear, or just a mood of the heart? – told him that somewhere across the huge arena, an acquaintance had returned to his seat at the ringside, and was now perched once again on some other wall before some other disarray of pebbles, casting his senses towards some other horizon, which, while not identical, was yet very much the same.

The Swiss Watch

Like many other Italian women whom marriage has passed by, Pia Chiantella had gone abroad to escape from the real or imagined miseries of her homeland, and to make her living elsewhere. Too sentimental for bitterness, she worked in Paris as a daily help in the house of a French banker, Monsieur Petiton, who ignored most of her qualities – he just didn't have time to investigate them – but appreciated her honesty, a virtue towards which bankers have an extraordinary sensitivity, more especially on the level of petty cash and minute gestures of confidence.

When Christmas approached, the Petiton family made preparations, as always, to move to their chalet in Switzerland, a new and rather vulgar building conceived in the fertile imagination of Monsieur Petiton himself, who, as many self-made men, believed he knew more about architecture than those trained in it. The chalet stood on a sunless slope watching over a sunlit village, with something medieval about its arrogance and hostility, lightened only by lavish use of modern wrought iron on a background of pink Mediterranean stucco and pinewood, and by grounds peppered with hideous dwarfs and gnomes in coloured stone, and a handful of monstrously stylized rabbits and gigantic squirrels.

It was Madame Petiton who suggested that on this occasion they might take Pia with them, both as a reward and in order for her to do a great deal of hard work, helping to look after the four rebellious children which the banker had sired almost negligently in the midst of his multifarious activities. Monsieur Petiton agreed at once, and several days before Christmas the caravanserai left Paris, the family by fast train, Monsieur and Madame Petiton in their chauffeur-driven Cadillac.

Pia had the children all to herself on the first day up in the mountains, aided only by Madame Demoruz, a local lady who cleaned the chalet the year round, two hours a day. A kind of firm friendship was struck between these two, who had nothing in common; but then, the world over, firm friendships are formed for no reason at all except loneliness, especially if there is the cement of a sensed mutual unhappiness to lend poignancy to the unspoken moments.

The Cadillac had become ignominiously stuck in a snowdrift some sixty miles away, and Monsieur and Madame Petiton had been reduced to spending the first night of their holiday in a hotel on the banks of Lake Leman. The Dutch chauffeur, who might have been a hero in saving the huge car from a flood, was completely nonplussed by conditions in the mountains, which he had never seen before. It was typical of Monsieur Petiton to place his trust in foreign servants, believing in a remotely uneasy way that he sensed criticism from those of his own nationality, and allowing this complex free reign by declaring that the French could no longer be honoured with his esteem.

It was during this first evening alone in an overheated kitchen that Pia felt the exasperating solitude of all great public holidays. They tend to bring people together, and thereby leave people who are alone with nowhere to go. The children had been put to bed. They were running about upstairs with wild shrieks, but, officially, they had been put to bed. The parents were away, and they were not Pia's children. There was a Christmas tree in the village, lit with coloured lights. The snow was falling. A lump formed in Pia's throat. She had agreed to go to Switzerland with a show of willingness and even of excitement, but that was merely her instinctive devotion to anyone who was kind to her. It had meant leaving her man in Paris. Her man (she called him *Il mio uomo*) was a spendthrift, reprobate ne'er-do-well of an Italian waiter who could never keep a place. Nothing really passed between them except money, of which she always had a little and of which he had none, but they talked in Italian and she felt sure of herself and even safe in his company.

There was something of the mysterious relationship between prostitute and pimp in their attachment, and now she wondered what he would be up to in Paris without her. He would

probably get drunk, and in his festive stupor find another
girl to protect.

In her mounting rage at these nagging thoughts, she
switched on her little transistor radio, and found that the
Italian network was broadcasting a performance of *Cavalleria
Rusticana* in its entirety direct from La Scala. This didn't
help matters. During the affecting scene in which Turiddu bids
farewell to his mother, Pia broke down and wept, and, having
wept, she prayed. Deriving a little solace from the act of
prayer, she began to think against the background of dramatic
verismo at its most untrue.

She thought of her sister Margherita, who had been such
a good companion until her marriage, but who subsequently
seemed to adopt a condescending attitude towards her unmarried sister, and resented any contact, however formal, between
her sons and their 'aunt in domestic service'. They were fine
boys, Giorgio and Manlio, aged twenty-eight and twenty-six,
even if they had not yet chosen professions for themselves. Of
the two Manlio was easier to forgive for his indolence, because
he was very handsome, while Giorgio was frankly ugly, but
the fact was that both tended to lie about in the sun, little
golden medals half embedded in their hairy chests, waiting
for something to happen. While they waited, they dreamed
of emigrating to Australia, they dreamed of opening snack
bars in Rome, they dreamed of winning the Giro d'Italia on
their bicycles, but neither of them had the energy to cycle the
distance of a block without lying down again and dreaming
of something else – as often as not of the misery of Italy's
deep south, with its ancient jealousies and age-old habits, its
sickeningly blue sea and sky, and its servitude to the sun. Poor
Italy and poor us, and yet, as is the way with those who are
good for nothing, they never seemed to lack pocket money,
although nobody ever knew where it came from or how much
it amounted to.

Now, under the influence of Mascagni's musical excesses,
Pia began to form a fierce and unreasoning love for these
two boys who were of her blood by proxy, and who would
surely have been hers if a capricious God had not decreed
otherwise. She also developed a fierce hatred for the snow,
that slippery apparel of the earth in high places, which hides

its malice behind a show of innocence. She longed for the hot cracked earth which burned her bare feet, for the pungency of warm pines, and for the harsh smell of dried fish and herbs in the shops.

She retired to bed at the end of the opera, and entertained angry and emotional dreams.

The next morning, after the arrival of Madame Demoruz, she took the opportunity of slipping down to the village. There was a shop at the other end of it which sold practically everything from coat hangers in the shape of reindeers' antlers to ski boots, and from lesser Swiss watches to wooden souvenirs. Here she bought Manlio a Christmas present, with a hundred and eighty francs and all her love. She didn't buy one for Giorgio for a variety of reasons. First of all, he was ugly, and, if it came to the pinch, she would gladly surrender him to her sister, even in her imagination. Secondly, if she had to cater to Giorgio as well, she couldn't afford to buy a really fine present for Manlio. Lastly, Giorgio was the older of the two, and could look after himself.

With the help of Monsieur Knüsperli, the shopkeeper, she selected an octagonal wristwatch which not only told the date, but had an alarm system as well. He packed it in a handsome box, decorated with a recurrent holly motif, and she mailed it to her nephew.

The Petitons arrived a few hours later, and life took on a routine: Monsieur Petiton going for long walks of a few hundred yards, armed with a stick and wearing a green alpine trilby studded with shaving brushes and lucky favours; Madame Petiton, who was younger than her husband, skiing in the eternal company of a celebrated alpine guide; and the children creating havoc on the nursery slopes, with the forlorn figure of Pia, dressed awkwardly in her city clothes, holding a sledge and an armful of garments at the bottom.

The days passed quickly, and soon the time came for school to begin again. Pia was asked to take the children back to Paris, where Miss Frazer, the Scottish nanny, was waiting for them after home leave for Christmas. The Petitons decided to stay on a little longer – she because the great guide had promised to show her some new tricks on the remoter slopes, he because he had found a non-skiing companion of the opposite sex in a neighbouring chalet. The Cadillac obediently awaited their fancy in the plain, so that Pia was compelled to take the squealing rabble back to the stern gaze and hard palm of Miss Frazer by night train. She arrived in Paris in a state of physical and mental exhaustion to find a packet awaiting her. It was her watch back again, with an apologetic and uncertain note from Manlio, asking her if it were possible to exchange it for another model which didn't have an alarm, since this one had woken him up on occasion when he had least expected it, and he feared it might prove bad for his heart.

The note was as short as one would expect from a person of his limited stamina, and he forgot to thank his aunt for her gift. She bore him no malice, since men don't have to remember such things as gratitude, but she racked her brains to think how she could possibly replace the watch now.

Eventually she put it back in an envelope and addressed it to Madame Demoruz, the only human contact she had made in the village. Cheerfully, she asked Madame Demoruz to take it back to Monsieur Knüsperli's shop, and to exchange it for a watch without an alarm. She said she was willing to honour any adjustment in price, but stated that, in her opinion, a watch without an alarm should logically cost less than a watch with one. On the envelope she declared the contents of the envelope to be a 'Gift of No Value', as she had been taught to do in Italy.

When Madame Demoruz received the watch, she took it to her husband to deal with. Since he was a man whose profession was officially that of a farmer, but who had always gone to great lengths not to possess a farm, he had more time on his hands than his wife, who slaved away cleaning four or five chalets a day in order to keep her family in pocket.

Monsieur Demoruz cast his great envious black eyes on the watch, and rattled it. He set the alarm, and derived visible pleasure from hearing it ring. After he had repeated this process for over half an hour, Madame Demoruz permitted herself to warn him that he ran the risk of breaking it.

'Shut up,' said Monsieur Demoruz, and downed another glass of Lie, a white liquor made from the sediment of grapes. His spirit fired, he put on his heavy farmer's boots, and

walked down to the village to see Monsieur Knüsperli. There
was no love lost between the two men. This had little to do
with their characters, but more with tradition. For centuries
the Demoruz and Knüsperli families had peopled this alpine
valley, with its indeterminate and special character, hemmed
in between German, French and Italian worlds, and with the
residue of lost Roman legions thrown in. They had inter-
married and interdeceived each other, and yet, preposterously,
they had maintained their own proud identities, together with
a handful of other families. The phone book was dominated
by six names. All the rest were outsiders or latecomers.

Now Monsieur Knüsperli looked up from his counter
with undisguised displeasure as a Demoruz, never mind which
one, entered his shop.

'What d'you want?' he asked, or rather, 'What dost thou
want?' to emphasize his annoyance.

'It's a question of this watch,' replied Monsieur Demoruz.

'What watch?'

'This one,' said Monsieur Demoruz, opening the packet. 'It
was bought here by an Italian maid who works up at the
banker's.'

'Yes?'

'It's not what she wants.'

'How d'you know?'

'She wrote my wife. She wants one without an alarm. I
think she's crazy, mark you. It's a nice watch. I wouldn't mind
having a watch like that.'

'You could never afford a watch like that.'

There was something about Knüsperli's tone which aggra-
vated Demoruz, but that was nothing new.

'It's none of your business what I can and what I can't
afford,' he countered, 'and you can be sure that if one day you
see me with a watch like this, I won't have bought it here.'

'What does this Italian woman want me to do?'

'I told you. What's the matter, you deaf or something?
She wants to exchange it for one without an alarm.'

'A cheaper one?'

'She said in her letter that she'd be willing to make an
adjustment, but thought one without an alarm ought to cost
less.'

'That's not necessarily so,' said Knüsperli, shaking his head. 'No, not at all. Your white-gold Vacherin, biscuit-thin, hasn't an alarm or even the date, and yet it comes out about twenty times the cost of the Zona Wakemaster. It's a different class of timepiece altogether.'

'I'm not saying I don't agree with you,' declared Demoruz with a sly look, 'but an Italian maid wouldn't want to go overboard, would she? And then,' he added, with gratuitous malice, 'you don't stock the really good watches, do you?'

'I have only to send a cable to any one of the major manufacturers to have any watch in any catalogue here tomorrow morning,' snapped Knüsperli, riled.

'I'm prepared to believe you,' replied Demoruz with his mocking sidelong look, 'but you don't *stock* them, do you? I mean, the Italian maid couldn't come in here, could she, and say, give me that Vacherin or that Piaget out of the window, could she, I mean?'

'She could if I showed her the catalogue. Yes, she could.'

'But she didn't, did she? I mean, you didn't, did you? Show her the catalogues, I mean.'

'What are you driving at?' asked Knüsperli coldly.

A wild look of innocence burst on Demoruz's face.

'Driving at? I'm making conversation!'

Knüsperli frowned, and there was a long pause.

'You know what she did?' Demoruz went on in a voice suddenly small and moralizing.

'Who?'

'The Italian maid.'

'No.'

'She sent the watch back in an ordinary envelope – unregistered, that is – and written on it was "Gift of No Value".'

Knüsperli emitted a low whistle of disbelief.

'I've got the envelope here! I've brought it with me!' Demoruz cried, as he dug in his pocket for the evidence.

Knüsperli smoothed out the envelope, and then looked up, his own eye as dramatic in its smaller, sourer way as Demoruz's.

'Attempting to deceive the Swiss customs,' he said.

'That's a federal offence!'

'I mean if they'd opened the packet, it'd have meant confiscation, at least.'

'Or a fine,' added Demoruz, 'or even prison. They're getting very tough these days. Or even all three of them, running concurrently. That's what happened to my wife's sister Edith. She got it concurrently. First time ever in the canton anyone ever got it concurrently. And she's a woman at that, although you'd never know it. What's more, your name's on the packet, see? That's the way they got my wife's sister too. She used to take things out of shops. What got her was the name of the shop on the bag. And such things get around. I mean, they get distorted. It starts out someone smuggled a watch bought at your shop, and by the time it's been the rounds, it's you who's been smuggling watches into your shop.'

'I'll tell you one thing,' said Knüsperli, after a moment of dour reflection on these verities, 'I'm not taking the watch back. It's been abroad. And it's come through customs with a false declaration of content. I'm not going to soil my hands.'

'Quite right,' agreed Demoruz. 'And yet it's a lovely watch.' He produced it and fondled it. 'Though it seems to be dented . . . Look here.'

'No,' said Knüsperli. 'That's a feature of the design. It's got a dent on the other side too, see?'

'Mm, I admit that, but this dent seems a bit bigger, doesn't it? The longer you stare at it, the bigger that dent becomes . . .'

The two men looked deep into each other's souls.

'Can you afford forty francs?' asked Knüsperli.

'Can I afford forty francs?' laughed Demoruz.

'Don't try to pull the wool over my eyes. I know you for what you are – a drunk . . . a wastrel . . . a disgrace to the entire valley.'

'I can afford whatever I want for whatever I want whenever I want it,' said Demoruz at the top of his voice. 'The point is, do I *want* to afford forty francs?'

'Well, do you?'

'For this watch? Yes, I do.'

'Right. Take it. But there's one condition.'

'What's that?'

'Here's a watch worth forty francs. It's a Pomona Evergo,

in a shockproof chromium-type case. For the price, it's good value. You send it to the woman, and tell her you picked it out yourself and that it's of equal value to the one she sent back. That's your responsibility.'

'Done,' whispered Demoruz, forking out forty francs in change which became smaller and smaller towards the end.

Knüsperli counted the money twice, and put it in the till.

'There's only one thing—' said Demoruz.

'Yes?'

'Who pays for the postage?'

Knüsperli thought quickly. He had made a good deal and wished to appear generous.

'We share the postage.'

The two men shook hands.

Three days later, Pia received the substitute watch in Paris.

It had travelled in the same envelope, which had been re-addressed. Her claim that it contained a gift of no value was still written on it in her handwriting. The new watch looked suspiciously cheap to her, and when she tried to wind it, the winder dropped out. She took it quickly to a watchmaker, who told her it was hardly worth repairing, since the repairs, which would be frequent, would quickly amount to more than the cost of the watch. She asked him to put a value on it, but he told her he had had no experience with merchandise of that nature. When pressed, he thought twenty francs would be exorbitant.

Pia returned home in a fury, and in her desperation she wrote a long letter to Monsieur Petiton, explaining the nature of the deceit to which she had fallen prey. Monsieur Petiton read the letter at breakfast, at first with amusement, but eventually with a welcome anger. Frankly, Monsieur Petiton was bored being up in the mountains. He disliked the snow. What made it tolerable was the manner in which the women dressed to face it. He had a predilection for the smart blouses they liked to affect, and especially for the skin-tight après-ski pants, which featured the female figure in a way that was at once subtle in repose and gross in motion. He was the kind of voyeur who would never stoop to a keyhole. But even this innocuous pastime had now begun to pall. The telephone and the telex were not sufficient to engage his attention or to challenge his acumen. However, his profession was one which had made him conscious of fraud and transgression – in fact, he often fancied he recognized symptoms where none existed. Now Pia's letter came to him like a chance bone to a somnolent dog. He decided to deal with the problem and mobilized all his vast and bitter experience in the field of mortal duplicity in order to carry out his delicate charge.

He entered Knüsperli's shop just before lunch, when Madame Knüsperli was helping her husband out.

Knüsperli quickly abandoned a couple of other customers, and smiled at his distinguished client.

'It isn't often we have the honour to see you in person, Monsieur Petiton,' he said. 'I trust there is no complaint about the ski boots for your son?'

'I didn't even know they had been purchased in this shop,' Petiton replied.

'Oh, yes ... we have fitted the entire family. In fact, Madame was in here only yesterday with her monitor, selecting some more advanced skis. I suggested Lone Eagles – the Champion's favourite ...'

Petiton looked at him sharply.

'I am not here in order to effect a purchase,' he said. 'On the contrary, I want some money out of you.'

'Out of me?' Knüsperli paled.

'There is the question of a watch,' Petiton went on, in his quiet, efficient way.

'A watch? I don't seem to remember—'

'On the contrary, I have reason to believe you know exactly what I mean. My maid bought a watch here—'

'An Italian lady? Oh, yes—' Knüsperli's affected innocence compelled him to be as helpful as possible.

'Precisely. An Italian lady. She bought a watch here for one hundred and eighty francs.'

'It actually cost one hundred and ninety-eight francs, Monsieur, but I made a special price for her.'

'That was most generous of you, I'm sure. We will now consider whether your subsequent actions were motivated by the same spirit of generosity. I understand that the watch in question proved unsuitable, and so she sent it back to you with the idea of exchanging it – a practice which is normal in all the better shops.'

'I agree, Monsieur.'

'I am glad to hear it. In fact, you proved your point by sending her in exchange a watch worth about twenty French francs ... about eighteen Swiss francs at the present rate of exchange—'

'Oh, Monsieur, I protest! Who valued the watch?'

Monsieur Petiton consulted a piece of paper on which he had prepared his brief.

'The firm of Augier, Dupont et Fils, 118 Boulevard de la Victoire, in Paris, the official agency for at least three reputable Swiss watches.'

'But, Monsieur, the watch is a Pomona Evergo!'

'I've never heard of such a company,' said Monsieur Petiton, 'and I do a great deal of work with the major companies in Geneva and in La Chaux-de-Fonds. However, it is always possible that there is a deficiency in my knowledge. In that case, all you have to do is to produce the Pomona catalogue, and we will see together how much you owe my maid.'

Knüsperli faltered, especially now that his wife was listening.

'The Pomona people don't put out a catalogue,' he said.

'Why not? Isn't it usual business practice?'

'I don't know, Monsieur. They're a curious company in many respects.'

'I can well believe it. Perhaps you could give me their address and telephone number so that we can clear this matter up.'

'I don't have their address on me.'

'Then how do you get the watches?' asked Monsieur Petiton. 'You don't make them yourself, by any chance?'

'I'll be frank with you, Monsieur—'

'Ah, at last.'

'What's the matter, Heinrich?' asked Madame Knüsperli.

'Nothing. Nothing's the matter.' He leaned forward. 'You have in your employ a certain Madame Demoruz, who cleans your chalet in your absence.'

'That is correct.'

'When your Italian maid selected the one hundred and eighty-franc watch—'

'And paid for it!'

'I'm not saying she didn't! I never said that! Never, Monsieur!'

'All right, go on . . .'

'She – the maid, that is – sent the watch away to Italy, I believe, as a present. This present turned out not to be suitable. Instead of sending it back to me, as she should have done, she sent it to Madame Demoruz, who gave it to her husband, whose name is Monsieur Demoruz.'

'That seems logical.'

'Now this Monsieur Demoruz came down to see me, and point-blank refused to surrender the watch. He said it wasn't a new watch any more, since he was wearing it. He also pointed out that it had been dented in transit. What was I to do? I couldn't afford to be out of pocket. I told him to buy the maid another watch and to sort it out with her, since she had sent him the watch in the first place. He selected the Pomona Evergo, which he said was suitable. He paid for it. Both watches have been paid for, and as far as I am concerned it's a closed chapter. People come in here all the time and buy things, and so long as they pay I'm not going to concern myself with what happens to the merchandise once it has left the shop. After all, I'm not a charitable institution!'

'Very well,' Monsieur Petiton said quietly, 'I have your story. All I can tell you is that someone will be compelled to pay up the difference between eighteen and one hundred and eighty francs, and the next time you see me I may well be accompanied by a gendarme.'

'The watch cost forty francs, Monsieur, not eighteen!'

'I prefer to believe the assessment of a reputable watchmaker especially since you seem unable to put your hands on any official Pomona price list. *Bon appétit.*'

'Damn Demoruz!' shouted Knüsperli after Petiton had gone, but his show of fire didn't prevent him from being scolded by his wife in a most degrading fashion.

Petiton lunched at the ski club, and watched the elegant ladies parade before him. After lunch, he returned to his chalet, knowing that Madame Demoruz would be cleaning there.

'Your husband has a handsome new watch, I am told,' he said, apparently reading *Le Figaro*.

'A new watch, Monsieur? I really haven't noticed.'

'Oh, come, come, Madame Demoruz – of course you've noticed. By the brilliant manner in which you winkle out every speck of dirt in this chalet, I can see that you notice everything.'

'He may have a watch, but it isn't new,' said Madame Demoruz doggedly.

'Not new? How old is it? A couple of weeks, shall we say?'

'What are you getting at, Monsieur?'

'Just this, Madame Demoruz,' he replied, looking straight at her, almost kindly. 'Pia sent you a watch she had bought for her nephew and which had been found unsuitable, didn't she?'

'That's right.'

'Perhaps you'd care to continue telling the story yourself from there on?'

'Why, what's up?'

'I'll tell you when you've finished.'

Madame Demoruz shrugged her shoulders. She certainly behaved in a less suspicious manner than Monsieur Knüsperli, but then she was a woman, Monsieur Petiton reflected, and even if there is not enough beauty to be shared by the sisterhood, the art of lying is a mine of inexhaustible profusion.

'When Pia sent me the watch, I gave it to my husband, naturally. I haven't got time to do more than my work. That evening, when I saw my husband, I remarked on the watch on his wrist, and asked him how he'd got hold of it. "Well," he said, "Knüsperli refused point-blank to take it back." "Oh," I said, "so he gave it to you." "No," he said, "its been paid for. He can't keep it, especially since he won't take it back, so somebody's got to have it." "Well," I said, "Pia paid for it – she ought to have it." "But she doesn't want it," he said. "I've got a letter telling us that much." "That's all very well," I said, "but she wanted another one." "I know that," he said, "and out of the goodness of my heart," he said,

"I bought her one. It cost me all of forty francs." "Forty francs!" I said. "Well, thirty," he said. "You can't buy a decent watch for thirty francs," I said. "Well, forty," he said. So he needn't have bought Pia anything, you see, Monsieur. It was, as he said, out of the goodness of his heart. He didn't wish her to go empty-handed, she being a foreigner, you see, Monsieur, and not Swiss.'

'In other words, Madame Demoruz, you maintain that Monsieur Knüsperli refused to take the watch back?'

'That's what my husband told me,' said Madame Demoruz, one of her lips quivering in premature outrage.

'Well, Monsieur Knüsperli maintains that your husband refused to give the watch up.'

'Oh! Oh!' cried Madame Demoruz, searching for an inflection which would do full justice to the sacrilege.

'I am not calling anyone a liar,' Monsieur Petiton remarked coolly. 'All I am interested in is the reimbursement of a sum which I estimate at one hundred and sixty-two francs, and I will go to the gendarmerie this afternoon.'

Monsieur Demoruz was with Monsieur Knüsperli when Monsieur Petiton arrived with the local gendarme, Broglio, who was a cousin of Knüsperli and a nephew of Demoruz, and who had reason to mistrust both. Madame Demoruz had hurried home and told her husband what Monsieur Petiton had said. Monsieur Demoruz, who could always be found at home during the day, bestirred himself and, bellowing with rage, rampaged down to the village. Now he and Knüsperli were frozen like statues at the height of their argument. They both greeted the gendarme by saying 'Adieu, Jules,' rather sullenly. The gendarme took off his cap in order to keep the row within the family.

'Shall I start?' asked Monsieur Petiton.

'I already have cognizance of the facts, Monsieur,' said the gendarme.

'You have cognizance of the two different stories, Monsieur le gendarme. It is up to us, to you, to unravel the facts,' corrected Monsieur Petiton.

'As you wish, Monsieur,' said the gendarme, who struggled to hide his slow-wittedness behind an affectation of weariness. Slowly he took out a pad, licked his finger, and found the

appropriate place after a lengthy examination of a blank sheet
of paper.

'Where is the watch?' he inquired.

'Which watch?' asked Knüsperli.

'I understand this contention is on the subject of a watch,'
said the gendarme.

'There are two watches.'

'Two watches,' agreed Monsieur Demoruz passionately.

'Two watches?' The gendarme looked at Monsieur Petiton
as though he had been told an untruth. 'If there are as many
as two watches this may be a matter for headquarters,' he
said.

'I told you the whole story in your office,' Monsieur Petiton
remarked with elaborate patience.

'I know that, Monsieur. I'm not an imbecile, you know.'

'Of course not.'

'You stated that an Italian lady, Chiantella, Pia, in service
with you at Number 91 *bis* Avenue Foch, Paris, Seine,
France, had bought a watch – *one* watch' (he emphasized
powerfully) — one watch, at the shop of Monsieur Knüsperli,
Heinrich, for a sum of one hundred and eighty francs—'

'Swiss francs,' interrupted Monsieur Petiton.

'Since we are on Swiss soil, Monsieur, francs will be taken
to mean Swiss francs unless specified as being French. On
receiving the watch, she decided that it would be unsuitable,
and sent it to Madame Demoruz, Irène, of the Chalet
Souriante Colline in this village, for her to take and exchange
for a watch of similar value or less without an alarm attachment. Whatever transpired, she received in return a watch
in a chromium-type case claimed to be a Pomona Evergo,
estimated by the firm of Augier, Dupont et Fils of 118 Boulevard de la Victoire in Paris as worth twenty French francs,
without any reimbursement for the difference in price. The
watch in question, when wound, refused to go, and the winder
fell to the floor. Is that correct?'

'That is correct,' agreed Monsieur Petiton.

'Then it is a question of only one watch,' said the gendarme,
'since it was not the intention of Mademoiselle Chiantella,
Pia, to purchase more than one.'

'She hardly expected to receive one at the cost of another,

more expensive one – therefore the case involves two watches,' argued Monsieur Petiton.

'Did she expect to own two watches?' asked the gendarme.

'Of course not.'

'Then it is a case involving *one* watch,' he insisted. 'You wish her to pay the correct sum for the Pomona Evergo?'

'Yes.'

'Then that is the watch which concerns us here.'

'But she has already paid for the more expensive watch!' cried Monsieur Petiton, losing his composure.

The gendarme sighed. 'Who is conducting this inquiry, Monsieur, you or I?'

'You are,' agreed Monsieur Petiton, with evident regret.

'Very well, then.' The gendarme faced Knüsperli and Demoruz. 'Now, when Demoruz, Albert, brought in the watch to you, Knüsperli, Heinrich, did you refuse to take it back?'

'I did not,' stated Knüsperli, categorically.

'That's a brazen lie!' shouted Demoruz, banging his gnarled fist on the glass counter.

'Take that back,' flared Knüsperli, 'or leave the shop!'

'Nobody's leaving the shop while I'm here,' said the gendarme. 'You were willing to take the watch back?'

'As Monsieur Petiton correctly pointed out, it is normal business practice.'

'Then why didn't you take it back?'

'Demoruz refused to surrender it.'

'As God is my witness,' roared Demoruz, bringing down his fist again, and this time breaking the glass on the counter, 'as God is my witness, that is a stinking lie. The Italian woman sent the watch back in an ordinary envelope marked "Gift of No Value" in an evident plan to defraud the federal customs.'

The gendarme's eyebrows shot up to meet his hairline. 'Are you making this part of the record?' he asked.

'Yes, I am!'

'Prove it!' cried Petiton.

'I *can* prove it, and will!'

'Produce the envelope!'

The steam suddenly vanished from Demoruz's boiler. 'Oh,

no,' he said, 'I used the same envelope to send the other watch back . . .'

'Still allegedly marked "Gift of No Value"?'

'I . . . I don't remember.'

'So much for the high moral principles of these people,' Petiton declaimed.

'At least it was a cheaper watch!' yelled Demoruz. 'A much cheaper watch! It really was a gift of no value.'

'Ah, you agree!'

'Of course I agree.'

'An admission at last,' said Petiton, satisfied.

'I never denied it was a cheaper watch,' warned Monsieur Knüsperli.

'You evaded the issue every time I asked you its worth,' accused Petiton.

'Forty francs he charged me, while you tell me, Monsieur, it's only worth twenty!' Demoruz howled.

'And who's going to pay for the damage to my counter?' Knüsperli roared back.

'Gentlemen,' said the gendarme, with that pained dignity which schoolmasters use in order to impress on their pupils that they are disappointed in them, 'gentlemen, what is at stake here, as I see it, is not so much a few francs as the honour of the commune.' With an instinct shrewder than his conscious thought, he made a move to shift the discussion on to the plane of pride and away from the facts, of which he understood not one. Knüsperli was the quicker of the two litigants to realize that an escape road was being opened for him.

'I'm not a fool,' he said, suddenly reasonable. 'I value Monsieur Petiton as a customer more than I value a slight extra profit, and I care for my reputation even more deeply. This shop was opened in 1902, by my grandfather—'

'You take after him, the old bastard,' said Demoruz.

Knüsperli brushed aside the insult with a sadly indulgent smile: '—and we have served the community faithfully ever since,' he went on, 'so that I am prepared, if all the parties are willing, to reimburse the difference in price myself. The sum in question is one hundred and forty francs. Is that agreeable to everyone?'

'You can't do that!' cried Demoruz. 'Don't you think I can

see through you, you hypocrite? You're trying to put me in the wrong!'

'Perhaps you're willing to join me? We'll put down seventy francs each,' smiled Knüsperli.

'You think I'm an idiot or something?' growled the cornered Demoruz. He looked at the others, and then back at the hated Knüsperli, who was smiling still, a meaningless, fixed, maddening smile. 'I won't pay a centime,' Demoruz said in anger, 'but you're all mad if you think I'll continue to sully my wrist with this tainted watch!' He took it off, and placed it on the cracked counter. 'There!'

'I wouldn't touch that watch now. You take it right out of here, and I never want to see either of you again.'

Demoruz looked hunted and outdignified. Suddenly, foolishly, he held it out to the gendarme.

'Are you trying to bribe me, Uncle Albert?' asked the gendarme coldly. 'I'm on duty, you know.'

Desperately Demoruz presented it to Monsieur Petiton, who waved it away impatiently. 'I've got more watches than I know what to do with,' he said, 'and of better quality than that.'

'All right!' shouted Demoruz, who suddenly saw daylight. 'Tell you what, I'll send it back to the Italian woman, and I'll declare what it is and its value on the envelope. That's what I'll do. The rest of you do what you damn well please!'

'Does that satisfy you, Monsieur?' the gendarme asked Petiton.

Petiton was frankly a little disappointed by these unexpected fireworks of generosity. He had not foreseen them, since they never occurred in the field of investment banking. 'I suppose the solution is reasonable,' he said, 'although the palpable attempt to defraud a domestic servant is going unpunished. If I hadn't taken the matter in hand, we could today be confronted by a grave example of social injustice.'

'How much do you pay the Italian?' asked Demoruz, his eyes huge and ironical.

'That is, I suggest, none of your business,' Petiton replied cuttingly.

'While we're talking about social injustice, I thought I'd bring it up,' Demoruz added. 'I just hope it's a bit more than the miserly pittance you pay my wife. Six francs an hour. He's stinking rich, rolling in money, and he pays the lowest wage in the whole damned village. And my wife's been far from well recently. Easy on the social injustice, Monsieur. Easy on it.'

Petiton flushed with anger.

Knüsperli came to his help. 'Six francs an hour? That means it took your poor wife over six and a half hours to buy you that watch. You'd better go easy on the social injustice, too, Albert.'

'I'll kill you if you call me by my first name! I'm Monsieur Demoruz to you, you scum!'

The gendarme separated them, and frog-marched Demoruz unsteadily and elaborately back to his chalet. That evening he got really drunk. There was a ferocious sense of frustration on the boil in his heart. He hated everybody, hit his wife, and drank his Lie straight from the bottle. The front of his shirt was wet from the times he missed his mouth. When his wife put his meal before him, he threw it across the room. He lit a vile cigar, and it soon made him sick to the stomach, so he threw it out of the window. It landed on a pile of straw, which soon began to smoulder and then burn, in spite of the cold. Madame Demoruz was the first to smell the burning, and she rushed out with a pail of water, but the wind blew some bits of flaming straw against the walls of the old barn, which quickly took fire. The local firemen, volunteers all, appeared on the scene when the barn was already an empty shell. They were never very quick off the mark on these occasions, because of their insistence on appearing at the scene of a conflagration in uniform. All they could do was to abandon the barn to its fate, and to throw snow against the walls of the chalet in case the wind should change direction.

Demoruz stood and watched, a fiendish expression on his face. He muttered the one word 'Knüsperli', relieved himself on the embers, took an axe out of the woodshed, and reeled down to the village. There he destroyed the window of Knüsperli's shop, and offered no resistance to the gendarme when the latter came to arrest him.

Relatively sober the next morning, he refused to believe that Knüsperli hadn't set fire to the barn. 'He had it in for me, because I showed him up for what he is!' he repeated endlessly.

Knüsperli proved that he was in the café playing cards with relatives, but Demoruz insisted that these relatives had to be liars if they were relatives of Knüsperli. He even claimed he had seen various suspicious characters flitting about in the twilight while he was eating his supper, and remembered that he had said to his wife, 'That's funny. Those people running about in the dark outside look like Knüsperli's relatives. They've no business out there.'

Madame Demoruz agreed rather shamefacedly to everything her husband alleged, and explained her black eye by saying that she slipped and fell while trying to identify Knüsperli's relatives in the dark.

Knüsperli resorted to the law in his exasperation, but while these due processes were tortuously under way, Demoruz was manhandled in the dark and left bleeding one night on his way from the café, an empty bottle of Lie in his hand. Soon after, the tyres of Knüsperli's car were found gashed in the morning. It became clear to the gendarme that factions had been formed, and that the venerable hatreds of the valley had been revived. Rather than resorting to Lausanne, and dragging all these sinister happenings into the open to the degradation of the village, he convened a meeting of the elders.

The *doyen*, Monsieur Willy Demoruz-Knüsperli, who was related to everyone's relatives, and who was ninety-two years old, put forward his views at this meeting. He stood up, his sparse hair standing like a field of exclamation marks on a red and freckled soil; his alpine eyes, blue suns setting in rivers with scarlet banks; his nose, a crystal drop trembling among the hairs of its prow; his carelessly shaved neck rising to his jaw in a series of corrugations; his toothless gums biting on memories; and he spoke.

'To destroy each other's goods is as blind as destroying one's own. We are here, by God's will, to live in peace. We fought all our wars at the beginning of history. We have learned to do without. God, in his infinite mercy, gave us high mountains to protect ourselves, good cows to milk, good wood to build with. And, as if that were not enough, He even sent us foreigners to exploit. We have everything we need, and more.

But I tell you, if now we have fallen out among ourselves, it is only because there are two uneasy consciences at the root of the trouble. I won't say who is right and who is wrong. It takes two uneasy consciences to make the kind of unpleasantness we've been having. One is not enough. I've no more to say, except that it will serve us right if the Almighty, whose wisdom passeth all understanding, takes away the foreigners. Then we'll be reduced to exploiting each other as we did when we still had wars.'

'Why do we see you so rarely in church?' asked the priest, smiling, when the meeting was over.

'Don't like it. Bores me. Sleep better at home,' murmured the old man.

Meanwhile Pia, in Paris, was amazed and gratified not only to have her money refunded, but to receive both watches as well. She sent the valuable one back to Manlio in a fresh envelope marked 'Gift of No Value', explaining to him that the shop refused to take it back, and that it had cost her a lot of money, and that every time the alarm rang he should think of the love which had motivated its being sent. The other watch she sent to Giorgio.

When she went back to Italy in the summer, she noticed that the two boys hadn't changed. Giorgio was as ugly as ever, Manlio perhaps even more beautiful. Only the bicycles seemed to have aged a bit.

'Well, and how are the watches?' she asked.

The boys looked at one another.

'Mine arrived broken,' said Giorgio.

'*Porca la miseria*,' Pia grumbled, 'you can't trust the posts. It left Paris in perfect condition.'

'Zannonelli said it wasn't worth mending.'

'As bad as that?' moaned Pia. 'Madonna. And yours?' She smiled winningly at Manlio.

'Mine? I lost it.'

'Lost it! You're lying!' Pia accused.

Manlio shrugged his shoulders in a noncommittal way.

In a fury, Pia took him by his bare arms, and shook him. 'Where is it?' she screeched.

'I sold it,' Manlio said, only half apologetic. 'I needed the money more than the watch. I sold it to an American sailor.'

'How much for?' Pia whispered dramatically.

'Four thousand lire.'

Pia slapped his face so violently that it had to be a gesture of love. '*Mascalzone*!' she cried. 'You sold it for less than I paid for it!'

Manlio shrugged his shoulders again, and lay down in the sun.

Dreams of Papua

Willard C. Holm had not been President for very long. It had all come unexpectedly, as though destiny had pointed an enormous finger from among the clouds, and singled out a particular ant from the anthill. Whenever this happens, the victim recovers from his surprise with suspicious rapidity, and begins to wear the mantle of office with that aggressive form of humility which inspires confidence in countries which flatter themselves that they are free.

Mr Holm, as he was now called, or Senator Holm, as he had been called before his ascendance to the ultimate rung of the ladder, was a man of simple tastes, who had developed a devious and calculating mind in the process of dealing with his fellow men. Instinctively he knew that his tastes hardly mattered, but that it was their simplicity which commanded respect. The voter had acquired a degree of sophistication as a result of television, and a politician of too austere a natural bent could quickly give a holier-than-thou impression when under the infernal scrutiny of the lens. Consequently, Mr Holm took care to drink in abundant moderation with hard drinkers, to swear efficiently with hard swearers, to be overprepared to laugh in the company of wits and comics, and, of course, to be solemn in the presence of religious leaders. He looked youthful when confronted with youth, humble with those of great age and experience, and utterly free from prejudice when dealing with those of other races or colours.

He was originally of Swedish stock, which had its advantages. It suggested cleanliness, decency, independence. It also suggested that he was unencumbered by dangerous inspiration, flashes of genius, or a sense of paradox, anathema in those who guide men's destinies. Beginning his life delivering newspapers in Minnesota was about as auspicious a start as a potential President dare have. The fact that he had been bad at school, a newsworthy item heartily plugged by those in charge of his public relations, was calculated to endear him to all those millions of other citizens who had shared this sterling quality with him.

His parents did not have the resources to send him to university, and he did not have the brilliance to go for a scholarship. He went to work instead as a clerk in a fountain-pen company. Here it was his eminently likeable and unspectacular qualities which assured him promotion over more turbulent men. He became a professional henchman – the devotees of all sides of an argument finding in him an aloof but thoughtful ally. Confidences were not hard to share with such a man, for he talked little, and seemed always to be thinking of solutions to knotty problems.

The only positive action he took during these long formative years was a vital one for a potentially successful politician. He married his childhood sweetheart, Grace Lines Collins. It was almost natural that during a period of intense political rivalry between two outspoken and florid rivals, he was chosen as a compromise candidate for the Senate, and was sent to Washington in triumph.

Here he worked long hours, and soon knew the eccentricities and habits of the Senate as well as he had known those of the fountain-pen corporation. Once again, his qualities of thoughtfulness and restraint earned him a reputation for being an upright and trustful confidant, and his unwillingness to commit himself on any subject soon gave him an air of power, as though he were in the possession of some knowledge which was not generally shared, and which made even the simplest problem a little mysterious, worthy of second thoughts.

The Forsyth administration was ill-starred from the beginning. On the eve of the elections, the vice-presidential candidate, Senator Godfree, succumbed to a heart attack. In the last-minute search for an uncontroversial and solid running mate, Senator Holm was selected. President Forsyth, a dynamic and forceful man, never cared for Bill Holm, but alliances at the top of the tree are not love matches; they are attempts to satisfy the majority. Forsyth was intelligent enough to know that with his own highly-charged and sometimes volatile personality at the helm, it needed a different quality to set him off. The radiant picture required a discreet frame.

The great finger in the sky had not done with Bill Holm yet, however. Not by a long chalk. While flying to talk to a Convention of Women for Democracy, the presidential plane carrying Austin G. Forsyth flew into the side of a mountain, and in a wave of national mourning Bill Holm entered the White House almost unnoticed.

After a period of necessary adjustment, during which he allowed the disturbed waters to settle by doing as little as possible, he suddenly and spectacularly developed a personality quite other than the one by which he had been known. The age of sixty-one is perhaps a little late in life to prove to the world that you're a born leader, especially when there isn't time to prove it to yourself first, but men change when they feel their mark on history has become inevitable. The mirror becomes more friendly in secret, more agonizing in public.

Without warning, Bill Holm brought in as Secretary of State Morland E. Crust, an investment banker from Denver, and made several other dramatic changes. In a cabinet of unknowns, President Holm was soon the best-known figure. So far so good. The international situation was chaotic at that time, as was the internal situation. This had the undoubted virtue that it was possible to switch from one to the other when necessary and use one chaos as a smoke-screen for the other. The Communists were active in Burma, the war in Vietnam was in its twenty-fifth year, Northern Laos had seceded from Southern Laos, although President Ming-Tu-Phot claimed the opposite to be true. At least fifteen United States ambassadors were generals, seconded to the foreign service. It was reckoned by statisticians that, at that rate, the military would outnumber businessmen in the foreign service within half a century.

The world was crippled by treaty organizations which had sprouted like weeds, peppering the newspapers with ever-increasing strings of initials. Their interests overlapped, their functions were nebulous, their jealousies were rife. Everywhere men in uniform wished they were elsewhere, but nothing seemed quite as dangerous as a vacuum, even in places where a vacuum had existed happy and unmolested since the beginning of time.

One evening, Bill Holm held a Brains Trust. General Ruttledge B. Hooker was asked to report on the situation in Northern Laos. A huge panel on the wall lit up to show the President where Northern Laos was to be found.

'We have word from Ming-Tu-Phot that the situation out there has gotten suddenly worse, sir.'

'I don't see that name on the map, Rut,' the President observed.

'No, sir. Ming-Tu-Phot's the name of the President, sir – their President, that is – the President of South Laos.'

Mr Holm didn't smile. He regarded the other experts with a baleful eye.

'I wish you people would specify, when your turn comes, whether we're dealing with a man or a place. With all these goddam foreign names, it'll save a hell of a lot of time – and patience,' he added grimly.

'I'm awfully sorry, sir. I thought you knew Ming-Tu-Phot, sir,' General Hooker said.

'Rut, I hardly remember the names of the people in this room,' the President smiled.

This evidence of his humanity was greeted with a ripple of warm laughter.

'Go on, Rut, I'm afraid I interrupted you—'

'Well, sir, the Northern Laotians are evidently using the territory of Northern Vietnam to infiltrate into Northern Cambodia and cut us off.'

'Cut us off from what?'

'Northern Burma, sir.'

'Let me get this straight, Rut,' sighed the President, passing a weary hand over his forehead, as the slides on the panel changed with lightning speed. 'Where are we and where are they?'

General Hooker cleared his throat in anticipation of a superhuman effort.

'In a general sense it's true to say, sir, that any time North is mentioned, it represents where they are, while every time South is mentioned, why, that's where we are, although as often as not that only represents half the truth, since they've succeeded in infiltrating into large sections of the South, while in the areas of Ky-Mang, Phing-Dot, and Mien-Det-Sing (those are place-names, sir), we've got far into the North. The situation is further complicated, of course, by the fact that South Laos is, in fact, North of Northern Cambodia.'

The President smiled slowly, infectiously. Then the whole assembly rocked with laughter, and tension was relieved. While it was going on, Professor Szasz, the white-haired Hungarian who had invented Escalation, was heard to declare admiringly, 'Only in America could this happen!'

Sobering up, the President asked, 'What are we going to do about this, boys?'

The Secretary of State spoke.

'Ambassador Glimpf suggested replacing Ming-Tu-Phot by Ming-Kam-Phot – I'm sorry – replacing General Ming-Tu-Phot by Marshal Ming-Kam-Phot.'

'Why?'

'Well, they're brothers, but they hate each other.'

'I don't see that's a reason.'

The Secretary of State kept his head admirably.

'I don't know that we can understand the reasons at this distance, but I'm sure that if Ambassador Glimpf recommends a change, he has a very good—'

'I don't understand how a democratically elected government can keep changing the way they do out there, and still hold a mandate from the electors,' the President declared, suddenly sure and conscious of all that's finest in American life.

'The government was democratically elected twenty-one years ago, sir, but there haven't been elections since we went in there in force to protect those very institutions against the Communists.'

The President's jaw hardened, and his eye was impregnated with the cold light of mission.

'It's good to remind ourselves of these facts every day, fellows. I guess it's as important as prayer. It reminds us why we're out there at all.'

There was a moment of silence. The President brushed away the pious thought, and returned to the fray with his habitual buoyancy.

'What party holds the power out there – in our terms?'

'That's a tough question,' murmured General Hooker.

'Broadly, broadly,' insisted the President.

'Well, sir, it's nominally a coalition between the People's Rally, the Neo Lao Hak Sat, the Unionists, the Peace Party, and the Democrats.'

'How many Democrats?'

'Three, sir, nominally, but they're not Democrats in our sense.'

'Only three Democrats?' asked the President incredulously, and then asked, 'Why do you keep saying nominally, Rut?'

'Because in fact the government is entirely military. It's made up of sixteen generals, sir, and four field-marshals. They don't represent any parties, sir.'

'How about their Congress?'

'The National Assembly, sir. That's been turned into the Nineteenth General Field Hospital, sir.'

Once again a cloud passed over the President's forehead.

'That's what happens to democracy, fellows, when its fundamental principles are neglected and undefended. Can you imagine Congress or the Senate turned into a hospital? It could happen. It could too, if we're not ready at all times to fight for those fundamental liberties which are the heritage of this great land.'

'We are witnessing the birth of a statesman,' murmured Professor Szasz.

'OK, Morland, we'll give the new man a chance to prove himself, and if that doesn't work, we'll have to try something else,' said the President lightly, glancing at his watch. 'Any other business?'

'Haiti, Mr President,' replied Mr Crust, firmly.

The President turned to the illuminated panel.

A map of Haiti appeared.

'What's that on the right? The unshaded area.'

'The Dominican Republic.'

'On no, not again. Say, what's the report from the Organization of American States?'

'Peru says she can't go on paying for her ten-man infantry unit indefinitely, sir.'

'It's not indefinitely, for crying out loud,' shouted the

President. 'It's only as long as we haven't got a government in there.'

'It's been twelve years already,' insisted the Secretary of State.

'Twelve years?' muttered the President. 'My God, doesn't time fly though.' He knew when it was expedient to change the subject. 'What's up in Haiti? Communists?'

'The French.'

'That's worse. At least you know where you stand with the goddam Communists.' He suddenly flared up. 'What business have the French in there?'

'The Haitians speak French, sir.' It was Elliot Koslowsky of the State Department who replied.

'Since when?'

'They always have. It's a kind of Creole, in fact, but the basis is French. And the French have always been very sensitive about their language. They even have a term for countries that speak their language, "*des pays de langue francophone*".'

'I must congratulate you on your erudition,' said the President sarcastically, 'but I don't intend to make a study of their prejudices. I got enough with my own.'

There was a little laughter.

'What are they up to in Haiti, Morland?'

'Mr Koslowsky has the facts, Mr President.'

'Mr Koslowsky?'

'There's a report from several American businessmen involved in the OABC—'

'What's that, one of our treaty organizations?' snapped the President.

'The Organization of American Businessmen in the Caribbean, sir – a kind of semi-official vigilante chamber of commerce type of organization,' replied Mr Koslowsky. 'And they say that they are encountering real sales resistance to some of our products, and they further declare that this is due to a meaningful effort by French businessmen to invest in that country.'

'There's nothing wrong with that, except it's the French doing it.'

'Well, sir, these men claim they've been molested by Haitian police while trying to counter French offers.'

'Molested? I don't understand that . . .'

'I think the insinuation is, sir, that the French government and the Haitian government are in cahoots to buy French wherever possible ever since Olympio Pastorale's visit – I'm sorry, Mr President – President Olympio Pastorale's state visit to Paris – there's the draft of a trade agreement in existence, sir – we don't know the exact nature of this agreement—'

'Why not?'

'We haven't had time, as yet, and then . . .'

Mr Koslowsky faltered.

'Joe,' said the President briefly.

Joseph E. Shales of the CIA nodded economically, like a bidder at an auction, and made a note on a piece of paper.

'It is believed that the agreement is for French machinery and technical assistance against Haitian sugar,' went on the discountenanced Mr Koslowsky gallantly. 'In fact, knowing what Haiti produces and what she needs, I don't see how the agreement could be about anything else.'

'Never mind, Mr Koslowsky, in a few days we'll have that agreement.'

Mr Shales nodded imperceptibly again.

'I want you to investigate these allegations, Morland, and if free trade is being interfered with, we ought to get back at the French in some way. Who's our ambassador out there?'

'Lieutenant-General Harvey Rice,' said Mr Koslowsky.

'Don't know him,' said the President.

The Secretary of State smiled in his usual stony fashion. 'I feel we ought to bear in mind,' he purred, 'that France is essentially an *ally*, and irritation with her mustn't blind our eyes to the fact that our number-one enemy is communism. North Laos, North Korea, North Burma, North Cambodia are real problems, which tomorrow could lead to North Nepal, North Afghanistan, North Iran, North Turkey . . . as far as the French are concerned, there are always valid countermeasures to use against a friend, which enjoy the status of irritants . . . We've already gotten at them by serving California wines in our embassies . . . now we could extend our countermeasures into the field of the garment industry by enforcing restrictive penalties on French woman's clothing, or hit them where it hurts in the field of cosmetics and deodorants . . . but all that is really more an amusement than a serious endeavour ... Our number-one problem is certainly how to continue escalation while lessening the risk of war. On the face of it, there may seem to be a contradiction of terms here, but there is a school of thought that doesn't believe so. We have now reached Stage Twenty-two of escalation in Laos, Twenty-seven in Vietnam, a mere Twelve in Cambodia and somewhere between Eight and Nine in Burma—'

'Refresh my memory about these stages of escalation, Professor,' requested the President, fatigued.

'Stage Twenty-seven is ze attack against military targets vis nooclear veapons,' said Professor Szasz with his heavy Central European accent. 'Stage Tventy-two is ze declaration of nooclear vohr mit limited obtchectifs. Stage Tvelf is conwentional vohr on an expanded scale. Stage Nine is confrontation of armed forces on a large scale, mitout any owert hostile act.'

'Would you translate that to me, please, someone?'

There was once again a little good-natured laughter, in which Professor Szasz failed to join.

'No, seriously,' the President went on, as though someone might have been guilty of a lapse of taste, and he was covering up, 'if I understand the situation, we can either let this thing drift as it has been drifting for the last fifteen years, in the hope that we, with our superior resources, can outlast the opposition, or else we can take the risk of further escalation while conducting a vigorous peace offensive at the same time – a pincer movement in the heart of the Communist conspiracy.'

'Well, I'd feel safer with the first solution, naturally,' remarked the Secretary of State almost wistfully, 'but then I'm not a soldier.'

'Oh, come on, Morland, as long ago as 1965 better men than you or me were saying we could go on like this for ever. So we can, but there's no policy inherent in attrition – it's the weak way.'

'It's the safe way. We've gotten used to the situation. We can live with it. People don't even look at the front page of the newspapers any more. They turn straight to the sports pages or the comics. And meanwhile we're keeping the

Communists from internal development – our industrial sea erodes their agrarian rock.'

'I don't go for that, Morland – I don't see it that way,' the President said, his eyes narrowed in determination and concentration. The Holm term was not going to be a festival for Rip Van Winkles. 'Barrett?'

Barrett O'Hehir was the Defence Secretary, a man with a reputation for an extraordinary ability to grasp almost anything, a family man, and a corporation lawyer. He had a pleasantly rational style about him, unforced and civilized. He was at all times approachable, and he had an admirable capacity for reducing the most complicated problems into terms of crystal oversimplification. The President liked him, relied on him. The Secretary of State was, by comparison, devious, with a vocabulary of unnecessary elegance and the kind of humour people tended not to laugh at. In other words, let's be blunt, an intellectual.

O'Hehir smiled before answering. He had taken no part in the debate so far, preferring to be produced as a trump card. Invariably, when the President tired or got himself lost among the welter of accurate facts, he would bark the one word, 'Barrett'.

'There's only one course left open to us, compatible with our responsibilities as the most powerful nation in the world, and the protector of parliamentary institutions—' (Oh, it was all right to use long words, on condition these long words were those long words the man in the street uses when he wishes to demonstrate that he is in command of his subject.) 'We have to show we mean business. Right? The only way we can manifest our intentions in the general area of the fields of conflict is by action – conciliatory and eager for negotiated solutions in our diplomatic endeavour, but in order to prove how ready we are to negotiate, it'd be crazy not to step up our combat potential and move one point up in escalation in the battle area.'

'You said that yesterday,' remarked the President.

'I haven't changed my mind,' retorted O'Hehir cheerfully.

The President smiled warmly. He liked the kind of guy who knew how to stand up to him. And then, he talked good.

'What if they should escalate back at us?' asked Mr Crust, smiling like the wicked fairy at the wedding.

'Zey don't haf escalation!' cried Professor Szasz, jealous of his invention. 'Listen, zey don't haf industrial potenshel ze vay ve do, zey don't haf sophisticated veppons, zey don't haf neezer ze vairvizawl neezer ze know-how for escalation.'

'They could retaliate,' suggested the Secretary of State.

'Retaliation is not escalation,' replied Professor Szasz finally, his blue eyes brilliant in defence of logic.

'You can't win, Morland,' smiled the President, and then addressed O'Hehir again. 'What would this mean manpowerwise?'

'Very little, Mr President. In the case of North Laos' – they all turned to face the screen again, where Laos reappeared automatically at the mention of its name – 'this would entail the immediate hitting of military targets with tactical nuclear weapons. For this we would require – General Scheidemeyer?'

'The transfer of Number 118 Tactical Nuclear Combat Group from Concord Field and the 415th Special Disruptive Strike Force from Fort Peluskie. A total of twenty-seven thousand men.'

The President nodded. 'I don't want to get involved in higher figures than that at this stage,' he said.

'The problem in Vietnam is somewhat more complex escalationwise,' O'Hehir went on. 'Here it will entail moving up one notch to Phase Twenty-eight, which – I'm sure Professor Szasz will correct me if I'm wrong – is the tough one of limited nuclear attacks on industrial plants not necessarily producing war material: collective farms and government buildings would fall into this area.'

'Quite correct,' nodded Professor Szasz.

'Hm. What does that involve?' asked the President, gloomily.

'General McAteer?' asked O'Hehir.

'No changes momentarily, sir,' replied the general. 'It merely involves switching from military to civilian targets. There is no reason at this time to believe the enemy to be well enough equipped to counter-escalate – I beg your pardon –

retaliate on us. In any case, we don't have civilian targets out there to retaliate against.'

'That's right,' said the President.

'Now in Cambodia, we feel we ought to move straight from Phase Twelve to Phase Fifteen,' said O'Hehir.

'That's a pretty substantial phase leap, isn't it, Barrett?'

'Yes and no, sir. Phase Fifteen is the one where a nuclear weapon is utilized for the first time, seemingly by accident, and apologized for.'

'Like when we bombed the Buddhist monastery at Phing-Aung,' said Mr Crust quietly.

'Not at all,' replied O'Hehir tartly. 'That was a real accident, not a simulated one.'

'The result is identical.'

'For them, not for us.'

General Goldsmith E. Cartwright now spoke up.

'You see, Mr President, it unnecessarily complicates our supply problems if we have to run a conventional war and a nuclear war at the same time. It means that a vast quantity of different armaments and munitions have to be continually ferried from our Taiwan and Hawaiian bases. By eliminating conventional weapons, or at worst confining them to Burma, we could streamline our entire operation, and draw away as many as fifteen thousand men for other duties.'

'This would be good public relations-wise,' added O'Hehir, 'as we could make a press release that we are withdrawing a substantial number of combat troops to coincide with our diplomatic peace offensive.'

This was constructive thinking. The President nodded.

'In the light of this, I suggest we go easy on Burma.'

The President took a quick glance at Burma on the wall, and assented.

'Now what form is this peace offensive going to take?' he inquired.

'Well, we haven't had a Summit for a long time,' sighed Mr Crust.

'Invite them here, you mean?'

'Meet at a place of mutual convenience. Geneva, for instance.'

'I don't like going abroad.'

'The Soviets have just changed their set-up again, Mr President. In a sense, they have a new President also. The two of you'll just have to make contact sooner or later,' Mr Crust insisted.

'A dictatorship just doesn't have the right to change its government as often as that,' grumbled the President. 'Who is this new guy, anyway, what's his name?'

'Mr Shcheparenko,' said Mr Crust.

'What do we know about him, Joe?'

Mr Shales consulted a file, and read with the dull intonations of one who either is not used to reading, or who has learned late in life.

'Ignaty V. Sch . . . Sh . . . Pa . . .'

'Shcheparenko,' said Professor Szasz, with apparent facility.

'Thanks,' smiled Mr Shales, 'born at Novo – something or other . . .'

'Skip all that crap,' snapped the President, 'and let's have the salient facts. What's the guy like? What's his background?'

'We know very little about him as of now, sir,' said Mr Shales balefully. 'The Reds conceal their top men real good on their way up to the Central Committee. He's believed to be an automotive engineer, and he put in a stint as Deputy Third Secretary of the Byelorussian People's Republic's Light Industry Committee in the early thirties. Then we lost sight of him until now.'

'Actually, although Shcheparenko occupies the top post,' Mr Crust interrupted, 'we have reason to believe that Mr Taburov is the real power right now, under the leadership of Mr Kastalkov, of course, who is himself under permanent pressure from the more theoretical wing of the party, represented by Mr Ovsepian and Mr Klutchko . . . and we feel it unwise to ignore Mr Griboyedov, who has made a sensational comeback since his last disgrace.'

'Sounds exactly like Washington,' laughed the President, amid general merriment.

Once again Professor Szasz threw up his hands in admiration of his new fatherland.

The President indicated that he was in need of rest, since he had to dine with a pressure group. The meeting broke up inconclusively, as such reunions often do after a climate of merciless efficiency has compelled men's minds to wander long before they are called upon to translate their findings into policy. One or two of the military blew their noses as they went out. The air conditioning had played its usual havoc with the sinus cavities.

The Secretary of State attempted briefly to take the President aside for a moment, but got a viciously playful thump on the back to send him on his way.

'I'll have those reports,' said Joe Shales briefly, 'and send them up with G-14 or one of his ADC's.'

'Great, great,' replied the President, who didn't know G-14 from G-13, or any other G for that matter.

'What's G?' he asked O'Hehir confidentially.

'G-14? O'Hehir answered, guessing instinctively to which G his chief must be referring. 'He reports directly to the CIC without having to go through Red Arrow.'

'Oh,' the President nodded, sagely.

It was reassuring to feel a vast machine working with maximum efficiency in back of you and all around you. It made a man feel like a passenger in an airliner, with sweet violins filtered through a grille to make even danger seem like part of a cradlesong for adults. The organization was hurtling on a predestined orbit. The temperature was cool and sterile. The mind was lulled in a hermetic cask of discreet good taste, and colours selected by experts in obscure but necessary sciences for their restfulness.

The last general closed the door and the President was alone, suddenly alone among his Currier and Ives prints of the early American scene, hirsute pioneers galloping all over the deep green walls. No ray of sunshine found its way through the slatted blinds. Here, in this room, there was eternal night, and nothing broke the silence but the occasional burp of the machine containing spring water, or, every now and then, a change in the electronic note of the air conditioner.

The President glanced at his watch, and there came into his lined face a strange and febrile expression which few had ever had occasion to notice. Dr Jekyll must have looked like that when he felt the first stirrings of Mr Hyde within him. It was a look of irresistible vice, of searing desire, a look of unappeased violence, demanding release. He crossed to the door like a madman, and locked it. Then he rushed over to the other door, linking his office with those of the secretariat, and locked that as well.

For a moment he stood surveying his room, wild-eyed and panting. Then he moved silently and swiftly over the pile carpet, and fell to his knees by his wastepaper basket. Furiously he looked through the envelopes which had accumulated there in the course of the day. Apparently not finding what he was looking for, he cursed roundly, and for the first time something pathetic came into his eyes. Like a disappointed child he looked aimlessly around him, without the apparent energy to rise from his knees. Then something cunning began to grow in him, and he rose and moved rapidly to the door leading to the secretariat, unlocked it silently, and opened it.

The offices were empty. The specially screened charladies had not yet arrived. The coast was clear. Moving like a television detective, the President eased himself towards the wastepaper baskets. He had to work fast. There was a patrolman for ever on the prowl. There was the staff. There was his family.

He worked through the envelopes with the speed of a bank sorter. Once or twice he hesitated when something caught his eye, and he stuffed the desired bits of paper into his pocket with febrile fingers. Before he could reach the last wastepaper basket, the patrolman came in. The President immediately felt guilty, with the guilt of a child.

'Mr President,' said the patrolman, with a note of kindly reproof in his voice.

'I was ... I was wondering if Miss Grininger was still around.'

'Miss Grininger left early. That old mother of hers is not getting any better.'

'Is that right?' remarked the President, with real solicitude in his voice. 'Too bad. I'm sorry to hear that.'

'Yeah. She's a wonderful and lovely person, our Miss Grininger.'

'I don't know what we'd do without her, George.'

George's name was Elbert, but he was willing to be George if Mr Holm wanted it that way.

'Had a pretty tough day, Mr President. Them crazy Commies aren't giving you a moment to yourself,' the patrolman stated.

'You never said a truer word, George.'

The President made a move to leave, but the patrolman was in a talkative mood.

'I can always tell from the faces as they come out, see. That Mr O'Hehir, he don't give much away, and Mr Crust, why, he always looks kind of ornery, not that he is, it's just the way he likes to look, see, but General Scheidemeyer, he don't hide much.'

'Is that right?'

'Yes, sir, I had the honour to serve under General Scheidemeyer . . . he was Colonel Scheidemeyer then . . . in the 614th Special Combat Detachment which disembarked at Cape Esperance, on Numa-Numa atoll on the eighteenth September, sir, 1944—'

As the patrolman began to delve into his enormous breast pocket, bristling with notebooks and as many ball-point pens as a cossack has cartridges, for some pictorial evidence of his association with General Scheidemeyer, the President prised himself free from the grasp of this melancholy camaraderie.

'He's a great gentleman and a great soldier, is General Arnold B. Scheidemeyer,' the patrolman was able to call out to the retreating President as his loneliness closed about him again, leaving him prey to that lugubrious sentimentality which usually attacks men when in the last stages of inebriation, but here solitude was sufficient.

The President locked the door again on the world of shared experiences, and walked over to his bookshelves. Slowly he eased out a volume of Ralph Waldo Emerson's writings, and reaching behind it, pulled out a tarnished red album.

He carried it to his desk, and slowly, like a criminal examining the spoils of the day, he delved into his pocket and brought out the envelopes he had taken. The first one gave him no pleasure, and he discarded it. The second one he spread out, and examined closely. Then he turned to a page in his album, and he allowed himself a small shout of joy.

'A three-riyal black Saudi Arabian!' he said aloud, and,

withdrawing a pot of adhesive substance from a drawer in his desk, he prepared to stick the stamp into the appropriate page of his album.

He found a ten-baht Thai airmail with temple dancers on it, and an irritating sixty-franc French stamp celebrating an anniversary of the creation of France's nuclear deterrent. He was just in the process of easing from its envelope a handsome twenty-five-kip South Laotian depicting a baby in a gas mask when there was a knock at the door. He pretended to ignore it. The second knock was more insistent.

'What is it?' called the President.

'Bill, it's Grace.'

'For God's sake, Grace, I'm resting.'

'What are you doing in there?'

'I'm resting!' shouted the President.

'Open the door.'

The President tried to ignore the command. The handle began to rattle. Angry, the President rose impulsively and threw open the door.

'Why've you locked the door?' asked Mrs Holm gently, and then, looking into the room, her tone changed to one of deep disappointment, as though she had caught a reformed drunk with a bottle.

'Oh, no,' she said.

'What do you mean, "oh, no"?' hissed the President. 'You behave as though you've caught me reading a dirty book or something.'

'Ssh! Ssh!' implored Grace, and closed the door behind her. 'You know what Don Rosco said.'

'What did Don Rosco say?'

'About your image.'

'Listen, Grace,' said the President with finality, 'I'm a man, and I've got a right to a life of my own—'

'You're the President, Bill,' she interrupted, 'and you're not like other men any more. You can't be. It's what you wanted, even though you never thought it possible. Well, it is possible – it's happened, Bill, even if it's hard to realize. I sometimes come out of a day dream, and say to myself, "Is this really you, Grace Lines Collins, from Clambake Heights, Minnesota, is this really you, in the White House, as the first lady in the land?" Well, it is, Bill. It's no dream, we've got to realize it. It's a reality, and it's a very wonderful reality and a deeply inspirational reality, and many real and wonderful people contributed to this reality, and we've just got to live up to that very great and wonderful dream which put us where we are.'

When faced with idealism of such unaffected purity, especially when it flowed in a pristine stream from the lips of a woman who had given him two fine sons and three wonderful daughters to make up a lovely family, the President was lost and chastened. He listened to her, and communed with her as a religious man communes with his God.

She sensed her victory, and with that psychological sense which makes clever women refrain from pressing home their advantage, she changed her tone to one more intimate and friendly.

'You remember when Don Rosco first came here, and we had that conference about your image. He said that golf was a fine hobby, although Mr Eisenhower had almost brought it into disrepute, but that was so long ago, everyone's forgotten about it now – and it's a great sport public relations-wise on account of it's restful and thoughtful and reflective and it takes place out of doors. Tennis, I remember him saying, had an effeminate image, and was a risk in the cardiac area.' She smiled affectionately. 'I remember you asking about table tennis. Don Rosco said that was not considered a serious pastime, and anyway the Red Chinese were too good at it. Cards are fuddy-duddy, and anything that smacks of gambling is out. Yachting is too risky for a man of responsibility. Fishing is fine, fishing and golf and watching baseball and football.'

'I don't care for golf and I like Ping-Pong. I'm good at it,' the President said self-pityingly.

'I know,' his wife consoled him, 'I know. But that's the price we have to pay, Bill. Read a lot, Rosco said, because that gives the impression you're not averse to taking advice, but don't write, that could mean you're not a man of action.'

'I remember all that,' he agreed, ruefully.

'And when I told him you collected stamps, why he really hit the ceiling. "No one," he said, "no one must ever find out about that! That's childish, retarded. It's like collecting post-cards or bus-ticket stubs or the tops of tins or silver paper." I don't agree with him. I think it's a fine and dignified hobby, but Don Rosco's the highest paid public relations man in the business, and he's brought an awful lot of popularity your way.'

'Stamps relax me,' declared the President without in-sistence. 'I've always been crazy for them. When I was young and didn't believe I'd ever be able to travel, to Minneapolis even let alone New York, stamps were like a window on the world, Grace. We'll never be able to travel again, my dear, you know that, as the ordinary decent couple we are. We'll only be able to travel as the President and his wife, or as the ex-President and his wife. We'll never see all those things I always read into stamps, whole ways of life, whole attitudes. You know my favourites, places I always wanted to visit? Papua was one, Uganda another, and the Bechuanaland Protectorate, and Manchuria, and then there was Upper Volta and the Maldive Islands and the Hijaz and the Trucial Coast and the Emirate of the Oman and the Faroe Islands, fabled names, all of them, for fabled places, storybook places which took firm root in a young man's mind fifty years ago, and which have never given him any peace since . . .'

The President's voice drifted away, and left him in a curiously lyrical and tender trance. Grace, who loved him without understanding too much about him, squeezed his arm affectionately, and left him with a half-sobbed, 'I'm sorry, Bill.'

The President replaced the album behind the works of Ralph Waldo Emerson, turned out the light, and closed the door of his study. He walked soberly to his apartments to shower and to change. The fever had passed.

The Summit was arranged for Geneva, but before leaving the President took the usual precaution – again, as he put it, 'under advisement from Don Rosco' – of visiting all surviving ex-Presidents and being photographed with them in their gardens. There were three of them left at that time, and they all smiled somewhat grimly on the photos, as though their greater wisdom had elevated them into some less temporal stratosphere from where they could observe the mortal scene with ironic detachment. Bill Holm refrained from smiling, not only because he felt ill at ease in the presence of these great men in the twilight of their lives, who liked to give him general advice which no longer had any bearing on reality, but also because Don Rosco had advised him against any levity on these occasions.

'We don't want to feel there's a kind of exclusive Presidents' Club which just exchanges anecdotes,' he had said. 'We want to feel that the presidency entails sacrifice, hard work . . . We want to feel you've given up a normal life – so that other Americans may enjoy it. Look tired, look sore, that's human, but never look happy. Leave the smiles to the others. They've earned them. They're retired, senior citizens.'

To further reinforce the patriotic aspects of the mission, Don Rosco arranged to have the President appointed as honorary chieftain of the Taktaminnehoe tribe of Blackfoot Indians in a reserve up in Montana. The Taktaminnehoes took a good deal of persuading to allow President Holm to become a brave, let alone chieftain, since they had all voted for the opposition at the last election, but eventually they relented when promised that some real estate claims from the time of the Indian Wars would be sympathetically considered in Washington. On the eve of his departure, the President was photographed wearing a headdress of plumes, a kind of shift covered with what appeared to be masonic symbols, and smoking an endless and repellent pipe. The more experienced braves rushed round him in enervating circles, swinging their tomahawks and leaping cautiously over a small fire while chanting for fertility in agriculture and courage in war.

Another successful image was launched. As Don Rosco put it to the President afterwards, 'I know it was tiring, but it was worth it for the coverage. We got one hell of a mileage out of that Taktaminnehoe story. The American public has gotten a guilty conscience about the American Indian. Have you noticed on television how the heavy is not the Indian any more, but the cavalry general, or the profiteer who sells them obsolete rifles? Negroes and Jews are too controversial for the image we want at this time – we're only just beginning to feel guilty about them on a national scale. I've no objection to you

appearing in a Yarmulke or appointing a few more coloured
rear-admirals or circuit judges ... I like it ... but after you
get back. At this time we need a feeling of solidarity and tradition.'

Geneva was upsetting to the huge American delegation,
since they had been conditioned to their own way of life,
which bore little resemblance to anyone else's. The villas in
which they were housed were old-fashioned and gracious, and
the service placed at their disposal by the experienced Swiss
was correct and highly efficient without for a single moment
being imbued with that humanizing relaxation which, more
than any other element, gives the Americans their sense of
identity and nationhood. On one or two occasions the President tried to crack a joke with the butler, but the latter either
failed to understand, or considered the contact as a momentary aberration which should be overlooked. Soon the President had the impression that he was surrounded by robots or,
worse, slaves. He began to think affectionately of the patrolman. There was a man without inhibitions, who knew he was
free.

Whenever the President rang for sandwiches and beer, they
brought a menu. Anything less than a three-course meal
seemed to be beneath these people's dignity. When he
eventually succeeded in making it clear that he wanted nothing
but a bottle of iced beer, it always arrived in a silver urn
embossed with half-naked wood sprites as though it were
champagne, served for the purpose of facilitating seduction.
The President's puritanical spirit rebelled against these impli-
cations, and horrifying visions of New Orleans in its wicked
heyday kept flashing before him as he tried to make himself
comfortable on the redplush and gilt chairs while the bottle of
beer crackled in the urn as the ice melted.

Only in the official Cadillac did he feel really at home. The
contours of the seat were familiar, and the air inside it was
cool enough to seem mentholated. Like a sporting fixture, it
was tough to meet the Russian team at home, even tougher
on neutral soil.

The conference began inauspiciously, since no sooner were
the delegates assembled in the hall than the entire Soviet delegation left the building – as a protest, it was afterwards

announced, against the new phases of escalation which O'Hehir, with his usual Machiavellian sense of timing, had put into operation that very morning. A small nuclear device had fallen on dock installations at a place identified as Tong-Aum. The Americans, through an understandable miscalculation in view of the difficulties of communication, had issued their apology for the incident three-quarters of an hour before the device had actually hit the ground. The government of North Vietnam claimed that a hospital, a school, a rest home for old people, and about a hundred houses had also been utterly destroyed. The Americans riposted with a communiqué describing this as 'an exaggeration', and further explaining that the device in question was no larger than a small transistor radio, that it had been thoroughly tested in Nevada before being made operational, and that it was entirely 'clean' as bombs go. The communiqué stressed, however, the difficulty of dropping a device as light as the one in question, since there was bound to be some deflection owing to 'wind and local atmospheric conditions', and admitted that it had not fallen precisely where intended owing to these considerations. The error lay in the fact that it was supposed to be a 'trial run', but an operational weapon had been taken on the raid by mistake. In the future, it declared, the North Vietnamese would only have themselves to blame if there were to be more damage than was actually intended, since their insistence on utilizing the latest Soviet-made anti-low-flying-aircraft ground-to-air missiles kept American raiders at extreme heights, from where 'the desired degree of accuracy with a device weighing only ten ounces was no longer possible'. The document ended by urging the North Vietnamese to forgo the dangerous luxury of defending themselves, and stated that a place at the conference table would always be open for them.

The Soviet delegation reappeared on the second day, largely because the New China News Agency had launched a searing attack on them for 'criminal inactivity in the defence of their brothers in the Socialist lands', and because China had sent several fresh brigades of 'volunteers' and 'pioneers' into the fray.

Without waiting for all the formalities of opening a conference of this scope and solemnity the Soviet Minister of

Defence, Marshall of the Soviet Union K. S. Pribalkov, a massive man with a shock of greying hair and a quizzical curl falling forward into his eyes, launched a vociferous attack on the 'further crimes of the capitalist bandits and imperialist savages'. There was no stopping him. Translators and advisors were brushed aside in the sustained violence of his onslaught. He repeatedly hit the conference table with his fist. Pens and inkwells shuddered, and blotters seemed to be breathing as the wind generated by his gestures penetrated between them and their leather frames.

The Americans were tempted to walk out in their turn, but Mr Crust urgently advised caution, on the grounds that it would be unseemly for the US delegation to cut short a speech which none of them could understand.

'Isn't it obvious what he's saying?' muttered the President. 'He don't like us.'

'We dare not take it for granted,' hissed the Secretary of State. 'The eyes of the world are upon us.'

Gallantly the Americans sat out the speech, as well as the applause from the entire Soviet delegation, which lasted a full three-quarters of an hour and in which the speaker himself joined, clapping his huge hands together rhythmically, while his eyes stared at his American counterparts in undisguised loathing. All that was missing was an inexhaustible Spanish dancer as a focal point for all this rhythm.

They broke for lunch after the applause was over. Mr Crust's speech after lunch was a tame and civilized affair, and the translators had some difficulty in finding Russian equivalents for its nuances and its irony. Occasionally the Russians discerned some pickings to get their teeth into, and laughed sarcastically.

It was difficult to imagine a conference held under less promising auspices. The next day, news reached the delegations that a Soviet, or Chinese, or North Vietnamese missile with a minute nuclear warhead had blown up a barge used as a PX store by the GIs. As this had happened at night, very few people had been killed, but the fall-out was notoriously dirty by American standards of cleanliness, and now huge quantities of life's necessities stored in neighbouring warehouses had become contaminated. The American military at the conference were beside themselves with anger, and strongly advised against going on with the talks.

'If that's the way they want to play it, OK, let's get on with it,' one general kept saying, like a damaged record.

Marshal of the Soviet Union K. S. Pribalkov looked entirely unrepentant at the other side of the table, which did not improve matters. The Secretary of State continued to smile in his awkward fashion, as though plagued with indigestion, and exuded a feeling of 'I told you so' with the stoicism of a Roman in the presence of a mad emperor. Mr Shcheparenko made a long statement, apparently finding it difficult to read his own notes. The translation bore out the fact that nothing original had been added to the deadlock, with the possible exception of a phrase, 'We will cremate you', which was seized upon by the Western press as the grimmest threat yet issued by a Communist leader, with its ghastly image of total nuclear war. Actually the phrase was a mistranslation of an old Ukrainian proverb to the effect that 'He whose house is burning will not speak with the voice of reason', which not even the most hardened arsonist would dream of quarrelling with.

That the conference endured at all was due to the rest of the world, with the exception of the Chinese, who saw no point in talking to the Americans, largely because the Americans saw no point in talking to them, and the French, who loved talking but didn't care for any talking which took place in their absence. The English were full of noble sentiments, and readily deluded themselves that their voice would eventually be listened to, for old times' sake.

Forced by the hopes invested in this doomed parley to drag it out, the contenders soon evaporated the main issue among numerous impotent subcommittees, and the President found himself alone with Mr Shcheparenko and a couple of translators. Evidently both leaders had been briefed and rebriefed about each other so thoroughly that they were now left almost completely without initiative, like boxers who have been told so much about the other fellow's style that they can no longer use their own with any freedom.

Platitudes about liberty were cautiously exchanged, and it became rapidly clear, at any rate to the translators, that each man fancied himself freer than the other. Shcheparenko looked like a small-time businessman from the Middle West. He had a very average face with a turned-up nose and rimless glasses. He also had a slight nervous tic in one cheek, and a mannerism which occasionally sought to free the neck from the constriction of the collar. His voice was soft, and he appeared to have some difficulty in framing his sentences, often having to correct himself in midstream and rephrase his thoughts from the beginning again.

It occurred to the President that what qualities of mind Mr Shcheparenko possessed were so well hidden that they only served to render the nature of the Soviet hierarchy more mysterious and more forbidding.

'This man is a front if I ever saw one,' he ruminated and then seemed to catch a momentary glint in Shcheparenko's eye which conceivably suggested that their thoughts about each other coincided at that moment.

The look, whatever its meaning, spurred the President to new efforts to bargain from a position of strength, which had been the American aim for many years now. It was no use. Shcheparenko and he had no experience in common. Whenever he spoke of democracy, Shcheparenko thought he was speaking about the people's republics; when Shcheparenko talked about peace, the President understood that the Russians weren't yet strong enough to talk in any other way. There was, for him, a dreadful warning contained in all this desperate talk of peace. It showed how a nation was compelled to speak when bargaining from a position of weakness.

'We believe in private enterprise and the dignity of the individual,' he ventured, as the subjects under discussion became more and more general and innocuous.

This was translated to Shcheparenko, who nodded seriously, and then countered, 'We, on the other hand, believe in public enterprise and the dignity of the state.'

This was translated to the President, who declared, 'A belief in private enterprise leads to efficient, competitive public enterprise, and the assured dignity of the individual on a nationwide scale culminates in the dignity of the state.'

This was translated, and Shcheparenko smiled knowingly. 'We think not. We know that private enterprise can never be free of corruption and that the dignity of the isolated individual is too often drowned in a sea of individuals who consider dignity to be a dead weight. Your system leads automatically to the corruption of the individual and the spread of war for motives of profit. Look at the way the New York Stock Exchange expressed optimism yesterday when you dropped your nuclear device. The Dow Jones average went up a whole point! The more you drop, the more the Stock Exchange rises!'

The President had understood Dow Jones, and waited agitatedly for the rest of the translation.

'It's you who are wrong,' he snapped. 'A belief in public enterprise denies man his competitive sense and enslaves him to the overall directives of a handful of leaders and party men, and the dignity of the state just isn't possible if man himself is denied his fundamental dignity!'

'What's all this about competitive sense?' asked Shcheparenko, once he had understood the President's contention. 'How did I reach the position I hold in the Supreme Soviet and Party of the USSR if I had not been spurred on by a competitive sense? Do you think this famous handful of leaders and party men you refer to are born into positions of authority? Do you think we inherit our power in the Soviet Union? I don't know how you started life, Mr President, but I started out as an apprentice riveter in the transmission shop of a truck factory in Krivoi Rog, in the Ukraine.'

'How do you think I started life?' barked the President.

'In the salons of Philadelphia perhaps?'

'Selling newspapers in East Grand Forks, Minnesota!'

Mr Shcheparenko held out his hand, which the President grasped. For a moment, the sun broke through the clouds, and even the translators smiled at one another.

'Even so,' Mr Shcheparenko said, slyly, still shaking the President's hand, 'from the beginning you were in distribution, I was in manufacture.'

'You can't have one without the other,' laughed the President good-naturedly.

Feeling on safe ground, the President pressed on.

'Agreeing to differ is already a great step forward,' he said.

'It's coexistence,' shrugged Shcheparenko.

'I don't care for the word, but that's what it is.'

'You don't care for the word ... because we coined it?'

'It's just ugly ... for a very beautiful and meaningful thing.'

'Better an ugly word than an ugly deed, like killing innocent women and children with nuclear devices.'

The President flushed.

'You know perfectly well that if you had any respect at all for treaties and fundamental human rights, these ugly deeds would not be necessary.'

'On the contrary, your economic system makes war inevitable. Your economy needs the permanent stimulus of war. So does your unemployment problem which is part of your economy.'

'What about Hungary?' cried the President. 'Was that a case of our economy causing the deaths of innocent and freedom-loving people, or was it just the naked aggression of a military dictatorship against an enslaved people who tried to choose freedom?'

'And what about the Dominican Republic?' asked Mr Shcheparenko. 'Do you treat people who try to choose freedom so very tolerantly?'

'What about East Germany?' countered the President, but before he had time to elaborate on the question, Mr Shcheparenko had slipped in.

'What about West Germany?'

'The Wall of Shame?'

'The Rearmament of the Wehrmacht?'

'The slave labour camps in Siberia?'

'Last week ten more Negroes were murdered by the Ku Klux Klan.'

'Oh, nonsense,' stormed the President. 'Where d'you get that from?'

'*Pravda*,' said Shcheparenko tersely, as though playing his trump card. 'And the news of the rise of the Stock Exchange when you dropped your nuclear device I got from the *New York Times*.'

'Let me tell you a story about the freedom of the press ...'

And so it went on, the President drawing Mr Shcheparenko's attention to the particular, and Mr Shcheparenko dragging the President back to the general, neither being equipped to comprehend the other.

A few minutes before the end of what was clearly going to be the last meeting between the two, Mr Shcheparenko suddenly changed his style, sending his translator out of the room. For a moment, the President didn't understand what was going on, and he became aware of how unusual it is to see a Russian alone. Mr Shcheparenko made a few curt gestures with his hand suggesting that someone ought to be eliminated.

'What does he want?' asked the President of his translator.

'He wants me out of the room.'

'Is that what he said?'

'He used rather more colourful language, sir.'

'How are we going to communicate if you leave?'

'In any case, I have orders not to leave you under any circumstances, sir.'

The President flushed with anger. This seemed about like a vote of no confidence.

'Who gave you those orders?'

'G-14, sir.'

'I'm sick and tired of G-14. Get out of here!'

'But, sir—'

'Get the hell out! Even if he wants to tell me something in sign language which may contribute to the peace of the world, I'm not going to be bound by orders from G-14.'

'OK, sir, but—'

'You heard me! What kind of impression are we giving the Russians if my own staff won't obey me? Is that an example for democracy, every man does what he thinks best? Come on, get a hold of yourself!'

Obediently, but with misgiving, the translator left them alone. Instead of speaking, Mr Shcheparenko walked purposefully to each door in turn, and locked it.

The President, who read spy stories for relaxation, became nervous in spite of himself, and began to wonder if there was not something in G-14's strictures. Instinctively he wandered to the window, and looked out. The fact that they were on the fifth floor did nothing to reassure him.

Once Mr Shcheparenko had finished with the doors, he

began prowling slowly round the walls, looking behind pictures, tapping panels softly, and examining the wall brackets.

'What . . . are . . . you . . . doing?' asked the President at dictation speed.

Mr Shcheparenko came towards him, and spoke softly, in imperfect but fluent English.

'I examine wall in case American microphones.'

'You speak English!' said the President, amazed.

'Between 1933 and 1936, I work at Buick motor division in Flint, Michigan,' explained Mr Shcheparenko with a smile.

'That's why the CIA could find no trace of you at that time!'

'There is old Manchurian proverb – safest place for flea is in lion's mane.' They both laughed, although the President didn't think there were any lions in Manchuria.

Mr Shcheparenko took a small transistor out of his pocket and switched it full on. The only programme available at the requisite strength was an inter-cantonal yodelling competition.

'What are you doing that for?'

'In case American microphones, we make it difficult for them.'

'American microphones? Who ever heard of American microphones? You must mean Soviet microphones.'

'Both, both,' Mr Shcheparenko reassured him, 'but all the time we find in our embassies, and also we put,' he admitted, and then, glancing upward, he indicated the pink Venetian glass chandelier.

'Look. That arm. A black shape, at base of candle.'

'Gosh,' said the President, 'is that one of ours?'

'It may be one of ours . . . or it may be——?'

'What?' the President asked dramatically. It was growing colder and colder in the shadow of the Chinese dragon.

'Swiss,' said Mr Shcheparenko.

'Swiss?'

'They clever than all of us. Got reputation good hosts, find out everything. Now.'

His mood became sentimental, and yet appeared to conceal an inner agitation. He looked deeply and almost embarrassingly into the eyes of the President, and held him by both elbows.

'I ask be alone with you, because I got present for you – and also wish – perhaps you do something for me in America.'

The President had fugitive visions of food parcels, aged relatives, cartons of cigarettes.

'President not big, for us impossible big present, because for so long isolate from other country – but I ask you accept in good spirit – it come with my heart.'

He withdrew a small envelope from his pocket, and gave it to the President.

'Be careful!' he urged.

The President shook out the contents of the envelope gingerly, and gasped.

'It's a ten-Kopek Nicholas II with a printing error . . . you notice eagle has four heads . . . very rare . . . not exist no more . . . other is complete set Azerbaijan People's Republic printed on first day creation republic . . . very rare . . . this set printed by Ukraine separatists . . . Petliura . . . between German occupation and Soviet power . . . very rare . . . and this set, unfortunately not complete . . . printed by White government, Koltchak, in Siberia.'

'How did you know—?' asked the President, deeply touched.

'Oh, is not difficult to see. We have instinct each other. When collector receive letter, he look envelope different way non-collector, even if stamp very ordinary. I observe. I observe all people from West, because they got more stamps than poor Soviet collector. I try find way acquire.'

'Well, this really is most gracious of you, sir, and I assure you, these gifts will form the prize possessions of my collection,' declared the President warmly. 'And now what is your wish, sir? What can I do for you?'

Mr Shcheparenko became highly emotional, which was a curious change from his glacial comportment during the discussion of political issues.

'I don't know how is possible . . . I don't know . . . we are prisoners, you and me, of our own entourage . . . is impossible be alone, like men . . . walk in forest . . . fish . . . discuss . . .

breathe . . . exist . . . I don't know how is possible . . .'

The President was not used to this kind of tearful outburst and he tried to give the conversation a more rugged, a more American tone

'It's up to us to make it possible,' he said.

'But how? How? Can you write letter me? Can I write letter you? Is all opened. Secretariat. Secret Service. Hundred peoples.'

'There's always the hot line.'

'Can send stamps on hot line?' asked Mr Shcheparenko deprecatingly.

'Oh, is that what you want, stamps?'

'Papua,' said Mr Shcheparenko, smiling through tears. 'Papua. I dream of Papua. I know it exists. A triangle. Black. Very simple. Very beautiful. Very artistic.'

'Papua,' murmured the President reverently, with the faraway look of a soldier recollecting an ever-absent friend.

'You got? Papua?'

'Yes, as a matter of fact I do have one, but you shall have it if I can get it to you.'

'No, no, keep. Find another for me.'

'It's tough.' The President couldn't explain why it was so tough, but a new dimension of human relations opened up as he began to understand the similarity of their positions and the structure of society. However a house is built, there is always a top floor, and the occupant still has to pass by all the other floors to reach the soil.

'Why Papua?' he asked, slowly.

'I cannot explain,' replied Mr Shcheparenko. 'It's something in the name, something far away. When I boy, in Krivoi Rog, I no father, only uncle, brother from mother, he sea captain Black Sea, and he tell me other places, far away. Russian land big and flat, like sea, with trees, like ships, and go on, go on, from one horizon to another . . . much fairy stories in flat countries always. Swiss country, many mountains, people little imagination, because not need. Live in Fairyland. Russian people, much imagination, because land flat, have to make own fairyland from clouds, reflections in water, noise of forest, moon . . . I dream always land which is not Russian . . . then uncle give book, atlas . . . and I only child, I imagine all places wonderful names ... different peoples, different alphabet ... Papua ...'

'Where else?'

'Oh. Tanganyika ... Yucatan ... Uganda ...'

'Uganda?'

'Yes, Mozambique ... Sumatra ... Iceland ... the Faroe Islands ...'

'The Faroe Islands,' the President repeated softly, entranced.

He suddenly came to life.

'I tell you what,' he said energetically, 'I'll see to it that you have the goddamdest collection of stamps in the Soviet Union. Don't ask me how I'll do it – I don't know – but I'll do it. Why, it's a national priority! Do you realize we've accomplished more in terms of sheer down-to-earth human relationships in the last five minutes than we have in a year of fruitless negotiation? Why, with our mutual interests, we've succeeded in finding a common platform, which is more than we've ever achieved through months of diplomatic palaver!'

Mr Shcheparenko agreed passionately, and even kissed the President very thoroughly to seal this emotional rapprochement.

The papers of the world, in their ignorance, announced the collapse of the Summit conference and with a sense of indolent relief the diplomats and the public returned to their comfortable prejudices and conditioned fears. Hope was too exhausting a novelty to be entertained for long. The one exception was the President, who had become noticeably short and bad-tempered with his aides.

The first of the weekly meetings after the President's return to Washington was most unsatisfactory. When the maps of the different countries under discussion were flashed on to the wall, the President never once turned to look at them. He told Professor Szasz he didn't want the word escalation mentioned again, which offended the great man. The only one to whom he showed a spark of tolerance was the Secretary of State. Mr O'Hehir and General Ruttledge B. Hooker grew white and tense and asked to see the President privately after the meeting. The request was denied, but the next morning the President had no alternative but to receive them. They brought with them Joe Shales.

'What is it, boys?' he asked them.

O'Hehir spoke up.

'We feel very strongly that you ought to go to Walter Reed for a checkup. We've already made arrangements with General Vandervliedeburgh, and there's a private room in readiness. We've had the hot line put through there.'

'Are you fellows out of your minds?' yelled the President.

'You've not been acting yourself since you got back from Geneva,' O'Hehir insisted.

'You're carrying a hell of a burden,' said General Hooker.

Shales nodded.

'And precisely why do you want to get rid of me?' the President asked slowly.

The three men looked at each other.

'Do you have any idea how the Russians work?' O'Hehir acted as spokesman.

'What are you getting at?'

'Remember the case of Major Schwalbmaker?'

'That dirty traitor,' muttered the President.

'Remember the facts, sir?'

'Sure I remember the facts,' replied the President. 'I've got a good memory.' He was suddenly and irritatingly on the defensive.

'You remember that he crossed into East Berlin, and said he wanted to work with the Commies against Yankee imperialism.'

'Sure. He'd been a member of a secret Commie cell in Pasadena for fifteen years, and you people fell down screening him.'

'That's the story we gave the press, sir,' said Jo Shales.

'You mean it wasn't true?'

'No, sir. Hopgood E. Schwalbmaker had never at any time been member of a Communist cell in Pasadena.

'Suppose you tell me why it was necessary to lie to the public – and to me?'

'The truth was too hot to hold, sir. Hopgood E. Schwalbmaker, to all appearances a good family man, with a lovely wife and six wonderful kids, was in fact a practising and vicious homosexual. When he was sent to Berlin on that special mission with General Catherley, he found himself far from home and domestic routines, and his old appetites were re-kindled – I'm quoting now from the report of Dr Frydlob, these are not my words – and he commenced a series of affairs with perverts in the Berlin area, these meetings often culminat-ing in whippings—'

'I don't care to know the details.'

'No, sir, but the facts are, the next thing we find out is that the Soviets have in their possession a series of photographs of Major Schwalbmaker dressed as a lady's maid being spanked by a nude man.'

'He's a disgrace to his uniform,' cried the President hotly.

O'Hehir took over the narrative.

'The next thing he knows, he's a sitting duck for blackmail, and so he hands over classified information in lieu of pay-ment, and when things get too hot for him, he crosses into East Berlin with a big ideological spiel.'

'Miss Inchbald, our archivist at the embassy in Moscow, was a similar case, sir,' said General Hooker.

'Good God, what was she, a dyke?' asked the President.

'No, a woman in her middle forties, unmarried, sentimental. She allowed herself to be seduced by an *agent provocateur*, and, once again, there were the photographs of her in her birthday suit, loaded, doing a cossack dance, and once again she bought time by handing over secret information.'

'Why are you telling me all this?' The President was begin-ning to suffer an awful, dawning suspicion about the reason for their action.

O'Hehir cleared his throat briefly.

'That's the way they work, sir,' he said evenly. 'They find out a man's weakness, and then attack at the point of least resistance. Oh, it doesn't have to be a sexual weakness – there have been cases where they've supplied heroin to an addict or liquor to an alcoholic – or even attacked in much more innocuous areas. The point to remember is that all of them, from the lowest labourer to the Secretary of the Communist party, are employees of the same machine, and they want to find out all about you, because all information can be useful eventually, even if it doesn't seem to add up to much at the time. Their main field of interest is not a man's work, or a man's duty, but his secrets, his relaxations, his vices, his hobbies . . .'

'His hobbies? How does a guy get to be vulnerable?'

'Well, sir, you know how sensitive we are about gifts from private individuals to politicians in office – Luther Leap had to resign because he accepted a used Turkish carpet for his beachhouse from Attilio Frigone, and then Frigone's corporation landed a large building contract with the Department of Agriculture.'

'I know all about that,' retorted the President, 'and let me tell you people that Frigone's corporation would have landed that contract in any case. He made the best offer.'

'No question. It was tragic, since Leap is one of life's great incorruptibles, and the carpet is of no value. Now let us say for the sake of argument that a high United States official should receive an unusual gift, by which I mean an object or objects of a more personal nature than caviar or vodka, from a high Soviet official, this would immediately put that United States official in a position of vulnerability.'

'One thing's for sure,' thought the President, 'old Shcheparenko was right. That mike in the chandelier was one of ours.'

'Thanks for an interesting twenty minutes, fellows, and you can give that hospital bed to a more deserving client,' he said.

After they had left, the President began thinking. He was now surrounded by familiar objects, and he was intrinsically less disorientated than he had been in Geneva. The Currier and Ives prints, the belching springwater, the moss-green carpet, the cool, humming night of his office were a solace.

'How did Shcheparenko know that I was a secret collector? That excuse of his was a pretty lame one, come to think of it. And then I can't remember ever having received any mail in his presence – messages, but not mail – messages with no stamps on them – why did I never think of that before? One doesn't think half the time – the benefit of the doubt's a habit in a democracy. And then, how about the Faroe Islands . . . and Uganda . . . and Papua. Papua! Coincidence just doesn't go that far . . . Tanganyika . . . I never cared for Tanganyika, never did want to go there, but that was just thrown in to make the coincidence seem natural. Only a handful of people knew I was a collector ... Grace ... the kids, perhaps, from the way I snatch the envelopes away from them at breakfast ... but none of them would be working for the Reds ... Don Rosco? ... I wonder if he's a fag? ... Makes some pretty elaborate gestures at times ... and Mrs Rosco doesn't seem a very adjusted person ... he uses a hell of a lot of after-shave lotion ... better have him re-screened as a potential security risk without giving specific reasons ... I'll have G-14 do it ...'

Locking the doors, the President withdrew his album from behind the works of Ralph Waldo Emerson, and examined for the first time his new and tainted acquisitions. Instead of sticking them into his album, he carefully tore out his prize black Papuan triangle with a kneeling headhunter on it, and then performed the same operation on a tenpenny Uganda with a profile of Edward VII on it, and on a ten-ore Faroe Islands stamp in imperial purple depicting a fishing smack in a rough sea. He placed the three stamps and Mr Shcheparenko's gift in one of his official envelopes, and addressed it to Mr Shcheparenko, c/o The Kremlin, Moscow, marking it 'Private', and giving it to Miss Grininger to mail.

Everyone was delighted to find the President his old self again, and the next weekly meeting passed off very well indeed, with considerable gaiety and a real spirit of efficient collaboration among all heads of departments. It was a most successful week altogether, marked by the stepping up of escalation by another two points in every theatre of operation, a trend which was reflected in the stock market. North Afghanistan appeared on the map for the first time, and with it, naturally, South Afghanistan.

A week later, the envelope returned from the Kremlin marked, in English, 'Address Unknown'. This was not surprising since Mr Shcheparenko had been replaced by Mr Stabavoi, about whom the CIA knew absolutely nothing.

Perhaps the microphone in the chandelier had been one of theirs after all.

The Assassins

At what age should assassins retire? This burning question was exercising Monsieur Ambroise Plageot, the newly-appointed head of the bureau of the French Sûreté entitled Eloignement. The purpose of this department is to safeguard the persons of foreign dignitaries visiting France by rounding up all potential assassins and sending them away for a while. Monsieur Plageot's brow furrowed as he looked up from the pile of documents before him and studied the figure of the man who was seated opposite him.

'You say that you had a pleasant relationship with my predecessor, Monsieur Latille?'

'Oh, yes, sir. It was a bit of a blow to all of us when he retired.'

'All of you? There are more of you?'

'Six in all. Members of the Nihilist International.'

'Nihilism went out before the turn of the century.'

'That's what many people think.'

Plageot sighed. He was half amused, half mystified, but being a good civil servant he could allow himself to show neither emotion. His eye roved once again over the documents. The earliest one was dated July 18th, 1903. It was yellowed and fragile. Attached to it was a dignified photograph of a youth with a vast shock of black hair whose long neck emerged from a butterfly collar several sizes too large. His name was Bratko Zvoinitch. The spindly, nervous hand of some long-dead policeman proclaimed that he had been detained at the request of the consul general of Montenegro as a suspected member of a terrorist organization.

Briefly Plageot fingered his way through the other papers in the Zvoinitch file. In 1910, when he was arrested again, he was called Bruno Silberberg.

'Why did you change your name to Silberberg?'

'Did I? Oh, you know, I've had so many names in my life,

I really can't remember why I adopted any particular one.'

Why choose Silberberg? You're not Jewish are you?'

'If I had been, I would hardly have called myself Silberberg. You have to be a Gentile to choose a Jewish name voluntarily. I think I occasionally choose a Jewish name in order to identify myself more closely with that great and victimized race. Revolutionaries can really exist only when they are in the minority. They are the living conscience of mankind. They are the forerunners of progress, the martyrs who lead the way. They act the dream instead of waiting lazily for the reality which may follow a century later.'

'I see.'

Plageot looked over his glasses and compared the face of the dark youth in the photograph with the wizened and asthmatic figure before him. There was no hair left, not a strand, not the trace of a root. The head was polished and locked into an awkward stooping position by some misfortune. His inability to move his head, the wrinkles at the back of his neck, and his great hooded eyelids, one of them billowing over three-quarters of his right eye like a sail, gave him the aspect of a tortoise, at once wise and ridiculous. The name of the maker of his jacket was clearly visible as the garment stood up of its own accord to enclose flesh which was no longer there. His perpetual smile was not humorous so much as ironic, as though he expected little of men, but the firm lines near the corners of his mouth suggested that he was used to taking more than they offered. There was something Levantine about the sultry sweetness of his expression, a resignation, a closeness to history, a somnolence brought about by years of intense heat, a low opinion of the value of tangible things, a weary exasperation with the ephemeral.

When he spoke, it was in a voice which was scarcely audible, clogged with dust and black tobacco. His words were formed delicately out of wheezy gusts of breath and sounded as though they came from far away. Plageot couldn't help liking the fellow. He had substance.

'Remind me of some of the other names I used,' he said suddenly.

Plageot obliged. 'Vladimir Ilikov, René Saboureau, Wolfgang Tichy, Antal Solomon, Count Napoléon de Souci ...'

At the mention of the last name, he broke into frank laughter, which was transformed almost at once into painful coughing. At length the fit subsided, and he looked up at Plageot, exhausted but dimly amused.

'I was always at my worst when I tried to be aristocratic,' he wheezed 'I could never think of a name. Napoléon de Souci ... What an idiotic idea! The Organization ordered me to infiltrate the royal family of Saxony from the inside in order to facilitate the murder of one of its members. We were aiming low in those days. They saw through me, of course. I no sooner presented my card than I was rushed away and reported. I didn't look like a Count Napoléon de Souci, you understand. Come to think of it, I can't imagine what a Count Napoléon de Souci would look like.' He grew more serious. 'No, I was at my best, at my most dangerous, when I was a man of the people.'

'Dangerous?' asked Plageot. 'And yet, looking through your file, I cannot find the evidence of a single crime you have committed. Certainly no murder. Always you have been arrested on suspicion.'

'I was never lucky in France,' said Zvoinitch, with a sigh.

'Then why did you stay here? You seem to have no family ties here, and certainly no ties of blood.'

'I love France,' murmured Zvoinitch. 'Unless you kick me out, I will never leave.'

In spite of himself, Plageot was moved. He closed the file and lit a Gauloise cigarette. 'Very well,' he said, 'let me recapitulate. I cannot reach any decision unless the problem is clear in my own mind. I took over this bureau yesterday, and you have consistently indicated by your insinuations that I don't know my way around yet. This I understand as well as you do. But put yourself in my shoes for a moment. A man of eighty-four enters my office—'

'Eighty-five.'

'Eighty-five; I beg your pardon. Far be it from me to shorten your life. You enter my office, supporting yourself on two sticks, and announce that you are a violent and notorious assassin. Because I am polite by nature, I ask you

to sit down. You do so with evident relief, having negotiated four flights of stairs. Then you produce a copy of this
morning's *Aurore*, in which the imminent arrival of the Imam
of the Hejjaz is announced, in order to promote better understanding between the French people and his people. I ask you
what this fact has to do with your visit. You express surprise
and tell me that my predecessor, Monsieur Latille, would
have understood. Since I insist, you explain to me that the life
of the Imam is in danger. I become interested and ask you if
you have any information which leads you to believe this.
You smile pityingly and tell me that you may be tempted to
kill him if I do not deport you for one week to Corsica. My
dear fellow, have you any idea where the Hejjaz is?'

'It doesn't matter where it is,' replied the old man. 'I am
against all autocrats, and the people of that unfortunate land,
wherever it is, deserve to be liberated. No despot is safe
while I am alive.'

'Tell me,' asked Plageot, 'what would my predecessor, Monsieur Latille, have done?'

'There was no argument with him,' replied Zvoinitch. 'He
recognized the danger which we constitute to the guests of
the Republic. He would have signed the authorization at
once, and we would have been on the plane tonight.'

'Tonight?' Plageot was frankly surprised. 'But the Imam
does not arrive until the day after tomorrow.'

'Monsieur Latille was not one to take risks where desperate
men are involved.'

'I see. By "we" I presume you mean yourself and your
five colleagues.'

'Yes.'

'And where are your five friends?'

'They are all packed and ready to go.'

'How is that?'

'When we read of the visit of the Imam in this morning's
paper we held a meeting, and I was sent as a delegate rep-
resenting our group.'

Plageot took out a pencil. 'Would you mind giving me the
names of your friends?'

'Is that necessary? Monsieur Latille—'

'Monsieur Latille is no longer here,' Plageot said sharply.

'Very well. Asen Popoff, of the Bulgarian Nihilist International. Yahuda Achron, of the Jewish branch. Professor Semyon Gurko, of the Ukrainian Separatist Nihilist Union. Lazar Perlesco, of the Nihilist Centre of the Banat. And Madame Perlesco, better known in nihilist circles as Rose Liechtenstein.'

'Well,' said Plageot, 'I can't give you an answer today.'

Zvoinitch made no attempt to disguise his annoyance.

'Tomorrow may be too late,' he said.

'That is a risk we will have to take.'

Zvoinitch rose with difficulty, seeming to think that he was more impressive at his full five feet eight. 'You are young,' he declared darkly. 'Anyone who is young in charge of a government department must be considered promising. Your career may well be ruined by your shortsightedness.'

'Do you know what I think?' Plageot answered. 'I think you should see a doctor.'

'Is that so? Before long you may find yourself in the position of being seen by a doctor.'

'Are you threatening me now?'

'I threaten anyone who stands in my way.'

He tucked his miserable suitcase under one arm, took a stick in either hand, and hobbled to the door.

'It may interest you to know,' Zvoinitch whispered, 'that the Imam of the Hejjaz arrives on Air France, Flight 178, from Baghdad at 7.48 on Wednesday morning. He is staying at the Hotel Raphael. He leaves on Sunday for Marseilles on the Train Bleu. Guard him well.'

He was gone. Plageot stubbed out his cigarette in irritation. He rang for Mademoiselle Pelbec, his assistant. After a moment she entered. She was one of those devoted functionaries who haunt French ministeries, walking hither and thither with bits of paper, for ever stamping something. An open pair of scissors hung from her belt on a chain. Her blouse was home-made and ill-fitting enough for one strap of her brassière to be permanently visible, gathered with the strap of her slip in the loop of a gigantic safety-pin. Her hair was dull red, her mouth twitched incessantly, and she had no eyebrows.

'You rang,' she announced, and made it sound like an accusation.

She had been eight years with Monsieur Latille, and she resented his retirement.

'Mademoiselle Pelbec,' Plageot said, 'what do you know of a man called Zvoinitch, who says he is a nihilist?'

Mademoiselle Pelbec became guarded and seemed to be choosing her words with some caution.

'Well, I know Monsieur Latille considered him a rather dangerous character,' she replied.

'If he is so dangerous, why was he not deported?'

'Oh, dear me, no,' Mademoiselle Pelbec blurted, and then steadied herself. 'While Monsieur Latille considered him dangerous, he did not consider him as dangerous as he considered himself, if you follow my meaning.'

'Frankly, no. From one meeting, I consider him a harmless crank.'

'You mean you are not sending him to Corsica?' Mademoiselle Pelbec asked in horror.

'Why should I?'

'Well, he never reports without good reason. The relationship between him and Monsieur Latille was quite remarkable. For as long as I remember, Monsieur Latille never had to send for them. They would report of their own accord whenever they read in the papers that anyone of any importance was visiting Paris. It was an extraordinary example of cooperation between the potential criminal and the potential pursuer. If all criminals were as public-spirited as the six of them, there would be no more crime.'

'Precisely,' said Plageot dryly. 'I believe them to be utterly harmless.'

'Is any of us utterly harmless?' asked Mademoiselle Pelbec. 'They never killed anyone in France, true, but in Macedonia their record is terrible.'

'How do you know?'

'Monsieur Latille told me so.'

Plageot grunted. 'There's no evidence of it here,' he said.

'Monsieur Latille wouldn't have invented such information. Why should he?'

'I wonder. That will be all, Mademoiselle Pelbec.'

She left on her dignity, muttering about upstarts and ingratitude.

Plageot stared out of the window, where a summer day was fading. Then he called another department of the Sûreté Nationale. In reply to his question about the Imam's arrival, he was told that the potentate was due on Air France, Flight 264, from Geneva at 9.12 on Wednesday morning, and that he would be staying as a guest of the President of the Republic. Smiling grimly, he replaced the receiver. He prepared to dismiss the matter from his mind momentarily when the phone rang. The man at the other end told him that he had been given the wrong information and that the Imam would not be staying at the Elysées but at the Hotel Raphael.

Plageot cursed. 'But tell me,' he asked, 'is he flying in from Geneva and not from Baghdad?'

'The information I gave you about the flight is correct,' said the voice.

'And where does the Imam go after Paris?'

'Monte Carlo.'

'Monte Carlo, not Marseilles?'

'No, no, Monte Carlo. The Imam is coming here to better the lot of his underprivileged people, but he is incalculably wealthy himself and likes to gamble.'

Plageot smiled. 'And I presume,' he added, 'that he will fly to Nice and then proceed by car.'

'No,' said the voice, 'he is booked all the way on the Train Bleu.'

'What? Thank you.' Plageot hung up and thought.

Two of the facts supplied by the old man were right, two were wrong. A policeman's function was to be suspicious, and yet it was far easier to suspect someone trying to allay suspicion than it was to suspect someone trying to attract it. It would be dreadful if the Imam did perish, blown to pieces by the traditional bunch of flowers containing the infernal machine in its scented bosom. His conscience would be indelibly marked if that should happen; he could never face Mademoiselle Pelbec again, that was sure. Damn Zvoinitch! With all his clumsiness, he knew what he was doing, setting little balls of doubt rolling. He was just too sinister not to be ridiculous, yet not ridiculous enough to be quite harmless.

Plageot called for the files of the people Zvoinitch had named as his collaborators. Their police records were remarkably similar. All had multitudinous aliases.

Plageot made some rapid calculations on his pad and came to the remarkable conclusion that their combined ages came to 508 years, Yahuda Achron being the youngest of the group at seventy-nine, Madame Perlesco the oldest at ninety-two.

It was more and more disturbing, more and more absurd. There was only one key to the mystery – Latille. Plageot searched his diary for the number and telephoned Latille at home.

'Hullo, is Monsieur Latille in?' he asked.

A woman's voice seemed hesitant.

'Who is speaking?'

'Ambroise Plageot. Is that Madame Latille?'

'Yes.'

'Ah, Madame. This is Plageot, your husband's successor. You may remember me from the little party the day before yesterday to celebrate your husband's retirement. It was I who was selected to present him with the commemorative inkwell.'

'Indeed I remember you, Monsieur. The inkwell is on my mantelpiece. It is very beautiful, as indeed was your speech.'

'I flatter myself that I chose my words with some felicity. Is your husband in, Madame?'

'Just a second,' she said.

Monsieur Latille came to the phone. 'Hullo, Plageot. How's everything at the office, old man?'

'That's just it, Latille. I have a question which only you can answer. Would you have a moment to see me?'

'Can't you tell me now?'

'No.'

There was a pause at the other end. 'Oh, very well. Come round at once, if you insist.'

'Thank you,' Plageot said, already feeling more a master of the situation.

Plageot was unmarried, but he had a mistress, who might as well have been his wife, because he was not entirely faithful to her. This happened to be her birthday. He called her. 'Annik,' he said in his most authoritative voice, 'I will be late – three-quarters of an hour. What's that, you're dressed to go out? So much the better; then you won't keep me waiting when I do arrive.'

He put on his rakish black hat and left the office for the day.

'My dear Plageot,' said Monsieur Latille, entering his humble drawing room, 'please excuse the disorder, but we are leaving tomorrow morning for Dinard.' He was a colourful personality, this Latille, with his unkempt grey hair, his tiny goatee, and his watery blue eyes, more of an artist, to look at, than a functionary. Plageot, so accurate, so dogmatic, so razor sharp, felt awkward in the presence of such floridity.

'I realize you must be very busy. I can only stay for a moment in any case, so I will come straight to the point. It is about a certain Zvoinitch.'

Monsieur Latille lost his geniality and sat heavily.

'Yes,' he said. 'I was afraid you would ask me about him. When I opened this morning's paper and saw that the Imam of the Hejjaz was arriving tomorrow, it spoiled my day. I became fretful with anticipation of the worst. I hoped to get away before the storm broke.'

Plageot sat down also. 'But what is the mystery?' he asked. 'Either the fellow is dangerous or he is not. It must be a relatively simply question to decide.'

'It is far from simple,' Latille said sadly. 'I feel at the moment like the head cashier of a bank, trusted by all, who is suddenly discovered to have embezzled millions of francs.'

'Why do you feel like that?' demanded Plageot in a strong voice.

'Because – because I could never make up my mind whether these superannuated revolutionaries were dangerous or not. Eventually, I could stand the uncertainty no longer, and I gave them the benefit of the doubt.'

'You mean that you acceded to their request and sent them to Corsica without due reason?'

'Precisely.'

Plageot's manner became very stiff and selfrighteous. 'You realize that you utilized the taxpayers' money in these caprices of yours, Latille?'

'Of course I realize it, my dear fellow, although I can't pretend that it caused me much anguish. The end result of most of the taxpayers' money is far less charitable and far less useful. Look at the amount of it which was poured into the Maginot Line, and a lot of good that did.'

'If everyone thought as you, there would be chaos!'

'There is chaos in any case, my dear Plageot, not because all men think like me but because all men think differently from each other. As Voltaire wisely said, it is up to each one of us to cultivate his own garden. Two bits of sound common sense placed in juxtaposition can easily lead to chaos. About that we can do nothing. All we can do is to keep our house in order.'

Plageot rose and paced the floor agitatedly. 'I did not come here,' he said, 'to indulge in a metaphysical discussion.'

'No,' replied Latille reasonably, 'you came here to ask if six old assassins are dangerous or not. I give you my answer. I don't know.'

'You surprise me, Latille, and you shock me. Now I understand why Zvoinitch told me he had a very agreeable working arrangement with you.'

Latille smiled. 'Did he say that? That was very kind of him, if a little tactless, seeing as he hadn't got your measure yet.'

Plageot stopped in his tracks. 'What do you mean by that?' he exploded. 'Are you now attempting to justify your actions?'

'I don't think they need justification. Up to yesterday your department was my department. I ran it for eight years, and I don't regret my decision in regard to these men. All I dreaded was the day on which I would have to explain myself. There is a difference between explanation and justification.'

'There is no time to dwell on fine points of interpretation,' cried Plageot. 'Explain yourself, then.'

Latille spoke softly and with amusement.

'I remember the first time Zvoinitch came to my office. He was called Zbigniew at the time. It was in 1946, when Paris was brimful of Allied generals. At that time, I was struck by his honesty. He told me he couldn't resist making attempts on the lives of foreign notables. I thought I might send him to a psychiatrist, but somehow it seemed a little eccentric to try to cure the foibles of a man over seventy, which had hardened, according to his file, into an ineradicable habit. Had he been a youth, I would not have hesitated. In view of his age, however, I decided to dispatch him to Corsica. Admittedly, I became a little suspicious when he suddenly produced as many as five friends, all suffering from the same peculiar temptation. Still, the last thing we wanted was a dead Allied diplomat or general on our hands, especially at a time when we were doing our utmost to make our battered country attractive for tourists. After a while, a degree of stability was re-established, and these old people were allowed to return to France.

'Then someone like Molotov came to Paris – I forget who, exactly – but suddenly the place was teeming with Russian security officers with the most alarmingly comprehensive lists of exactly whom they wished removed. When they used the word "removed", I suspect that they meant a more irrevocable course of action than mere transportation to Corsica. In my eagerness to show the Russians that their lists were far from complete I ostentatiously sent our six friends abroad once again. I didn't have to round them up. As usual, they reported of their own accord, and during the presence of General Serov in my office I was able to demonstrate to the Russian that opposition to the régime is civic-minded in a democracy.

'When Tito arrived, the same procedure was repeated, and it happened again when Adenauer appeared. Then one day they turned up for no particular reason. I asked them to what I owed the pleasure of their visit – and it was a pleasure, Plageot, I promise you. They combined the qualities of emotion and of ridicule, as good clowns do. They were, in short, a relief from the dreary parade of grim, ugly, charmless people who engage our attentions day in and day out.

'They explained, without batting an eyelid, that the Shah of Persia was due in France. I laughed. "You're not going to pretend," I said, "that you wish to assassinate the poor defenceless Shah. He has troubles of his own, finding out how to drag gasoline from the soil, without any more trouble from you."

'Zvoinitch took over at this point. He is their spokesman. His eyes gleamed with a cunning so transparent it was touching. "Look at Madame Perlesco's file," he said, "and see what happened in the late summer of 1912." I did so. She had been arrested in Ispahan and deported to France at the request of the Persian government for consistently shouting insults at the royal house in public.

' "The Persians must have been appallingly sensitive," I observed.

' "Shrewd, shrewd," he corrected. "They recognized danger when they saw it. In those countries it is not the practice to conduct assassination personally. Instead, you incite the mob, and they do the work collectively."

'The story was incredible but expounded so ingeniously, and they had packed their few belongings so painstakingly, that I gave in.

'Some nine months later, they really went too far. They came to my office, all packed and ready to go, on the pretext that the Prince of Monte Carlo was due. I told them to go home. They insisted that the consequences of my decision would be dire. I replied that they were abusing my kindness. Zvoinitch suddenly brandished a huge pistol of Arabic design, which he produced from his voluminous pocket.

' "Have you a licence for that?" I asked him. In moments of peril I always find courage in being lighthearted. He answered that the Nihilist International had no licence for anything and that this formed part of their general policy.

'I began to laugh. This seemed to enrage Zvoinitch, who pointed his pistol out of the window and pulled the trigger. There was a resounding report which set up an intense singing in my ears. Unfortunately, the dramatic effect was somewhat spoiled by Perlesco, who shouted, "Fool, there goes the last of the gunpowder!"

'I rose and pointed to the door with a trembling finger.
' "Out! Out!" I yelled. "And never come back!"

'They left in confusion, just as some people working in neighbouring offices came in to see what had happened.

'When it was announced some time later that the Emperor of Ethiopia was about to pay us a visit, I half expected them to return, but the days passed and they did not come. I was troubled by remorse, Plageot. Perhaps I myself was growing older and could sense the yawning cave of retirement before me, ever closer, ever closer. Whatever the reason, I felt myself the prey to a terrible compassion for these old idiots. By throwing them out of my office, I began to sense the kind of guilt I associated with kicking a dog or stealing a sweet from a child. In itself my gesture had been unimportant, but I suspected that it had assumed a vast importance to them, since their world was so constricted. I prayed for them to return so that I could clear my conscience.

'Then, only a few hours before the arrival of the Negus at Orly airport, the door to my office opened tentatively. It was Zvoinitch! I leaped to my feet and blurted out, "My God, where have you been? I thought I'd have to come and get you!"

'Zvoinitch smiled feebly and began to shake. "Then we can go to Corsica?"

'"Here are your papers," I said with a sigh of relief.

'That was the last I saw of them.'

Plageot stared at Latille as though he had just watched some military secrets being sold.

'One thing you have not explained,' he snorted. 'Why do these people wish to go to Corsica? Is it the meeting place of the Nihilist International?'

'Oh, no,' said Latille, with a smile of charming frankness. 'I don't believe the Nihilist International exists any more. No, I think they like the climate of Corsica. They regard it as a vacation. A vacation we pay for.'

Plageot hovered on the brink of physical disintegration. He was purple with outrage.

'This is the most scandalous sequence of events which has ever come to my notice,' he roared. 'You are a victim of your own weakness and sentimentality, Latille, and because of your approaching dotage you project your self-pity on to a group of harmless nitwits who—'

Latille held up a hand to stay the avalanche.

'Harmless?' he flashed. 'If that pistol had been aimed at a man, it would have taken his head off. They do not lack imagination to the extent that you do, Plageot. They may be mad, but they are imaginative. At this moment they may be seated in some garret, concocting some diabolical device in order to dispatch the Imam of the Hejjaz – not, Plageot, because they have anything against the Imam, but because it is their way of telling you that it is time for them to go to Corsica.'

'Arrest them, then! Throw them into prison! Teach them a lesson!'

'That's your way, isn't it? Prison. It's still at the public expense, Plageot. It may be cheaper at the Cherche-Midi, but the food they eat is paid for by the taxpayer. The people of France must pay for either my tolerance or your intolerance.'

'Deport them, then.'

'Where to? Who would take them? My dear boy, you have a very low opinion of France and of her traditions.'

'France is not a charitable organization!'

'France is the home of the cultivated mind. You're so ambitious that you will rise to the top of the tree and scatter the seeds of your personal misery far and wide. Thank God I am not your contemporary.'

Plageot trembled. His mouth worked meaninglessly and his eyes stared. 'What the hell are you talking about?' he cried.

'Why was I so civilized in regard to these curious characters? Because I am happy in myself, and he who is happy is generous. He wishes to give others the secret. I have been married for forty-one years, and no cross word has ever passed between my wife and myself. We had humour and resilience. I knew I would never rise to the top, and I was reconciled to my mediocrity. I could even joke about it when the occasion demanded it. Our daughters are not very beautiful. They have my wife's face and my figure. Consequently, they found husbands who married them for the most subtle of their qualities, and they are all as happy as we are. When my wife drove our car into a tree last year, I welcomed the opportunity of walking again. There is some advantage to every disaster.'

'What has this to do with me or with the efficient administration of the department?'

'Everything,' said Latille. 'You are a thoroughly miserable character. Your humour is sarcastic, as though all your thoughts turned rancid in the filter of your mind. Head of a department in your early forties, you are deemed one of the most promising men in the police, and it is to be expected that you will end up as prefect of Lyons, or Marseilles, at least, making life difficult down there with your dreary little pettifogging decisions. Or else you may end up as resident in one of our minor possessions, confusing the natives and passing the time by altering the traffic regulations from day to day. I know your sort. Life is a dossier, memory is a file, ambition is a badge, love is a regulation. You are a bachelor. Why? Because you are selfish. You need women more than you like them, and you like them more than you love them, and you love them more than you can love one of them. At the moment you are living with a second-rate actress. Again, why? Because you have reached a grade in which it is *de rigueur* to live with a second-rate actress. You never take a spiritual risk. You are dead. You see what you want to see, feel what you want to feel, and your charm goes about as deep as eau-de-Cologne. Mind you, I only say this because I like you. Unlike those unfortunate nihilists, you are still redeemable. We can make a man of you yet.'

Just then Madame Latille entered. She was of surprising ugliness, but her smile radiated warmth and amusement. 'Jules,' she chided, 'you haven't offered our guest a glass of port!'

Plageot, sobered by the presence of a lady, said, 'I regret, Latille, that I will have to ask for a thorough investigation of your activities and bring this case to the attention of the prefect.'

Latille shrugged his shoulders and grinned sadly. 'Do as you wish, but don't be surprised if the Imam is blown sky-high while you are engaged in your corrective measures and the Arab world rises against us in vengeance simply because you were dealing with matters of greater importance.'

Plageot stormed out and proceeded to a most unhappy birthday celebration with his mistress. Annik did what she could to cheer up her lover, but all he could do now was to think of her as a second-rate actress. He argued over the bill with the waiter, the proprietor was called, the car wouldn't start, and when they reached his apartment, a fuse had blown out. Annik dressed in a brief, transparent pair of black pyjamas and lay around on her pink sheets, exuding desire, but he sat grimly on a chair, facing the wall.

Suddenly he phoned the Sûreté. 'Inspector Bréval,' he said, 'are you on duty tonight? This is Plageot. Eloignement. There are six people I want followed. This is urgent, top priority. I will give you their names and addresses.'

When he had finished his conversation, he lay down on the bed and closed his eyes. Soon he was asleep. His dreams were peopled with murderers. Everyone carried some lethal instrument. Mademoiselle Pelbec tried to stab him with her scissors. He couldn't open a door without finding Latille there, followed by a battalion of happy and hideous daughters. When he went to the cubbyholes to fetch his mail, he saw that many tiny naked women were filed there, one for every grade. The prefect's cubbyhole contained one of the most distinguished actresse in France, six inches tall. '*Bonjour*, Plageot,' she said with a captivating smile. 'One day you will be a prefect and you will inherit me.' He awoke, covered with perspiration and on the verge of tears.

'Curse Latille!' he cried aloud.

The next morning two detectives were waiting to see him. 'Well?' he asked. 'Did you find any of them?'

'No, sir,' replied the detective.

'Fools!' Plageot brought his fist down on the desk.

'With all due respect, we are not to blame for the absence of the suspects.'

'No, no, of course not. I didn't sleep very well. I am nervous.'

The day passed slowly. Plageot could do no work. At four o'clock in the afternoon, a phone call from His Excellency Djamil Al-Haroun Ibn-Ibrahim Al-Salaoui, chief economic adviser to His Serenity the Imam of the Hejjaz, announced the fact that a threatening letter had been received by the delegation in Geneva on the eve of their departure. Apparently the letter, postmarked Soissons, was brief and to the point. It said 'Death Awaits You in Paris.' There was no signature, but an amateurish picture of a decapitated head and a gory scimitar.

In a way, Plageot was relieved. Now there was no more

ambiguity, no more fear of looking ridiculous. He informed all relevant departments of the nature of the threat. At six o'clock a man walking with the aid of two sticks was arrested but released after an hour of questioning. He turned out to be a retired colonel with a glorious record. He also intended to sue the police. The operations proceeded under an evil star.

The Geneva police called at eight to report the arrival of a menacing telegram at the hotel of the Arabian delegation. It read: WE MEANT WHAT WE SAID IN THE LETTER. THE SCIMITAR OF VENGEANCE IS POISED. It had been sent from Bordeaux. Bordeaux? Plageot examined the map. Soissons was quite far from Paris, Bordeaux much farther. This must mean that the organization was larger than he thought. He looked at his watch and became nervous. Time was running short.

At eight o'clock the prefect, Monsieur Vagny, held a conference, which Plageot attended.

'Gentlemen,' the prefect said, gravely, 'we are taking every precaution to ensure the safety of the Imam of the Hejjaz. Obviously what I tell you here is of the utmost secrecy. At the last moment, the Imam and his party will be switched from the Air France plane which was to have taken them to Orly on to a Swissair plane which will land at Le Bourget. The Swissair plane lands ten minutes earlier. From there a Citroën car bearing a false Imam will proceed directly to the Hotel Raphael, while the real Imam will go in a Deláge by a more circuitous route. The floor waiters on the second floor of the Raphael have all been replaced by policemen. The elevator operator will be Detective Vaubourgoin, one of our best men. We will infiltrate the kitchen staff with our lads. If the assassins strike, they will find us waiting. We cannot afford to underestimate the threat to the Imam's life or over-estimate the importance of his survival to our country. That will be all, gentlemen. To your posts.'

Just before the Air France plane was due to leave Geneva it was searched by the Swiss police. A bomb with a timing device was found aboard, gaily ticking away under a seat. Most of the passengers had already taken their seats when one of them, a distinguished gentleman of swarthy appearance, collapsed. He was taken off with suspected appendicitis. It was under his seat that the bomb was found. He was promptly arrested by the Swiss authorities and turned out to be a member of an Arabian secret society in favour of a return to power of the Imam's deposed uncle, a dissipated gentleman who lived in Rome. The French were informed of these findings when the Swissair plane was already very close to Paris. The Swiss also added that, while the would-be murderer was still believed to have been a bona fide appendectomy patient, he had used the phone in the airport clinic and was talking agitatedly in Arabic when the police broke in to arrest him. He may have realized that the Imam would not be a passenger on that plane and may have warned the other members of his conspiracy about this.

The French police prowling through Orly Airport noticed a suspicious group of Arabs who were drinking coffee nervously at the bar and chatting furtively. Plageot walked up and down with Inspector Lagnon but saw no trace of the nihilists.

'Is the plane late?' he asked suddenly.

'Didn't you hear?' Lagnon replied surreptitiously. 'They got a message through just now. They found a bomb aboard. The plane won't be coming at all. They caught the man, but they think he had time to warn the other members of his organization that the Imam would land at Le Bourget.'

'What?' cried Plageot. 'Why didn't you tell me?' He ran out, waved to his car, and set out in the direction of Le Bourget at full speed.

He arrived at Le Bourget just as the Imam and his party were sweeping out of the plane in a flurry of white, their dark glasses sparkling as brightly as their teeth.

Inspector De Valde met Plageot. 'It's all right. They've just phoned through from Orly. They've captured all the assassins. Eight of them. Arabs.'

'That's what they think!' cried Plageot. There among the crowd was Zvoinitch with five old people. 'Arrest those people!'

'What for?' asked the baffled De Valde.

'Those are your assassins!'

'But, I tell you, they telephoned—'

'Do as I say!'

Discreetly, the six nihilists were rounded up and bustled away. Zvoinitch looked triumphant. 'Oh, please let me hear the thing explode,' he pleaded with Plageot, as the little group stood on the pavement.

'What thing?' Plageot screamed, shaking Zvoinitch mercilessly by the lapels.

Zvoinitch rapped him painfully on the knuckles with one of his sticks. 'The bomb,' he said.

'Where is it?' Plageot was nursing his hand.

'Will you send us to Corsica?'

Plageot caught sight of the Imam and his party approaching their car. Customs formalities had been dispensed with in the interests of hospitality.

'Very well,' he hissed, 'but where is it?'

'Under the rear wheel of the car. When the car moves off – *pouff*!' Zvoinitch made an eloquent gesture.

Like lightning, Plageot ran off and dived under the Imam's car. Running madly with a black box in his hand, followed by two of his men, he threw himself into the gentlemen's convenience. To the consternation of the old attendant who stood there, he filled a sink with water and dropped the black box into it.

'Get out!' he cried to the attendant, and to his men he gasped, 'Cordon off this area. Bring the bomb removal people.'

On the way back to Paris, he gave in to dreams of glory. He heard the congratulations of ministers, read the envy in the eyes of his colleagues, and was tinglingly surprised at his own incredible courage. Half an hour later, he sat at his desk. Napoleon could not have felt more sure of himself when he seized the crown from the Pope's hands. The six assassins were lined up before him. He did not offer them seats. It was better for them to stand. He had called in De Valde to witness his triumph.

'What was the name of your contact in Geneva?' he asked.

'Geneva? We have no contact in Geneva,' Zvoinitch said.

'And in Soissons?'

'Nor in Soissons.'

'And in Bordeaux?'

'No.'

'You're lying.'

Zvoinitch shrugged his shoulders. He didn't care for boors.

'Perhaps the name of Mohammed-Bin-Mohammed will refresh your memories?' Plageot barked.

The assassins looked at each other, then shook their heads. 'It's not a name any of us have ever used,' said Zvoinitch.

'You choose to joke,' said Plageot with an unpleasant inflection. 'I advise you to take this examination more seriously, for your own sakes. The game's up, you know. Mohammed-Bin-Mohammed is arrested. He has confessed.'

'I don't understand why you are asking all these meaningless questions,' Zvoinitch remarked gently. 'You promised us we could go to Corsica.'

'Corsica?' Plageot laughed harshly. 'I think you are more likely to end up in a shadier place.'

'But you promised!' Zvoinitch was indignant.

'Shut up!'

There was silence, and the receding echo of Plageot's rudeness.

'I will tell you what occurred, since you refuse to tell me,' Plageot murmured. 'You were expecting the Imam at Orly, but we forestalled you. Your contact in Geneva, Mohammed-Bin-Mohammed, entered the plane as a passenger and carefully placed his bomb under his seat. Then he looked around and realized that the Imam would not be travelling on the craft. He quickly feigned illness and was carried to the airport clinic. While the nurse was out of the room, he telephoned you at some prearranged number and had time to tell you to go to Le Bourget before the Swiss authorities arrested him. You moved quickly to Le Bourget with the bomb you had prepared in case the attempt in the airplane failed. Quickly identifying the car destined to carry the Imam by the quantity of policemen surrounding it, you stooped to tie your shoe and placed the bomb under the back wheel, and then retired amid the crowd to watch the results of your lethal handiwork. Can you deny this?'

De Valde looked at Plageot in admiration. For lucidity, for shrewdness, for grasp, this assessment of a situation would be hard to equal. It was a model of police work.

'We went to Le Bourget because we guessed that the Imam would land there,' said Zvoinitch.

'Lies!' snapped Plageot. 'The other day you told me the Imam would land at Orly in an Air France plane.'

'Did I? I was guessing. One usually forgets a guess. That's why honesty is the best policy.'

'It is indeed. You even mentioned the flight number.'

'I made it up, knowing that you would forget it. As far as Air France goes, that was in the papers.'

'But the Air France morning flight from Geneva does not go to Le Bourget.'

'How was I to know that?' Zvoinitch replied. 'I relied on my instinct. If I had been wrong, we would have found our way into the Hotel Raphael.'

'Ah! At last a confession! And how did you know about the Hotel Raphael?'

'Oh, that's easy,' said Zvoinitch. 'The Hotel Lancaster puts out its refuse bins very early every morning. If you get there in good time, you'll find the reports of the celebrity service almost every day. They're a little late by the time we get them, but they're good enough for us. They announce imminent arrivals on occasion.'

Plageot smiled grimly. 'Never underestimate the ingenuity of the trained criminal mind,' he said to De Valde.

'Remarkable,' muttered De Valde.

Just then Monsieur Kellerer of the police laboratory entered. He wore a white lab coat.

'Aha!' said Plageot. 'Now for the incriminating evidence!'

'Are you sure this is the correct article?' asked the perplexed Kellerer.

'Positive,' said De Valde. 'I supervised its removal from the sink in the men's toilet myself and transported it here.'

'What's wrong with it?' Plageot demanded.

Kellerer opened it. 'It's empty,' he said 'It's just an empty box.'

'But that wire leading from it,' Plageot stuttered, 'does it signify nothing?'

'Nothing at all. It's just soldered on to the outside.'

'Could it not have contained something which dissolved under the water?'

'Out of the question.'

De Valde began laughing, at first softly, then hysterically.

Plageot's irritated question, 'What are you laughing at, De Valde?' only made matters worse.

Kellerer felt that the laughter would be contagious and prudently left with the evidence, a smile growing on his face.

'For God's sake, De Valde, pull yourself together!' yelled Plageot.

'The idea ... of your breaking the world's record for the two hundred metres ... in order to make an empty box harmless ... by immersing it under water in the gents' convenience. Oh, it's too good, too good!' De Valde sobbed, holding on to the side of the desk.

'De Valde! Return to your office!'

But it was too late. The laughter was sweeping like a forest fire through the assassins. De Valde left with difficulty. As Plageot stood before his desk, tears of rage filled his eyes.

'Silence! Silence! I demand silence!' he bellowed like a child in a tantrum. 'I shall arrest you,' he announced, when the noise had calmed down a little.

'On what grounds?' asked Zvoinitch.

'I'll – I'll find grounds ...'

'Presumably we'll stand trial, whatever grounds you find. The courtroom would be an ideal place for us to ventilate this story, perhaps even to immortalize it.'

'Are you blackmailing me?'

'Not at all,' said Zvoinitch. 'Blackmail entails a financial transaction. If we have to go to court, we will have to swear to tell the truth. I am only threatening to do exactly what I have to do on oath in any case.'

Plageot looked around like a madman.

'All right,' he said. 'I'll send you away, but it'll be to the Sahara, to the Chad – Ubangi-Shari, where the heat is unbearable.'

'Monsieur Plageot,' Zvoinitch replied calmly, 'we are very conscious of the fact that every time we are sent away from France it is at the public expense. If you wreak your vengeance on us by sending us to Equatorial Africa, it will not be we who suffer so much as the poor taxpayer. The fare is considerably more expensive. I should hate to think that our good-natured romp would end up as a burden on the man in the street, simply because your feelings are hurt.'

These particular sentiments, expressed with such solicitous nobility, were too much for Plageot, who just sat down and wept.

After a moment, he rang for Mademoiselle Pelbec.

'The documents, Mademoiselle,' he said wearily, 'for Corsica.'

'Here they are,' replied Mademoiselle Pelbec, laying them on his desk.

'You had them ready?'

'Oh, yes, since I saw in the papers that the Imam was arriving.'

'I am back-dating them to yesterday, before the Imam's arrival, for the record,' Plageot said, handing them the documents.

The situation was delicate. The assassins just nodded politely and left, not even deigning to express their thanks for fear of arousing another storm.

As Plageot sat alone, his soul was a desert. He heard laughter from the office next door, and he could not conceive that the reason for it might be other than the story of his disgrace on its journey round the vast agglomeration of buildings. He grew grim, and his mouth set into a powerful and melancholy curve. Such things are sent to try a man, to temper his steel. With a painful sob still in his heart, he gazed at the sky and knew that he would go far.

'Mademoiselle Pelbec,' he called militarily, 'bring me the deportation files nineteen and twenty-one, at once!'

It is only in fairy stories that chastening experience makes a lasting difference in a man's character. Monsieur Plageot became, if anything, harder and more disagreeable. He used every opportunity to discredit both De Valde and Kellerer without really analysing his reasons for hating them. His relations with Annik were cold, contrived, and artificial: when he wished to be hurtful, he called her a second-rate actress. Only in one regard did the incident of the six assassins affect him. Knowing that they would never retire and that he would have to wait for them to die, he never again opened his morning paper without a sickening trepidation.

The Gift of a Dog

Angela looked at herself in the mirror, and made a cool assessment of her market value. She was naked, and a few drops of bath water still sparkled on her shoulders and on her arms. Tomorrow she was to be married, and it was the last opportunity to look at herself with quite such detachment. She lowered the lights, since the white glare suddenly seemed to her indecent. Once the room was plunged into chiaroscuro, she took her place before the mirror again, and noticed how flattering photography can be when the art of darkness implements the craft of light.

Her husband would get more than he deserved. Her body was full and ripe, and yet discreet in its opulence. From all angles she was lovely, and she looked herself in the eye with a melting gratitude which appeared to her the very quintessence of ardent femininity. Then her gaze hardened, and she accused herself with a stare of undiluted breeding.

'Fool,' she said aloud. 'Fool.'

She was twenty-six, an age at which a person who suspects that they will never marry begins to feel the earliest confirmation of a lifelong solitude. Inversely, it is an age at which those who desire children more than any source of fertility begin to sense the first pangs of desperation. She had been engaged almost for ever to Bryan Upstreet. They had known each other as children, and detested each other. Their parents knew each other, and seemed to like each other. Then adolescent schooling had intervened, and they had gone their separate ways for a while: he to a celebrated public school in the Midlands, she to a Gothic academy on the cliffs of Kent. When they met again, they regarded one another with the shy affection which the love-hate of children can engender in young adults. Part of their relationship was already the result of longevity, a quality which is usually the monopoly of much older people. What they never realized, however, is that their schools had cunningly prepared them for just such a marriage, for just such a distant, sensible love. Their accents were the identical clipped one of the English upper classes, with its irritating distortions of the rough majesty of Chaucer's and Shakespeare's tongue, its whimsical short-cuts, its triggered vowels, and its sudden baroque overshoot, investing a single sound with a rainbow of colours where, grammatically and aesthetically, there is room for only one.

They held hands at dances until it became a habit, linked by their sense of belonging, not necessarily to one another, but to an established norm. But naturally, the upper classes would never have become the upper classes if they had behaved like that from the beginning. As all things must have a season, so must decadence keep rise and renascence apart. The elegance of today is merely the drift of yester-day's lack of scruples. It was the Honourable Gyles Car-chester-Fielding who proved the point, and that more than once. He was, of course, Lord Sparshot's heir. Of course.

He had yé-yéd his way into Angela's life, as he had rumbaed and tangoed and watusied his way into other more or less innocent lives, at one of those huge balls which still keep up the illusion of languid wealth in the mist-filled valleys of the English countryside. Looking at herself naked in the mirror, Angela remembered the absurd dash through the night in the open Italian roadster, on the crown of the road, ignoring the urgent headlamps of the cars driving in the opposite direction, ignoring the cold, ignoring everything. She remembered their registering at the hotel in Maidenhead (apt name), and Gyles's threatening to sign in as Mr and Mrs Smith.

'I dare you to!' she had laughed.

He had done just that, and the night porter, without batting an eyelid, had replied, 'Room twenty-four as usual, sir?'

She might have known it then, but she didn't care. She was full of champagne and night air and what she liked to think was madness. In the room, he had tried to undress her, but her breeding had come back to her in a sudden surge, an admonition from some faraway nursery. She had struggled, and he had lit a cigarette, a Turkish one specially made for his father by a firm of ancient artisans in the City. There was a look of amusement in his eyes as he studied her reactions, a look which was a challenge and a promise of forbidden delights.

Gently, but quite savagely, he began to tease her. Had she ever been abroad? Had she slept with many men before? Was she a virgin? The questions purred out as though they were part of an interview by a kindly doctor. Suddenly the embarrassment of ignorance outweighed the embarrassment of nudity, and with the controlled and automatic coldness she might at other times have applied to a domestic science course at school, she stepped out of her evening dress, let her slip fall to the ground, undid her brassière, and hung it on the back of a chair.

He made no move, since he still had half a cigarette to finish.

After an agonizing moment, he said, 'You have lovely breasts, d'you know that?'

'Have I?'

Comparison gave her a curious feeling of comfort, of confidence. He drew deeply on his cigarette, and ruined her effect by watching the smoke rings climb slowly towards the ceiling and disintegrate.

'You don't expect me to go the whole hog, do you?' she said in her clipped accent, sounding obscenely more dressed than ever.

He shrugged his shoulders.

'I tried to help you, but you wouldn't let me,' he replied, sitting down on a chair the wrong way as though it were a horse.

In a fit of anger (an anger she drove herself into; she couldn't have done it otherwise), she removed her shoes and stockings and struggled out of her girdle. Her contortions made him laugh good-naturedly.

'What are you laughing at?' she asked, hostile.

'Woman is the loveliest bloody thing in creation,' he chuckled, 'and yet to keep up appearances she has to imprison herself in the most ludicrous damned garments a perverted mind could invent. You look as though you're some obscure African animal during the mating season.'

She stood there in her panties, holding her girdle in her hand, where it now looked like some monstrous ring of crumpled Elastoplast, fit for a blister on a giant's finger, and stared at her seducer, still fully dressed in his white tie and tails, laughing behind a cloud of blue smoke, and it was too much for her. She burst into tears.

'Let's go home,' he said, wearily, preparing to rise. 'Where d'you live?'

She was crying bitterly, but the tears only came with difficulty, so that she made the pathetic noises of one who is trying to restrain all emotion.

'You're hysterical,' he added gratuitously, 'or else you're far too young for this sort of thing. I'm sorry. I made a mistake.'

Her fury returned. She shouted something to the effect that he had done nothing of the sort. Half turning her back to him, she pulled off her panties with the panic of one who is diving for the first time.

'Gorgeous,' he said.

'What's gorgeous?' she cried, her back still towards him, and then, turning to face him, she went on in her peremptory, violent tone of voice, 'Is that all you can bloody well say, "gorgeous"?'

While she stood there as God and Mrs Symington-Stobart had made her, her body shaken by spasmodic sobs, he smiled, calculatedly stubbed out his cigarette, and began slowly to undo his tie.

She was naked again now that she remembered it, but in quite a different frame of mind.

'You've got a lot older, and a bit wiser . . . perhaps,' she told herself. It was no use linking yourself for life with a man like Gyles Carchester-Fielding, even if one day it meant being Lady Sparshot. That was inviting unhappiness. That was locking yourself away in the bosom of some county where people had nothing else to do but speculate on who's sleeping with who, and where the endless movement of the horses under them turns idle minds to thoughts of copulation. Marriage was a base from which sorties could be made into dangerous waters, but it was un-English and, above all, un-Victorian to confuse the functions of husbands and those of lovers. After all, it was to avoid just such confusion that the architecture of country houses possessed such labyrinthine networks of corridors, in defiance of logic. She thought of Bryan, with his schoolboy glasses and his slight tendency to stutter. He had passed the Foreign Office exam with exemplary doggedness, and already he dressed with the flagrant sobriety of an embryo ambassador. His head rose like a great lozenge, covered with a generous coat of pomaded yellow hair, parted just off centre with incredible accuracy, the white line of his scalp showing damp and clean and healthy. Already he affected the slight forward stoop of the inquisitive, kind, helpful old man, one eyebrow always slightly higher than the other in an eagerness to be titillated by humour, receptive to all manifestations of subtlety. This tendency towards social grace was underlined by a nervous habit of repeating the word 'yes' with metronomic regularity while someone else was talking, until such time as a negative response was called for, when the 'yes' would abruptly change to an understanding and compassionate 'no', usually just a fraction too late to convince the talker that he was really listening.

And this was the man to whom she was surrendering her half-awakened femininity, a man who would no doubt display on the carnal couch all those qualities of tact and politeness which had made him a natural for the Foreign Service.

Her reverie was interrupted by the entrance of her mother, a lady with a face resembling a flowered porcelain plate chipped in places. Her eyes had almost disappeared in the creamy folds of age, and her tiny nose stood like a crooked finger, in the centre of it all, powder clogging the pores, so that it radiated an unhealthy clownish whiteness.

'What are you doing there, darling, in your birthday suit?' inquired Mrs Symington-Stobart.

Angela ran for a towel, and draped herself in it. For some unaccountable reason, she felt an embarrassment in front of someone who had seen her undressed more often than anyone else.

'Nothing, Mother,' she replied with some annoyance.

'Isn't it all *too* thrilling?'

'No. Frankly it isn't. I'm wondering if I'm not making the silliest mistake of my life.'

'Oh, we all wonder that just before our wedding day – still, it's better that you should say that to yourself now than later.'

'You sound just like Bryan, Mummy,' Angela grunted.

'What *do* you mean?' asked Mrs Symington-Stobart, who was a great one for emphasis.

'When I came back after that adventure with Gyles Carchester-Fielding—'

'Oh, don't talk about it!'

'Bryan said exactly what you just said, or almost – "better get it out of your system now, old girl, than later, when we're married".'

It was a cruel imitation of her fiancé, and it made Mrs Symington-Stobart sigh, but the ever-present and tremulous smile quickly returned as a barrier against the shocks of existence.

'When you reach my time of life,' she muttered, 'you begin to know a little about the value of things. Well, good night, my dearest wedding girl. I just came down to kiss you, and to have a chat if you wanted one, that's all.'

Angela accepted the kiss with stony resignation, and, as she was obviously in no mood for a chat, her mother left, on the wings of a deeper sigh than usual.

In deference to her imminent marriage, Angela slept well and dreamlessly.

The next morning was entirely hateful. First of all, a large and throbbing spot began to develop on her cheek, a place where no jewellery or displacement of her coiffure could possibly conceal it. Her wedding dress no longer seemed to fit as it had at the dressmaker's. Mrs Symington-Stobart was on her knees behind her daughter, pushing and pulling, and the occasional appearance of Major Symington-Stobart, half dressed and already wearing the hideous, humourless grin of one with a stiff collar half a size too small, did nothing to alleviate the tension in the house. Younger brothers Oliver and Eric flitted about in their underwear, imbued with an irreverent sense of occasion which led them to crack a few lewd jokes at the expense of their sister, who began to feel like a fatted calf prepared for the sacrifice.

By the time the cortège arrived at the church, tempers were

frayed, and it was with a real shock that Angela saw a small Italian sports car parked just in front of them. She looked furtively among the ranks of romantic spinsters and sentimental housewives who hover around weddings with the same clinical attention which better equilibrated people apply to traffic accidents.

'Cuckoo,' said Gyles Carchester-Fielding, outflanking his quarry.

The Symington-Stobarts looked at the intruder with displeasure, and Angela, as virginal as a newly launched yacht before her despoiler, said,

'What are you doing here?'

'I can't stay for the ceremony, alas,' murmured Gyles in his most seductive manner, his eyes brimful of mischief. 'I'm not much of an ornament in church in any case – and Dad's up from Howth – he's got a new popsy in town – but I have brought you this—'

He opened his overcoat, and produced an immense puppy of some obscure breed. In spite of herself, Angela smiled, and the sentimental ladies cooed with pleasure.

'Oh, it's adorable!' she cried. 'Is it a he or a she?'

'I wouldn't be caught dead giving you a she,' said Gyles. 'It's a breed Dad's trying to develop, and which he calls a Leominster hound. It's very rare. As rare as you are. There he is, with all my love.' And he ran over to his car, and drove away.

There was a quick conference as to what to do with the unexpected wedding present. Brother Oliver volunteered to try and smuggle him into the church, to sit near the entrance, and to take him out at the first sign of trouble. The major wasn't comfortable enough to object, although he did hiss something about it being a 'poor show', and Mrs Symington-Stobart openly asked if 'that gay Lothario' had not done enough harm.

'Mother, please!'

The clergyman succeeded in conveying in his address that marriage was a massive drudgery, a state of thankless self-sacrifice, a banquet of bitter pills, ended only by the parting of death, which, in his bleak voice, sounded like a blessed relief after the drab epic of misunderstood gestures and fragmentary joys. The first and only one to protest this jeremiad was the dog, who started howling in a deep Dantesque diapason far beyond his years. People looked around in scandalized amazement, while the parson's granite eyes filled with water. Oliver, seeing that the dog had not yet reached the age of control, rushed it out of the church, but the breed had been conceived by Lord Sparshot for use in pastoral sports, and now the poor anchorless animal gave full voice to its unhappiness as the contradictory and bewildering odours of the street began to tease its nostrils. Oliver was quite unable to gauge whether the howling could be heard in church, but it seemed hardly likely. He was wrong.

Bryan became more and more agitated, and shot Angela some sideways glances suggesting that she must be responsible for this mockery of his wedding. Angela took refuge behind an expression of simple piety, but when one or two of the younger members of the congregation began to giggle, she felt her control deserting her. It was a nervous reaction. Her diaphragm was pulsating by itself, and there was nothing she could do about it. She began to laugh. The clergyman, whose well of austerity was bottomless, only uttered in the intervals between her outbursts, and the consciousness of being waited for only made mattters worse for her. When Bryan eventually turned to her with the ring, she thought he was going to break her finger. During the ceremonial kiss, she could feel the heat of his fury in the tension of his lips.

At last the ceremony was over, but the puppy was not to know that. He punctuated the muddy music of the organ as they all filed out with an even more desperate insistence than before. The reception took place in one of the larger and more impersonal hotels, and here the dog was able to run around freely, and try to find a familiar aroma among the forest of legs. Occasionally he would look up with an expression of tragic gratitude as a kind hand moved to pat his head, but then he would stagger off with the uncoordinated clumsiness of a very young thing, and yap at the entire roomful with unbearable stridency. There was an unpleasant quality to Major Symington-Stobart's voice as he read out the telegrams to which the puppy was evidently allergic, for he began to howl. Such is the masochism of the English when faced with the unhappiness of lesser creatures who are forced to exist without the comfort of verbal communications that all sympathy quickly went to the unhappy little dog, and an atmosphere of hostility developed towards any human interference with the dear little animal's peace of mind.

By the time the cake was cut, it might as well have been the dog's wedding – in fact, he seized the first slice from the plate in a movement as fast as it was ruthless, and tore it apart on the floor as though it were alive. The guests found his voracity quite irresistible, while Angela screamed as her hand was caught between the handle of the knife and Bryan's larger, hotter hand, pressing down in fury on the cake. The speeches and toasts were all of a quality which serve to make of weddings the real tests of the truth of love. Dr Upstreet was, if anything, less inspired than Major Symington-Stobart. In place of the latter's endless hesitations and protestations of inadequacy at this sort of function, Dr Upstreet brought an assurance, a power, and a clarity which were wasted on the subject at hand. He reminisced at length about the first childhood symptoms which led his wife and he to deduce that their only son had the makings of an ambassador. One anecdote after the other was presented for the delectation of the assembly, anecdotes which had lost their savour, and even their point, with the passage of time to all but the devoted biographer, who now laughed heartily, and alone, as he recalled each and every one. It was Angela's turn to glance with cool hostility at her new husband, who could willingly have strangled his father during the long half hour of his discourse. Eventually the time came for the young couple to leave. They waved goodbye to the party as graciously as possible.

'Do tell me, what are you going to call the dog?' asked a lady who was covering the wedding for a woman's magazine.

'Casanova,' replied Angela, without thinking.

The honeymoon took place in a hotel at Folkestone. There was no question of going abroad because Bryan was working very hard at the Foreign Office, and expected to be posted overseas in any case. The hotel staff was brimming over with that odious complicity which surrounds honeymoons – they were full of winks and smiles and sugary understanding, even if they were rather taken aback by the arrival of the dog, since pets were strictly forbidden in the hotel, even on a leash.

Nevertheless, rather than cast a shadow over the affecting picture of intact illusions, the administration stretched a point.

'Keep the little fellow as quiet as possible, though,' exhorted the head porter. 'Otherwise we'll have other guests wishing to bring their pets.'

'That's what we call a precedent,' said Bryan, with a pedantic little snigger.

'Absolutely correct, sir,' snapped the porter, who knew a patrician when he saw one.

Angela wondered what she had ever seen in her husband. Her train of thought persisted, and when the door eventually closed on their cherished solitude, they failed to rush into each other's arms. She sat down in front of her dressing-room mirror, and looked at her tired face with its throbbing spot. There was something unhealthy in the relationship between her and mirrors in general. They seemed to be her counsellors, and, as always, the advice they gave was corrupt, slanted, impure. She could see Bryan hovering around in the background, pretending to busy himself with this and that. He was furbishing his ill-humour. The trip down in the rented limousine had passed in virtual silence, with a brief discussion about whether the window ought to be closed or slightly ajar as the high point in this first meeting of minds destined to last as long as life itself. Suddenly Angela felt a wet nose against her knee, and she vented all her frustrated love on Casanova, whose uncertain orange eyes shifted hysterically in both thankfulness and a desire for more and yet more affection. Bryan began to feel the pangs of jealousy, which grew no matter how intensely he told himself not to be ridiculous. Eventually he tried to alienate the affection of the dog by squatting at the other end of the room and attempting to look playful.

Casanova had been bred by the savage peer to know only one master, however, and the fact that he had been placed in Angela's hands was more than a token. He embarrassingly ignored Bryan, who continued to bounce up and down on his haunches, and make discreet dog noises. Discreet because Bryan was a great one for order, and the request of the hotel authorities had already become law as far as he was concerned.

Casanova shot him one or two suspicious glances, then suddenly barked a great bark from somewhere in prehistory, and flew at Bryan.

'He bit me!' Bryan rose to his full height, and his dignity closed over him like an envelope.

'Oh, darling, he's only a puppy!' cried Angela.

'Look, he's drawn blood!'

'Let me kiss it better.'

Angela stopped on her way to her husband to deal Casanova one or two accurate blows on the muzzle. Casanova winced, and gazed at her with adoration.

She kissed Bryan's finger, and then they kissed each other on the mouth. The dog, outraged by the sight of such harmony, began to bark.

'Quiet!' commanded Angela, and Casanova dropped to the floor like a small sack.

'I'll ring for some iodine,' said Bryan. 'The bloody thing's probably got rabies.'

They dined in their room, because every time they tried to leave in order to go to the dining room, Casanova howled. They toasted each other dutifully in champagne, and when the time came to go to bed, they undressed as though they were changing into bathing costumes. Angela had never consciously seen Bryan without glasses before, and he looked quite different. His features for the first time resembled those of his parents, and she had a disturbing vision of all the relatives who were sharing her marriage bed in spirit. His underwear was not of the most modern kind. There was a baby-blue and silky discretion about it which was more eloquent about his mind than about his body. His pyjamas were striped, red and black, and it seemed to her that even for the night he wrapped himself up in loyalty to a club.

She fluffed out her hair, so that it fell in virginal simplicity and abundance round her shoulders, and slipped discreetly into a diaphanous froth of lavender and lace, garnished with little bows of innocence. A hissing noice attracted her attention, and she turned in time to see Bryan using a breath-sweetening spray.

'Oh, it's cold!' she said, as she eased herself into bed.

'We'll soon alter that,' he replied, and then visibly blushed, feeling he had gone too far. Timidly, he moved towards her, and toyed for a moment with her fair hair.

'You're the loveliest woman I've ever seen,' he said, rather formally.

'Thank you,' she said.

After a moment, he asked if, in her opinion, there wasn't a little too much light.

She agreed, and turned out her bedside lamp.

Under cover of darkness, he approached her stealthily, and she felt the proximity of his mouth as she was inundated in a haze of peppermint and cloves. Then she felt a great weight upon her, but it didn't feel like the weight of a man.

'Get off the bed!' hissed Bryan. 'Down! Down! Go to your cushion!'

In the dark, Angela felt the same high-strung reaction she had experienced in church, and she began to laugh helplessly.

'You're laughing again,' said Bryan, in a reproachful and bitter voice.

'I can't help it.' She only laughed the more when she felt a paw on her breast, and a hot and glutinous tongue began to lather her face.

The lights went on on Bryan's side of the bed. He put on his glasses, and stood up, absolutely furious.

'I'll have it put to sleep!' he shouted. 'Get down! D'you hear me?'

'Oh, darling,' she pleaded, 'he's only a puppy!'

'You'll be saying that when he's ten years old, and sharing your bed, and I'll be in the kennel!'

This made her laugh again.

'It's not funny!' he yelled. 'It's a tragic truth. Now get that damned hound to obey you. He won't listen to me. He only bites me!'

'Down! Go cushions. Go shut-eye,' said Angela.

Guiltily, Casanova dropped off the bed, and loped over to his cushion. Bryan followed him with his eyes, and suddenly shouted again.

'Look!'

There was a huge puddle on the floor, and the ornate bauble hanging on the end of the curtain cord had been masticated out of all recognition. Chips of wood and bits of material lay all over the place.

'I'll have to pay for all that!' screamed Bryan. 'And he's only just started. We're here for a week. He'll have time to destroy the hotel!'

There was a peremptory banging on the wall.

'D'you hear?' whispered Bryan.

'What?'

'The neighbours. It'll be the manager next. Turn out the lights.'

'It's your light that's on.'

'Oh, yes.' Bryan turned to the dog.

'Now stay there!' he commanded, with an admonishing finger.

Casanova growled, and Bryan turned out the lights. Almost immediately there was a crash of glass. They both knew that a vase of expensive flowers had been placed on a small occasional table with the compliments of the management. Angela started laughing again, a mixture of laughter and tears, and Bryan hadn't the heart to turn on the lights again. In his practical mind, he hoped that the water from the flowers had fallen on the dog's puddle, and that the whole might be put down to an accident. After all, accidents can happen to anyone, and the manager might even be constrained to apologize for having placed the flowers on such a fragile table.

The night was ruined, and with it, the honeymoon.

Back in town, in their new little house, they tried a new system, impossible in the hotel. They put the dog's basket in the corridor. Their morale was boosted by a sense of ownership. There was a little garden to make plans for, furniture inherited, given and bought. They were at home.

The first night, Bryan was absolutely charming. He was determined to make his marriage work in spite of its disastrous start. A day at the office, away from domestic problems, had put him in a good mood, and he had rediscovered the feeling of being his own master. He brought Angela a gift of roses, and he even listened to her woes with admirable serenity. They had apparently lost Mrs Bradlock, the daily help, because she didn't like the way the dog looked at her.

'Never mind, I'll do all the washing up until we find a dog-loving daily,' said Bryan.

Angela was touched by this wonderful resilience, and began to trust her own judgement again. She cooked dinner, which they ate congenially and even happily, and Bryan dared to speculate on the arrangements they would have to make if there should be an addition to the family.

They went to bed aglow with good will and a sense of adventure without which love is an empty thing. The striped pyjamas now looked gay and enterprising, while the waft of peppermint was like a breath of spring.

They turned out the lights, and found each other in the dark with joy and with relief.

Then the scratching started – scratching and the falling of a heavy object.

'What's that?' asked Bryan.

'Oh, darling, who cares?'

'I care.'

The magic had gone again.

Bryan opened the door, and when he came back, he announced with self-righteous economy, 'The Queen Anne grandfather clock your dad gave us is scratched all the way down its front, and the top fell off. It's in smithereens.'

'The clock Dad gave us?' Angela cried, and tumbled out of bed. She found Casanova, and whipped him hard. He whimpered a little and crawled into his new basket, which was already only half a basket, since gnawed wickerwork could be found all over the house. Guilty, Angela had to take it out on someone.

'Who ever left the door to the dining room open?' she asked.

'I expect to live in a house, not in prison.'

'It's only logical, isn't it, when there's a puppy around – to shut the doors, I mean.'

'Logic is a very relative advantage when dealing with a mad dog – I beg your pardon, a mad puppy.'

'Oh, for Christ's sake, you're at home, not at the Foreign Office!'

'At all events, it wasn't I who left the dining room door open.'

'Are you accusing me?'

Another night was evidently written off, and it ended in the early hours of the morning, when Bryan issued an ultimatum. She would have to choose between him and Casanova. There was no other way. The dog would have to be given away or destroyed.

The fact that, in his mental and physical exhaustion, he had suggested that the dog be destroyed revolted Angela, and she held it against him at the climax of every argument from then on. As a compromise, they tried sending it away for a while, and Mrs Symington-Stobart, with a mother's instinct that all was not well with her daughter's marriage, agreed to try and take Casanova in.

He was fetched by the chauffeur, and succeeded in destroying an armrest and half a seat in the family Rolls-Royce during the short trip. The Symington-Stobarts did what they could, putting up with every inconvenience, only coming to the end of their tether when Casanova killed Mrs Symington-Stobart's Pekingese, and brought the corpse to her in his mouth like a well-trained hunting dog while she was playing bridge in the drawing room with three other ladies. She had to enter a nursing home for a complete rest after the tragedy, but her husband, furious, could find Casanova nowhere. He had run away.

During his absence, there was a strange, oppressive silence in Angela's house. While Bryan was at the office, she began to miss the dog, at first surreptitiously and unbelievingly, then overtly. Now that she was free to do what she wished with her day, she wished to do nothing. She began to wear that hard, brittle look on her face which unsatisfied women have, and there was something forced about her casualness. Even her relaxation seemed to be carefully planned, and her conversation was forbiddingly cool.

When Bryan came home, her unhappiness found a target. It was as though, by now, the dog was almost more conspicuous by its absence than it had been before. There were now no disasters to deflect their attention from the long silence of their suppers and the stillness of their nights. They were not married. They were not even living together. They were living under the same roof.

It was while Bryan was away one day that Angela knew

temptation. She dialled Gyles' number, and replaced the receiver before anyone had had time to answer. Her cheeks were burning with a sense of danger, and she experienced a kind of nefarious exaltation by the rashness of her deed.

The next day, cold as ice, she went further, and was informed that he'd be back about eight. Would she leave a number? No, she wouldn't. Eight was a little late for her. She'd try again tomorrow.

She did. Gyles appeared to be delighted, but not surprised, to hear her voice.

'How's the pup shaping?'

'Oh, very well, thank you. He's grown a lot. He's in the country at the moment.'

'He's essentially a country dog.'

'Yes. I know.'

'Treat him roughly. They're very capricious dogs, and they love ill-treatment. It's turned out a very feminine breed. Incidentally, what did you call the brute?'

'Casanova.'

There was a moment of silence.

'Peculiarly apt,' Gyles said. 'Incidentally, how's married life?' he went on.

'What's it to you?' replied Angela.

'I want to know, in case I'm ever tempted to continue the line.'

'It has its pros and its cons.'

'What's he like in bed?'

'You are the limit, honestly,' said Angela, flushing with excitement.

'Why? Isn't it important?' asked Gyles, innocently.

'It is, very important. If you must know, he's absolutely great.'

'I shouldn't have asked you that question.'

'Why on earth not?' Angela was abruptly broadminded.

'Because it's very disappointing if it's true. And because it's very sad and very brave if it isn't.'

Once again there was a pause, a long one.

'What's your phone number?' asked Gyles eventually.

'Typical.'

'What is?'

'You're too lazy and too conceited even to look me up in the book.'

And she replaced the receiver, and imagined his voice calling, 'Angela . . . Angela!' at the other end.

Her reverie was cut short when the phone rang.

'It can't be him already,' she thought, 'unless he'd looked up the number before.'

'Hello?' she said.

It was her father, who chided her for spending her whole life on the phone. 'Simply couldn't get through to you,' he grumbled, and then told her the whole lamentable story of the death of the Pekingese.

'But where is Casanova now?' asked Angela, agitated.

'You really are extraordinary, Angela,' Major Symington-Stobart said. 'Li-Pong is dead, your mother's been transported to Smallwood Hill Nursing Home in an advanced state of shock, and your only concern is the whereabouts of that confounded whelp.'

'I want to know where he is, Daddy,' Angela insisted disagreeably.

'D'you know he's practically destroyed the Rolls? The tennis court's a complete mess, the petit point armchairs are beyond repair, the whole house is filled to the rafters with cotton-wool and smashed porcelain, and he practically took away one of Ambrose's fingers. If Ambrose hadn't been with us for such a long time—'

'Daddy!' interrupted Angela, with menacing insistence.

'What?'

'I asked you a question.'

'I haven't the faintest idea where the blasted dog is, and I care less! I've informed the police, as a public duty. I hope they shoot it.' And he slammed the receiver down.

Angela walked around the house in agitation for an hour afterwards. If there was any love in her, it was now devoted to Casanova. She felt needed, and helpless, and the tears rolled down her cheeks. When she lit a cigarette, she noticed that her hands were trembling. At length, she came to roost as usual at her dressing table, and in her mirror she saw the portrait of a mature woman deeply and unhappily in love.

She had not long to meditate before there was a soft scratching and whimpering at the front door. She rushed to open it. There stood Casanova, shivering, and wagging a contrite tail. Angela dropped to her knees and embraced him as Penelope must have embraced Ulysses. When she recovered her composure, she took him to the bathroom, and rubbed down his wet coat with the first towel which came to hand, which happened to be Bryan's face towel, with his initials in one corner. Then she gave him some hot milk and made him lie in front of the gas fire in the drawing room. He repaid all this attention by licking her face with feeble insistence, and by making an enormous mess in the entrance hall while in transit from bathroom to fireplace.

When Bryan came home, he stepped in the mess, but didn't lose his composure. He was in a blatantly good mood, and, leaving his soiled shoes by the umbrella rack, he entered the drawing room. The dog growled weakly.

'Dog's back, I see,' he said cheerfully.

Angela told him the saga as dramatically as possible, but he seemed to only half take it in, being remarkably undisturbed by even the most horrifying details of what had happened.

'Well, I've got some news too,' he volunteered, when he was politely sure that his wife had run out of steam. 'I've got a posting at last. Sir Norman Guildford-Nasmith is taking us with him when he goes to Baghdad as ambassador next month.'

'Baghdad!' Angela was amazed.

'Yes, Baghdad. It'll be two years at least. It's pretty hot out there, I gather. You'll have to do quite a bit of shopping. I've already ordered an Anglo-Arab dictionary.'

'Baghdad. Where is it?' Angela asked.

'Iraq, I believe.' Bryan sobered up, and assumed a tone of understanding with some difficulty. 'Oh, then there's the question of Casanova,' he went on. It was so unlike him to call the dog by his name that both Casanova and Angela looked at him.

'Obviously we can't take him with us,' Bryan explained, 'because of the quarantine laws. If we ever take him out of the country, we can't get him back in without six months in quarantine, and that's hardly fair on any dog. It represents three and a half years in a dog's life.'

'Oh, that's why you're in such a good mood,' murmured Angela.

'No, no, those are the cold facts, my dear,' he replied. 'After all, I know how attached you are to the ... to Casanova, and I'd do anything to make it possible for him to come too, but unfortunately ...'

'You're a bloody hypocrite,' said Angela, quietly. 'You hate that puppy, and you're absolutely delighted to be able to break the bad news to me. It gives you a sadistic pleasure to come in here and be able to have the inevitable on your side. Well, I've got some news for you. I'm not going to Baghdad. You can go alone.'

'You are my wife,' said Bryan, 'and you are coming to Baghdad with me.'

'No, I'm not.'

'And what is more, we are dining with Sir Norman and Lady Guildford-Nasmith tomorrow evening. It's a great honour to have been asked. That is the reason for my delight if you must know ... the reason for my alleged sadism.'

'You'll never guess who rang up today, right out of the blue,' Angela purred, changing her tactic.

Bryan left the room.

'Aren't you interested?' she called out hotly.

He reappeared with a rag and a pan.

'I'm doing my job as a domesticated animal,' he said softly. 'I'm going to clean up my rival's mess, which is smelling up the house.'

'Gyles Carchester-Fielding.'

'What about him?'

'He called.'

'The very man,' said Bryan. 'It's poetic justice. Casanova can go right back where he came from.'

Casanova looked over his shoulder at that moment and caught Bryan's eye. It may have been just the result of hearing his name, which he was beginning to recognize, but Bryan saw there a glint of almost human resentment. For a second Bryan felt like apologizing, but chased away the idiotic thought with irritation, and sank to his knees with an audible sound of effort.

Angela cried and fretted most of the night, protesting that

she wouldn't go to Baghdad although in her heart she knew very well that she would. The idea was more than exciting. He sat in bed, storming at times, and at others pretending to read a book he had already read and found boring. He was even tempted to hit her once, but contained himself when he visualized the chain of reproaches stretching into the indeterminate future. What was more remarkable than the family row, however, was the fact that Casanova behaved perfectly through all this, lying quietly on his cushion, and never once barking or even whimpering.

Breakfast was eaten in silence.

'I'll be back in good time,' said Bryan, as he left for the office. 'Just lay my dinner jacket out if you will, please. The Guildford-Nasmiths live in Chelsea. Dinner's at eight sharp.'

Angela spent her day telephoning her girlfriends, and telling them that she was off to Baghdad very shortly.

'Oh, my dear, how simply thrilling!'

'Isn't it? Bryan's landed an awfully good job there. It's only a first step, of course, but they say Sir Norman's an absolute dear – we're dining there tonight – and the word is that Sir Norman's an absolute natural for Paris or Washington eventually – and as he thinks the world of Bryan . . .'

At about half past six, Angela began to run a bath. She had laid out Bryan's dinner-jacket neatly on his side of the bed. Next to it, she had placed a clean shirt, underwear, his cuff links and dress studs, his evening socks, and his mentholated mouth-spray. On her way to the bathroom, she noticed Casanova standing near the front door.

'Do you want out, my pet?' she asked, astonished. He had never wanted to go out before, having been quite satisfied with the carpet. He wagged his tail. She opened the front door, and watched him go over to the hedge, where he lifted a leg.

'We'll make you a respectable dog yet,' she said, and added, 'you just stay there and guard the house while Mummy takes a bath.'

Bryan came home while Angela was in her bath, and no sooner had he closed the little gate leading from the street into the garden than Casanova leaped at him with such violence that he staggered, and his glasses fell off on to the gravel path.

In a blind terror, he sank on to all fours, conscious of the dog's proximity, and began searching for his glasses. The dog seized him by the back of the neck as its instinct told it to seize a wild boar or a stag, and once he was on the ground, it dug its teeth deep, and tore at the vulnerable flesh with the frantic discipline of an animal obeying the laws of nature. When its work was done, it sniffed with apparent disinterest at Bryan's motionless form, and sidled back into the house as though there were nothing better to do.

Angela came out of the bathroom naked but for her shower cap, and walked about her room. She didn't even bother to draw the curtains. Because there was no one else to talk to, she talked to Casanova, who looked at her with pleasure.

Carefully she made up her face for the soirée.

'The old boy's running it a bit fine, don't you think?'

Casanova wagged his tail again, once.

'A quarter to seven, and no sign of him. That's not like him, is it? Breakfast, seven-thirty on the dot. Key in the door, six-thirty PM, regular as clockwork. God, I look tired. Bloody silly. The night is meant for sleeping, or . . . oh well, let's not talk about that, my Casanova, even if it is one tiny bit your fault. Love. *Amour. Amour. Die Liebe.* What's it in dog, I wonder?'

Seven o'clock rang from a neighbouring church.

'We'll be late! Well, it won't be me to blame for once.'

Her annoyance began to grow, and, instead of putting on her evening dress, she lay down on her bed. It would be good for him to find her in the nude.

'What, aren't you ready yet?' he would ask, and then, as a scandalized afterthought, 'At least draw the curtains if you're going to lie around like that!'

While she was engaged in these attractively perverse thoughts, the bed gave an ugly wrench, and Casanova was up and looking at her, his head lowered.

'What are you doing there? Get down at once! At once!' The dog gave no sign of being willing to obey her.

She smiled, a little frightened in spite of herself, and said, 'All right, stay up here then, but lie down then, and don't let the old boy find you, or there'll be hell to pay. Neither your life nor mine will be worth living.'

Casanova lay down beside her, and stared at her, his orange eyes as bright and unblinking as those of an owl.

Idly she began playing with his ear, folding and unfolding it, while his mouth opened, and he began panting, his eyes now half shut in ecstasy. The warmth of his fur against her thigh was not unpleasant. It was oddly disturbing for her to be a little afraid of her slave.

'Oh, my Casanova,' she murmured, 'my wicked Casanova, you're only a puppy now . . . what will you be like when you're a dog?'

Life is an Operetta

It was in the winter of 1927 that Mitzi's dream came true. The little girl from the outskirts of Kekesféhervar made her debut in an operetta written by the great Imre Dobos himself. Malicious tongues whispered that, in order to attain her ends, she had had to give herself to Dobos, and, unfortunately, as is so often the case, the malicious tongues were quite right. However, she sang prettily, caused Dobos's fourth divorce, and the score, fired no doubt by love and a blaze of sudden youth in the afternoon of life, was acclaimed a masterpiece of its kind.

Mitzi had always been attracted by operetta, and even in her school days she knew all the tunes and all the words of the current hits. Her first sweetheart, Lajos Palotai, was a mild, long-haired fellow, painfully myopic, whose tastes ran to more serious music; but to oblige his black-eyed paramour he hammered out the frivolous melodies on the upright piano. Together, on the banks of lustrous summer rivers, in small cafés, they fabricated her dream. She would be a great, great singer. His role in the dream was never quite clear, but he was too much in love and too timid to lay claim to any definite pigeonhole in her ambitions. He was flattered just to sit and listen and hold hands.

When she was eighteen, she went to Budapest.

Lajos saw her off at the station, without misgivings but with a jungle of sadness in his heart, which he tried manfully to disguise with awkward gallantry. The audition led to the four-poster bed in the Dobos villa, by way of a candle-lit restaurant with gipsies and a night ride in an open Hispano-Suiza.

Lajos came up for the première of *Caravan Love* and sat alone in a box which Mitzi had charmingly reserved for him. The story of the operetta was not marked by the shedding of any startlingly new light on the gipsy problem, nor did the music show signs of any but melodic gifts. In the first act, a wandering Romany band encamped unwittingly on the estate of a prince, who happened to be celebrating his betrothal by allowing his disreputable hussar friends to behave badly in the ancestral halls. In the second act, the hussars went hunting and came across the gipsies. Their legitimate fury against people who don't live in castles stopped abruptly when the prince clapped eyes on the gipsy king's daughter, played by Mitzi. Against the background of a hummed czardas, he sang the aria *All Alone a Flower Bloom'd in Autumn,* which subsequently became a favourite encore piece for strident tenors the world over. Forgetting his own engagement to the Countess Etelka, a buxom blonde in white fur, he courted Mitzi with the relentless verve of a talented cavalry officer. The gipsy king admonished his daughter, in a resonant bass voice, *Beware of the Love of Princes,* imploring her to go on wandering and making clothes pegs and to choose a mate from her own kind. When his arguments proved unconvincing, he locked her in her caravan.

By night, the prince, dressed in tatters with a gay bandeau around his head, crept into the encampment and serenaded his beloved with the celebrated *Schatzchen, My Heart Beats in Your Breast.* Here Mitzi really came into her own by answering him in the world-shaking hit *Your Voice Is Like a Symphony.* It all ended happily with a variation on the Sabine women, a rhapsody to Hungarian integration, in which hussars carried joyously struggling gipsy maidens in their arms, while the grimly conservative king of the *zingari* found himself swept by the pervading mood of amatory abandon on to the heaving bosom of the Countess Etelka.

The applause was rapturous, and it was a trembling, tearful Lajos who clutched Mitzi's hands in the flower-filled dressing room afterwards. He was a little disconcerted by the fact that they could not dine together, but she had a prior commitment with the great Dobos ('Business, you understand, my heart's darling'). Still, he said he understood, which wasn't true, but he was the type to say so.

He saw little of her for the next week, since Dobos seemed to have an incredible amount of business to transact. After ten days the situation was further complicated, not by a hardening in Lajos's attitude or by an increase in her lover's attentions, but by the fact that she suddenly fell in love with Ferenc Ferensci, the high tenor playing the part of the prince in the operetta. She was not the kind of woman who could be serenaded and kissed every night without allowing it to affect her.

Dobos was livid, since he was both very important and no longer young. 'Damned ingratitude!' he snorted, and allowed the echo of his *cri de coeur* to richochet off every coffee-house wall in Budapest. Lajos felt for him.

One evening, soon afterwards, the young and dissolute Prince Szent-Mihaly sent an enormous bouquet of flowers to the stage door. It was followed the next night by one even larger. The inevitable ensued; more violins, a convenient moon, yet another hectic night ride – this time in an open carriage with a coat of arms on the door and a couple of bored dragoons galloping alongside – and a huge, creaking bed in which generations of Szent-Mihalys had died, made love, and been born.

Ferensci began to sing very flat in his depression, sharp in moments of anger. Both Lajos and Dobos felt for him. After a while, however, Prince Szent-Mihaly was severely reprimanded by his terrible mother and dispatched to Monte Carlo as a punishment. It was at this very moment that Dobos chose to be intoxicated by the beauty of another girl he had auditioned, and he declared to the press that he had discovered the voice of the century. The double humiliation was too much for Mitzi to bear. In an orgy of contrition, she confessed all to Lajos, and they held hands again.

Life, she reflected, is like that. What she meant was that life is like an operetta. The sophistication of an elderly roué's love, the wit and sparkle of his crooned conversation, the popping of champagne corks, the giggles charged with the hysteria of desire as the waxed moustaches of a prince tickled her naked shoulder, the heart intent on imminent surrender being led through the caverns of sensuality by the feverish strains of a tearful violin – did it all lead to happiness, to fulfilment? No, no, and no again. True love was to be found at the end of Act Three, in poverty, wrapped in the stained frock coat of a struggling music teacher, old faithful, who had stood by and suffered in silence while she, the volatile, irresistible fly-by-night, had drunk deeply from the spangled cup of illusion.

No sooner had she felt this profound sense of purification than she began to find the inarticulate, indecisive Lajos distinctly boring. He had served his purpose for the moment. She had blurted out her confession, and he had just smiled through his tears as though a prodigal spirit were returning to the fold. Her conscience was clear again. The Budapest triumph was repeated in Vienna, but with an Austrian tenor with whom she fell in love because it was part of the plot. She also captivated the notorious modernist composer, Manfred Von Ilch, who wrote to a thirteen-tone ladder of his own invention, thereby exciting the implacable hatred of those who were religiously addicted to a ladder of merely twelve tones. With the pathetic lack of discrimination shown by most great men when they fall in love, the otherwise unswerving Dr Von Ilch decided that Mitzi had exactly the right timbre for his troubled muse and wrote expressly for her his fragmentary *Vier Grausame Lieder* ('Four Cruel Songs'), based on the chants of medieval flagellants and scored for female *sprechstimme*, electric guitar deliberately distorted by low voltage, cheese grater, castanets, and four whips of different sizes. The only performance of the work was a disaster, since Mitzi, once confronted by an audience, could not resist imposing a most ingratiating expression on her face, and consequently this penetrating adventure into the gloomy fathoms of human subconsciousness became instead merely comical, a comment on itself from some *avant-garde* revue. The more the audience tittered, the more coy Mitzi became, and soon afterwards Dr Von Ilch took his life, leaving nothing but an enigmatic letter in Latin.

Once more the prey of a deliciously tragic feeling of guilt, Mitzi summoned Lajos to Vienna. She told him she was desperately alone, which was a feeling she always had when an attachment had just ended and before she had had time to establish another one. The long-suffering Lajos looked deep into her eyes and said to her: 'Mitzi, one day you will realize my worth. You smile now, because you are kind. But one day there will be no one – the princes, the composers, the tenors, they will all have gone. Then you will stir the pot of memory, searching for someone to whom you can turn. Suddenly your face will light up. You will call my name, and it will be for ever.'

'It is for ever now,' she said, her eyes wide and innocent, as though she had been unaccountably misunderstood.

'I believe you,' he lied, tears of emotion forming in his eyes, 'and I will stay with you, abandoning the little class I was building up in Budapest.'

'Class? What class?' She became coquettish. 'I never did know what you did in your spare time. I was absurdly jealous. What class?'

'Piano and Theory.'

'How interesting.'

'You're not serious.'

Mitzi flashed. 'I'll show you how serious I am tomorrow. We will dine together at Sacher's after the theatre, and we will make plans, huge plans, as we did in the old days.'

When Lajos arrived at the restaurant, he saw Mitzi dining with an elderly gentleman. He retired in confusion to the foyer and wrote a note reminding her of their date. Nervously he gave it to a waiter and sat down to await developments. After a seeming eternity, the waiter returned with a card, on which was written:

Dearest friend,

I tried to reach you everywhere, without success. *Not* tonight, my Lajos, not *this week*. I am with Mr Nate Schiffnick of *New York*. May be most important for *both of us*.

Your *little* goose,

Mitzi

Lajos left the restaurant sick at heart.

Caravan Love opened in New York late in 1931, presented by Wyant and Schiffnick and starring Mitzi and Diego de la Luna, a silent star who had drifted into musical comedy when it was discovered that his speaking voice was impossibly high for the villainous roles he was cast in, although his soaring lyric singing voice fitted him admirably for the part of the prince on Broadway. By the time the heroic Lajos had arrived in the United States on the Hungarian quota, Mitzi had not only triumphed in the operetta but had also had her affair with Diego de la Luna. In their transports of passion, he had murmured in Spanish while she had shrieked in Hungarian, since their mutual knowledge of English was quite inadequate for the purpose of communication.

Lajos arrived at the theatre on his first evening in America and was told that Miss Mitzi Somlos could receive no visitors. When he tried to buy a ticket at the box office, he was told that there were none, and if there were, they would cost the earth. Without the means of bribery, he loitered miserably around the building until the performance was over and then stood by the stage door with a couple of neurotic autograph hunters who had staring, imbecile eyes and who talked to themselves.

One by one the other actors emerged, interspersed with members of the orchestra carrying their instruments. Eventually Mitzi came out, drowned in expensive sables, drenched in a mist of perfume, on the arm of elderly, sallow Mr Schiffnick, who wore tails. For a moment Mitzi's eyes met those of Lajos, and she looked away quickly, more irritated than surprised, and bent low to step into the limousine which was to carry her and her bald Prince Charming to an evening of delight.

The very next day, at a quiet reception of some four hundred guests, Mitzi and Nate Schiffnick were married on the roof of a fashionable hotel. Everything was done in the best of taste and with that commendable restraint which marked all of Mr Schiffnick's artistic ventures. An organ was played by a lady in top hat and tails but little else. The lights in the organ changed colour according to the mood of the service. A cake in the shape of Mitzi was wheeled in, and Mr Schiffnick cut it, permitting himself lewd but friendly remarks to his many acquaintances with every incision of the knife.

That night Lajos was at the stage door again, and he managed to say the word 'Mitzi' as she emerged on to the pavement. This time she did not ignore him. She looked at him with the greatest coldness and annoyance. 'You understand nothing. Nothing,' she said.

Lajos trembled with an anger he had never felt before. 'I understand what you do not!' he cried. 'Life is not an operetta. It cannot be lived as though it were!'

'Is this man annoying you, honey?' asked Mr Schiffnick.

'Yes.'

'Burger!'

The stage door man appeared and passed a menacing remark.

'Remember,' shouted the retreating Lajos, 'you will suffer more than I! Goodbye, for ever!'

Two weeks later, as the direct result of recklessly attempting to live the life of a younger man, Mr Schiffnick died. His funeral, arranged by his erstwhile partner, Mr Wyant, was as majestic as his marriage had been devout. The music of his greatest hits was played by a huge orchestra throughout the service. Mr Wyant did his old pal proud. When the will was read, however, it was discovered, to the general surprise and to Mitzi's horror, that he had left nothing but debts. Schiffnick had been a spendthrift, a man excited by dangerous living from day to day, and a bit of a crook. Those closest to him were all agreed that he died just in time to escape the massive retribution which had been building up over the years to strike him. Some people even began to call him 'Lucky Nate Schiffnick' after his death.

Mitzi dressed from head to foot in black and wept frequently, as though to convince herself that her marriage to the man who had seemed to have been fashioned from yellowed ivory in both life and death had been the inevitable result of true love. Although she would never admit it, she always thought of her father's death when tears were called for. People were suspecting that she was a better actress off the stage than on.

The first flush of success began to fade, and soon *Caravan Love* was tottering along on the very brink of loss. The Budapest papers, which Mitzi's brother sent her, spoke of her great success in the New World. She was quickly caught between reality and legend. It was impossible for her to return now. As soon as the New York run ended, she went out on the road and milked the property until there was no more life left in it.

She still dressed in mourning out of reverence for the man she hardly knew.

Soon she was haunting the agents' offices, but gipsy maidens were no longer an everyday necessity, and her command of the English language remained doggedly unimproved. Money ran short, and her past love of goulash and Sachertorte began to take its toll. By the day she grew stouter, stockier. Men no longer fell for her. She fell for them, and in the chase she frightened them by her determined brightness, her brittle peals of artificial laughter, her languorous airs of fatal love, which seemed to be based on techniques rejected by Mata Hari as old-fashioned. She thought of suicide, not seriously but romantically.

One night, while she was sitting dejectedly in her one-room apartment, there was a knock on the door. It could only be a creditor, she told herself. At the third knock, she tiptoed to the switch and turned off the lights. No use. The knocking continued. Preparing some choice invective, she flung open the door.

'Lajos!' She hid her face. 'Don't look at me. I am old and ugly.'

'You are twenty-nine,' said Lajos, 'and more beautiful than ever.'

'Where have you been? And how did you find me?'

'I always knew where you were. Cleveland, Cincinnati, Columbus. I even knew that your marriage wouldn't last. I didn't guess that the end would be so abrupt, so terrible, but I knew something would happen.'

'How did you know?' she asked mysteriously, since she had a predilection for the occult, perhaps because she had depicted a gipsy for so long.

'I knew, because there is justice in this world,' he replied magnificently, 'and because I was waiting.'

Heartened by this show of generosity, she could afford herself a little bitterness. 'You know he left not a penny.'

'But why, why, did you marry him?'

This was what Mitzi had been waiting for, the question which provoked all her frustrated theatrical talents.

'Because I was a fool,' she hooted, 'a fool. Like a butterfly, I was drawn to the flame. I was a little Magyar Cinderella dazzled by the brightness of the ball, and I lived my dream to the full!'

For the next hour, Lajos could not manage to say a word, so torrential was the storm of conventional images which blasted his eardrums. She postured, she hid her face, only to reveal it again more dramatically, she played her version of *Camille* to a crowded gallery, she sang a few snatches in a carefully broken voice, she threw herself on a divan, rolled on to the floor in an act of nun-like self-mortification, then rose violently to her feet and defied the world, her mascara running down her face like the reflection of prison bars. At length, even her energy attained its limits, and she sat heaving on a kitchen chair, the hair on her forehead matted with perspiration, her buxom frame rocked with uncontrollable nervous spasms.

'Marry me,' said Lajos.

She held out a hand which was prematurely blue-veined, like an old lady's. 'Dearest boy,' she murmured.

Lajos rose and spoke in a pallid voice. 'I work as music critic on the Hungarian weekly paper.'

'You can't live on that.'

He stammered, 'I also wash dishes at the Come-n-Gettit Steak House.'

The tears welled into her dark eyes again.

Embarrassed, he added, 'I have written out my address if you should need me.' And, placing a piece of paper on the table, he left.

She stared after him vacantly, then gazed into the mirror. Quickly she tidied herself up, replaced the powder, the rouge, the mascara, the lipstick, and then examined herself with a look of enigmatic fascination.

'I am not old enough to marry Lajos,' she reflected.

Her road downhill was the more painful for being gradual. When money ran out, she took a job teaching Hungarian at a language school, but although her knowledge of Hungarian was adequate, her knowledge of English was not, and her pupils made no headway. Eventually she struggled on as an independent seamstress, coping with the overflow from other, recognized firms of clothiers. She called herself Mrs Mary

Schiffnick, since she maintained proudly that the name of Mitzi Somlos would be associated only with glory.

Lajos visited her about once a week and never failed to renew his proposal. There was something desperate about his restraint, something almost mad in his insistence. Time passed, and with it grew the bitterness. War was declared, but Mitzi had not yet brought herself to make a decision as momentous. She still went to auditions, calling herself Mary Schiffnick, dressing more and more eccentrically in clothes she made herself, but it didn't help. She tried the names of Mary Buda, Maritza Liszt, and Marimka Czardas, but there was apparently no magic in these sobriquets.

To humour Lajos, she used to say that they were more married than not, since neither had any other temptations. As far as he was concerned, she was right; but her eyes had acquired the habit of dropping suggestive hints left and right, a habit she regarded as indispensable to her calling. Never mind if her indiscriminate flirtation was becoming more and more pathetic; there was nothing about it to console Lajos, who had suffered too severely to be entirely rational in his appraisal.

During the war, Mitzi became curiously patriotic and wept copiously at the thought of her 'poor country' at the mercy of 'those Germans'. To listen to her, one might think that she was a deposed empress bemoaning the loss of her estates and her tiaras.

'The younger generation will never know the life we led,' she used to pontificate sourly: 'the hussars with their brilliant shakos, their fur-trimmed jackets thrown carelessly over one shoulder, their gallantry – ah, the compliments that used to flow. At the end of some princely banquet, they would ride their white horses down the long tables, missing the bottles of Tokay with such elegance, such elegance!'

There was nothing in this description of life at home which Lajos recognized. The truth of the matter was that Mitzi had taken to the bottle, since reality was too bleak for her, and in her cups she lived in the lilting world of musical comedy. On one occasion Lajos permitted himself to lose his temper and shouted at her, 'I told you once before, and I tell you now, life is not an operetta!'

He slammed the door, only to have the mortification of hearing her drunken voice embark on the sugared strains of *Your Voice Is Like a Symphony* in blurred, dill-pickle tones. Evidently his mention of the word 'operetta' had put her in mind of it.

The war passed, and Lajos became sullen. He was no longer in the best of health. He wished he had the strength of character to liberate himself from the intolerable weight of his obligation towards this woman, but a strange fatality bound them together. This useless romance had occupied so much of his life that he would now have felt quite lost without it, as though a man reconciled to blindness were threatened with sight so late in life as not to matter. His romance had become an illness the body could no longer do without.

He saw her more frequently – every day, in fact. He even cooked for her when he had a few hours off. Promotion had come his way, and the Come-n-Gettit had moved to a more respectable neighbourhood, changing its name to the Filet Mignon in the process. He was now deputy head waiter of the establishment and seemed to take a certain pride in being dressed in tails around the clock. Even when off duty, he wore his formal attire and carried his thin head high under its mop of wiry grey hair. The waiters called him 'the diplomat'.

The reason for this peculiar serenity was that Mitzi had drifted off into a half-helpless indifference. She allowed him to do things for her without protest. A melancholy had settled over her, a resignation. She no longer even talked much, and when she did it was without colour, without invention. They were married in all but name. They no longer held hands, but she allowed him to take hers in his without responding. The toothless lioness might still have her dreams of glory, but she kept them majestically to herself. She had mellowed.

It was only on occasion that Lajos fancied he noticed a disturbing sidelong look, with infinite cunning in her eyes, usually when she thought she was not being watched.

One day, when he had just cooked her some stuffed cabbage, he noticed this furtive, dark glance, at once calculating, malicious, and terrible.

'What are you thinking of?' he asked.

She woke out of her daydream. 'Revenge,' she answered, simply.

'Revenge? Against whom?'

'All of you,' she replied, in exactly the same way as before. There was a pause.

'Life is not an operetta,' she announced, dispassionately. 'You've no idea how you hurt me when you said that.'

'I hurt you? Why? I admit, I was very angry—'

'Angry? I have often been angry. It is nothing. But to be hurt ... that can last a lifetime. You allowed me to dream when I was young. You knew, didn't you? How cruel you were. How cruel.'

Her ruminative calm was far more disconcerting than the tantrums of the past. He washed up with trembling hands and left. She may have mellowed, but she was slowly going mad.

The Hungarian revolution broke out in 1956. Lajos heard the news with alarm but had an evening of service before him, and it was midnight before he could hurry around to Mitzi's room. There was no light under the door. He knocked without receiving any reply. He tried the handle. The door was open. The room was empty. It looked as though it had been ransacked. Her jewel box was empty and lay on the floor. Old letters were strewn all over the place. An apron lay on the bed. He looked around in horror. Suddenly his eye fell on a note leaning against the mirror. It was addressed to him. He tore it open. All it contained was the enigmatic phrase: 'Life is not an operetta?'

Distractedly, he wandered the streets, trying to decide what to do. He was not one to involve himself with the police for no reason. After all, this might just be part of that insane revenge she had talked about. The message might have been placed there in order to worry him out of his wits. He felt deeply resentful. Then it occurred to him that it might have been a suicide note. She might even now be floating in the East River. The police would want to know what the message meant. How could he ever explain it to them? He had left fingerprints all over the place. If she had committed some irrevocable act, could he not be suspected? How would his fingerprints have got on to the note if he pretended he had not been up to the room? He was a potential suspect, and there is only an inch between a suspect and a criminal. He saw himself under the blinding lights of the detectives, his story sounding more and more incredible and disjointed. It would be better to go to the police now – and yet, in doing so, he might just be falling into her cunning trap. There was no solution. He went home and sat up all night thinking of alibis. The farther he wandered from the truth, the unhappier he became. At dawn, he rushed out and bought the morning paper. There was no mention of suicide anywhere. He sighed with relief until it occurred to him that the body might not yet have been found. He was white as death and bilious with fatigue.

Mitzi arrived in Vienna that evening by air. Her American passport was stamped, and after a quick meal at the airport she took a taxi to the station. She was dressed in old clothes and wore no jewellery, for the simple reason that she had sold it all to make the trip possible – the platinum and emerald brooch from Dobos, saying 'For ever', Prince Szent-Mihaly's pendant of diamonds and rubies, saying the same thing, and the other battle honours of her horizontal conquests. At the station she reserved a third-class ticket on a slow train to a town which lies a few miles from the Hungarian frontier. Owing to the congestion on the line, the train crawled through the night, stopping frequently while officials on the line called to each other and traced mysterious patterns in the air with coloured lanterns. It began to rain, not gradually but with an almost insensitive intensity, as though a brigade of flamenco dancers had suddenly started a performance in the middle distance. Just before four o'clock in the morning, the train finally pulled into the station. There were some figures on the farther platform, and from their shouting Mitzi knew them to be Hungarian. She left the station hurriedly. There were several trucks and vans in the parking place; at least two were ambulances, with large red crosses on them, while another was evidently a mobile recording unit of some broadcasting station. There was considerable activity, and Mitzi heard English, French, and some Scandinavian language spoken as she walked quickly into the sleeping town. Soon she reached the point where the main road passed through the town, and there she found the inevitable signpost pointing to Vienna in one direction and to the frontier in the other. She glanced at an illuminated electric clock which hung over a closed café. It was 4.21. There was no time to lose. Gallantly she began to direct her steps towards the Hungarian frontier.

There would be no dawn that day. Perplexed roosters began crowing with unconvinced inflections over the desolate countryside. She was suddenly blinded by headlights. She rolled into a ditch. The car rushed by, splashing her with a shower of freezing mud. It was an Austrian military vehicle. Cursing, she rose to her feet, and, ignoring the fact that she was wet through, she bravely trudged on.

Soon some black figures became visible on the road before her. Hiding behind a clump of bushes, she waited, and because she was compelled to wait, she began to shiver. Her teeth rattled like a machine gun, and she held her mouth shut with her hand, convinced that the noise could be heard miles off. The dreary little procession passed – four or five men, several women, a crying child, a cart. They were talking in Hungarian. When they had gone, Mitzi resumed her journey. She heard some shots and then the barking of dogs; not the disorganized barking of some farmer's house guard but a more regimented sound, the deep-throated, disconcerting rasps of several large hounds of the same breed. The frontier. She turned off the main road and walked down a yellow cart track. After about a mile, she entered a marshy field and half fell, half staggered across it, following a route parallel to the main road. It was growing painfully light. The field led to another, seemingly endless. All of a sudden, in a clump of trees, she was confronted by a shallow stream swollen by the rain, flowing fast, leaving arrowheads of angry water where it met the opposition of protruding rocks. Without thinking twice, she plunged in, staggered, fell, and eventually reached the farther shore, a steep embankment rising to unknown ground. With tears of panic in her eyes, she struggled along the bank for a full half mile until she came to an innocent little path up the sharp incline. Moaning with exhaustion, she climbed it slowly, only to find a mass of barbed wire at the top.

She could not stop now. She took off her coat and laid it across the wire. Then she tried to crawl across it. Every time she had to retreat as the cruel barbs plucked her skin. Then she lost her temper and stepped on the coil, but as she did so the rest of the wire rose to meet her. She refused to retreat. Kneeling, falling, rolling, she passed through it. Her legs and hands were bleeding, but she was across.

After resting for a moment, she walked along the line of barbed wire on the east side of the stream, where the ground was high and firm. She was heading back to the main road. At length she could see a small house with a flagpole near it and a red, white, and green road barrier, gaily striped like a barber's sign. As she approached the house, she could hear evidence of some commotion inside it. A few dead bodies lying carelessly by the roadside did not reassure her. She paused, and as she did so she noticed how her wounds hurt her. She entered the customs shed.

A few terrified-looking peasants were standing around while a ferocious man in the uniform of a major in the security forces was walking up and down, brandishing documents and shouting. His eyes and his moustache were so black they had mineral tints of blue in them. Behind him stood two customs officials in attitudes of dismay and mute protest.

'We have shot eight of the swine this morning already,' yelled the major. 'There are six of you. That will make fourteen before breakfast – a fine catch of Fascist hyenas by any standards!'

Suddenly he caught sight of Mitzi.

'Who are you?' he cried, and went on without waiting for an answer. 'Aha, here is one fine lady who is so eager to leave the Socialist paradise that she even tries to escape in an unauthorized fashion. I can see from the state of her ladyship's legs that she attempted to negotiate the barbed wire which the state has thoughtfully placed along our frontiers for our protection, but when she found that the work of our engineers was too efficient, she calmly presents herself to the customs authorities and expects to be let through.'

'You misunderstand—'

'Silence!' the major thundered. 'These officials of the border control have been guilty of grave dereliction of duty and will be punished. Over a hundred citizens of our country have been allowed to cross into Austria. This is an intolerable situation.

You no doubt thought that such a criminal emigration was possible. I am here to tell you that you are wrong. Examples will be made of you all!'

'I am an American citizen,' said Mitzi calmly, producing her passport from her bag.

The major's eyes narrowed. 'Let me see that,' he snapped. 'Mrs Schiffnick. Born in Kekesféhervar. July 9th, 1908.'

'Do you have to read the date out to the assembled company?' asked Mitzi hotly. 'That should read 1918.'

'Kekesféhervar? For our purposes, you are Hungarian.'

'I am American, and the consul in Budapest knows that I am here,' said Mitzi.

'You had a heart attack in the early hours of this morning,' replied the major, with what he imagined to be a pleasant smile. 'The people's government will express its condolences to your friend the consul.'

The smile left his face. 'Take them out and shoot them!' he yelled.

The peasants showed panic, but Mitzi was remarkably calm. She knew of no operetta with such an ending. Just then the phone rang. The major picked up the receiver. As he did so, the noise of a motorcycle could be heard.

'What? Impossible!' bellowed the major. 'Repeat that at dictation speed. I don't believe it. What is that noise I hear? Shooting? Szilay – Szilay, answer! I order you to answer!'

During this halting conversation, a youth in a leather jacket had come in and had whispered excitedly to the two customs officers. As soon as the major laid down the receiver, he was seized by the three other men and carried struggling out of the room. After a momentary pause, there were three shots.

The customs officers returned, and the senior one, a tall, blond, ascetic man, announced that a full-scale revolution was sweeping the country.

'This is the business of the young,' he added. 'You are free to go.' Calling to Mitzi, he said, 'Mother, I advise you not to try any tricks with forged passports. If it didn't deceive us, it will certainly not deceive the Americans.' And so saying he threw her passport into the wastepaper basket.

'Why did you call me Mother?' asked Mitzi, deeply hurt. 'Do I look so old?'

That evening found Mitzi in a refugee camp on the road to Vienna. A Dutch nurse had tended her wounds, she was wearing warm clothes sent from Italy, and she had a cold she had supplied herself. It had not yet been decided what to do with the refugees, and they were sitting around a bare room, talking and smoking.

During the course of the evening, a photographer wandered in. His clothes and his manner declared him to be American, and there was something eminently successful about his dishevelment and the calculated way in which the gum in his mouth was helping him to think. He was garlanded with cameras and flash bulbs. He looked around the crowded room with an expert and a calculating eye.

Mitzi knew the curtain had risen, and without a flicker of self-consciousness she filled her lungs with a vast quantity of air, and it came out again to the tune of *Your Voice Is Like a Symphony*.

Every head in the room turned to listen to her. The flash bulbs began to go off, and the gum was being chewed at twice the rate.

When Mitzi sensed the camera pointed in her direction, she thought of her father's death and began to weep copiously, without for a moment allowing her crying to affect her voice or her breathing. When the performance ended, the applause was tumultuous. The photographer knelt by her side.

'That was just great,' he said. 'My name's Cy Endhouse, from *Be* magazine. Wasn't that a song called *Your Voice Is like a Symphony*?'

'Yes,' said Mitzi demurely.

Cy searched his memory. 'Wasn't that from *Caravan Love*?'

'It was, yes.'

'Wasn't that sung in New York by—?'

'Mitzi Somlos,' she interrupted. It would be too painful if he made a mistake.

'Yeah. Yeah, that's right. Mitzi Somlos. Whatever happened to her?'

'I am Mitzi Somlos,' she said, with immeasurable wistfulness.

'You! But, how – why are you here?'

'I chose freedom,' she replied, with a fatalistic shrug of the shoulders, and added, '*They* wouldn't let me sing, for political reasons.'

The next copy of *Be* magazine carried a full-page picture of Mitzi, shot brilliantly from an odd angle and captioned 'The Voice of Freedom'. The picture eventually won Cy Endhouse the Pulitzer Prize for Photography, and deservedly so. A week later Lajos received the following letter:

Dearest dreamer,

I am in Vienna, having escaped from Hungary after *many harrowing* adventures. I will tell you when I see you. I am waiting here to go to *America*, and I have given your name as a *reference*. I will, of course, come as a *refugee*. Now, my sweet Lajos, my childhood *lover*, I am in *terrible trouble*, and you *must help me* as only you can. As a result of a picture of me which appeared in the magazine *Be*, I have sold the story of my life under the *Communists*, who *prevented me* from singing because my *father* was a *landowner*, to the films for $100,000. Please, dear heart, don't let me down. *Dream* as you once did so *wonderfully*, and write down the story of my *life* without delay. I know I can *trust* you, as *always*.

Your own *little goose*,

MITZI

The letter reached Lajos as he was sitting in his hospital bed after a complete nervous breakdown as a result of his sense of guilt about Mitzi's presumed suicide. Before he suffered an unexpected relapse, he had just time to reflect that, for some rare, impossible, dangerous, and impervious people, life is an operetta after all, and can never be anything else.

God and the State Railways

In order to understand this story fully, it is necessary to have a working knowledge of the trade union movement in Italy. Since there are no Italians who have this knowledge, it could, consequently, well be that the story is incomprehensible, and yet God usually comes to the rescue in such cases, bringing an order which is perhaps a little rudimentary to a chaos which has seemed complete.

I have seen many Gods in my time. There is a Russian God with slim admonishing fingers and a brown look of disapproval, a terracotta phantom involved in angular chants, smelling of earth, damp cloisters, and incense, aglitter with traces of gold at the edges; there is an Anglican God, more reasonable and less dramatic, the victim of a tragic miscarriage of justice in which His only son fell foul of a legal system which had none of the advantages of British researches in the field of jurisprudence, a God eminently understanding and discreetly sad, prayed to with an intensity none the less solemn for being curiously casual; there is a Hollywood God, only seen from behind in the form of Christ, or as a disturbing palpitation in the sky too cerulean to be quite true, an apparition which stays the Roman whips in midair, which brings frowns of misgiving to the foreheads of procurators and centurions as they prepare for battles lost in advance, which is the signal for a hundred female voices to rise to the ceiling of their range in a rapturous vocalize, accompanied by the full resources of a mid-Victorian orchestra; there is the God of the minor-channel American TV Bible Belt, the Lord of the rimless glasses and the no-nonsense man-to-man approach, the Lord of the electric organ, the latter-day Gothic arch, the God in the street with no unnecessary predilection for the arts.

You don't have to be a Catholic to catch a glimpse of the Italian God – not the bearded figure portrayed by the

Renaissance painter, but the reflection in the upcast eye of the simple widow for whom events have become too complicated for assessment, let alone solution. He is the final appeal to sanity after the disillusionment with mortal justice, the ultimate voice which will invade the conscience of the police, the judges, the lawyers, the government employees, all those with papers to sign, with cards to punch, with stamps to stamp, the weight which every mortal carries Atlas-like on his shoulders for the span of his natural life, and the poorer the country, the greater the weight. Occasionally even the voluble Italians run out of arguments, and then a strike is called. Nobody is ever quite sure who called it, and those who called it are never quite sure if the call will be obeyed. Because the unions are without the resources for a prolonged protest, these strikes have only a nuisance value. They are a reminder to the government that unions do exist, but they also remind the government that unions are relatively weak.

On November 8th, a railway strike was decreed in the whole of Italy. Inflammatory posters went up, with much talk of bread, wages, and honour. Midnight was to be the hour of action. At 8.40 – or, rather, at 20.40 – every evening a train leaves Rome for Florence, Milan, Domodossola, and Geneva, with carriages for Dunkirk, Hamburg, Zurich, Brussels. Several sleeping-cars are attached to the regular wagons, and the occupants are invariably highly international. I can speak with authority only about the travellers in sleeping-car number three, bound for Geneva, because I was one of them.

I arrived in the station with about ten minutes to go. The majority of porters seemed sullen. They were either strike-minded or else just apprehensive. As I tottered away from my taxi under the weight of my baggage, one porter pointed to another, seated on his barrow, who pointed to a third, leaning against a wall, who pointed to a fourth. Then, out of nowhere, a fifth arrived, more helpful than a porter should be. Words were passed.

'Italy will remain a country steeped in ignorance so long as there are creatures like you about,' said the first porter. The second porter just spat. That was his eloquence.

My porter put down my bags. 'Let me tell you fellows something—'

'We don't want to hear from blacklegs,' said the third.

'Go to High Mass,' said the fourth, looking into space and munching a dandelion seed.

'The strike isn't called till midnight,' my porter went on, 'but you people are acting as though it's already started. That's not honest.'

'You're working extra hard to compensate for the time you'll lose during the strike. Call that honest?' The first porter had flared up.

'No use arguing with an idiot. Go to High Mass, that's where you belong – with the priests.'

'It's not a question of priests,' my porter retaliated angrily, 'but of honour, of making a *bella figura* in front of foreigners. It's by people like you that most of the foreigners judge our country.'

'It'll do the foreigners good to see our country as it really is,' said the third porter, 'and, in any case, to hell with foreigners.'

'Without the foreigners, where would our economy be?' said my porter. 'Answer me that!'

'We could all be rich if the wealth of the Vatican were divided among the people,' said the first.

I permitted myself to intervene. 'My train leaves in seven minutes.'

My porter picked up my luggage and threw it on to his barrow. 'The wealth of the Vatican,' he muttered breathlessly as he half ran. 'The Communists always think of a negative solution like that. Good, we distribute the riches of the Church. We'd all be rich for one afternoon, and then what? We'd all be poor again, including the church. It's better that someone's rich, it's reassuring. Eh! The secret is that it's tough to be rich and a Communist. I know nothing about the others, the Russians, but over here the hope of every Communist is to get himself a successful racket, so that there's no need for him to be a Communist any more. Communism's strictly for the have-nots, and everyone wants to have. That's how deep it goes.'

After all the rush, the atmosphere around sleeping-car number three was surprisingly quiet, grave even. So many cruel armistices have been signed in railway carriages that it takes very little to give them an aura of fatality and gloom. Now there was a little cluster of officials near the entrance, muttering to each other as the steam swirled up lazily from under the train and wound itself around their legs. They were consulting documents, making notes, scratching things out.

The controller looked me square in the eye and I already felt like a general in defeat. 'It is understood,' he said, 'that you leave at your own risk.'

'Yes,' I replied. It was unconditional surrender, but what alternative was there? 'How much do I owe you?' I asked the porter.

'Whatever you wish, *Dottore*.' He shrugged fatalistically, conjuring up a vision of destitute children who could do with a crust of bread. It was dishonest but brilliant. There is a fixed fee per bag carried. I knew this, but I still over-tipped him. I had no wish for anyone to lose his faith in capitalism at this particular moment.

'How does it look?' I asked the controller.

'Bad,' he replied. 'Half an hour ago it was better; then a quarter of an hour ago it was worse. Now it is just bad.'

He was a good-looking man, this controller, who managed to make his brown *wagon-lit* uniform appear military. He was young and dark, with the calculating aspect of one who enjoys initiative and who feels he has his finger on the pulse of events.

I entered the wagon to find most of the occupants in the corridor. The lady in the next compartment seemed both imperious and worried. I learned later that she was the Duchess of Calapiccola and that we had absolutely no friends in common. She held a diminutive dog in her hand which blended with her buff-coloured tweed like a chameleon. It was invisible until it barked, which it did occasionally in an utterly personal manner, a kind of bronchial belch of a very old and very large man. People who had heard this voice but who failed to see the dog tended to look at the duchess with surprise, a look which she met with a stare of melodramatic hostility. Farther down the corridor there was a senior nun of some rare order. The small portion of her face visible gave no indication of its true dimensions. She may have had a tendency towards stoutness or she may have been scrawny; I neither knew nor cared to know. What I could see was not so much pink as white with scarlet flushes, with an expression so enclosed and a smile so enigmatic and dogged that my only wish was to avoid all contact with her. She had companionship, in any case, in the shape of a thin, sour priest with dandruff on his shoulders. They conversed in whispers, he looking at her with a yellow, liverish intensity, she responding with the slightest movement of her lips, her eyes downcast so demurely that she seemed like a grotesque caricature of a well-behaved little girl.

There was, of course, the inevitable American individualist who had to be somewhere in a hurry, kept on checking his watch with other watches, consulted tickets which had been sold him back in Dayton, Ohio, and flicked over the pages of *A Hundred Useful Phrases in Italian* without finding anything to say which corresponded with his mood.

'Go by train to save time,' he said, without the guarantee that anyone could understand him, 'and you land right in the middle of a strike. I guess you can't win.'

Hearing a man speak with an unaccustomed timbre to his voice, the duchess's dog pricked up ears almost as large as itself, inclined its head to one side, began shivering like an epileptic, and barked. The American reacted like everyone else by looking at the duchess, then saw the dog.

'Hello, little feller,' he said, extending an affectionate hand with a huge fraternity ring on the fourth finger. The dog, seeing a vast five-pronged weapon advancing in its direction, embossed with a great golden orb, encrusted with a red stone and cabalistic runes, flew into a passion of defiance. It may have been small, but it still had the instincts of a dog, and of a fierce dog at that. Now it was at bay, defending its mistress. The duchess placed a blue-veined hand over its eyes, and with its world precipitately plunged into darkness, it whimpered feebly with frustrated blood lust and fell asleep in a matter of seconds, its dreams filled with violence and rampant hatred.

'I'm sorry,' said the American, confused. 'What is it? I thought it was a Chihuahua, but it seems too small for that.'

The duchess gazed at him with undisguised loathing.

'He's cute anyhow. Kind of hard not to step on, I should think.'

The duchess entered her compartment and closed the door.

Snubbed, the American looked at the priest, who stared back unhappily from sometime in the Middle Ages, the whites of his eyes almost as dark as the pupils. Even the smile of the nun had about it a trace of reproof.

Confused, wronged, misunderstood, the American retired to his compartment. I looked at the priest and didn't try to disguise my disapproval. He suddenly smiled back. His expression was quite shockingly pleasant and open. I found it impossible not to respond.

'Let us hope we all reach our destinations on time,' he said with a shrug. 'Trains and cars and aeroplanes have made us lazy – they gave us hope and made us negligent. With them we leave everything to the last moment. A thousand years ago we would have left on horseback with plenty of time to spare.'

'They didn't have strikes in those days,' I said.

'Oh, they had worse than strikes. I don't blame the railwaymen for airing their complaints.'

'It's all a question of communication,' I replied. The expression on the priest's face which the American took to be a reproach was, in fact, there only because the priest was thinking of something quite different. The priest probably never even heard the dog bark. As for the duchess, had the American been outrageously gallant and had he paid her some empty compliment instead of lavishing his playfulness on the dog, she would probably have slapped the dog hard for interrupting at the wrong moment. If life was difficult in its insignificant moments, how much more difficult was it in moments of importance. The nun probably had the right idea by avoiding contact with anything but the murals, the crucifixes, the cold corridors of her imagination, a static world without surprises. And yet, wasn't that a form of surrender, of self-gratification at the expense of life?

I looked at my watch. It was 9.12. The train was still in the station. I released the blind, which flew up, and wound down the window. The controller was alone.

'What's it look like now?' I called to him.

He smiled grimly. 'Had you asked me five minutes ago, I would have said worse. Now I don't quite know.'

The train lurched, then began creeping away.

'We'll reach Florence anyway,' he called, poising himself

with the elegance of one used to leaping on to moving objects. 'From there on, *beh*!' He grimaced and joined the train.

I tried to read now that I was alone. The nun, I suspected, felt quite at home in a train, since I imagined monastic life to be a little like existence in a sleeping-car: the embryonic warmth and intimacy, the isolation, the feeling of walking about in your own mind. If I were a monk, the one fear I would have would be to be relegated to a large cell. That would be the worst of both worlds.

The dog barked next door. 'Shut up,' I said aloud, but not so that the duchess would hear it. I put away my book and fell asleep.

When I woke up, the train was no longer moving. I looked at my watch. It was well after midnight. The strike was on. I became conscious of voices, not just the usual voices of a station. Someone was making a speech. There was some heckling.

I peered around the blind. It was like a scene from an early Soviet film. I could almost hear the searing sound-track which would accompany such a sequence, mainly brass, a semitone flat for technical reasons, but also with the burden of an epic sadness. The railway workers were gathered on the platform. It was cold. Whenever one of them spoke, explosions of breath would shoot into the midnight blue. The lighting was glacial, unkind. It made them all look hungry. There was paper on the platform. A trolley of refreshments stood abandoned – at precisely twelve o'clock, I imagined. Plump bottles of Chianti, bars of chocolate, all four wheels pointing in different directions.

'*Ragazzi*!' said the speaker. 'By order of the Central Committee of—' It was hard to hear; the contents of that kind of speech are always quite predictable. However worthy the cause, revolutionary resolutions invariably lose their drama in a fog of useless, predictable oratory. When people have a sense of occasion, they sink to it.

I no longer looked, just listened. There was very little opposition at first, merely isolated shouting. Then a new voice took over, a voice I quickly recognized as that of the controller of our sleeping-car. He spoke with a certain – for lack of a better word, I will call it 'majesty'. There was no effort of rodomontade; he fell into none of the temptations which the Italian language prepares for those endowed with voice too rich or vision too baroque. He spoke simply, like a foreigner, and it was probably because he sounded like a foreigner that they listened.

The strike, he contended, was calculated to annoy. It had been prepared carefully enough to do anything but that, nor could the unions, with their present structure, even hope to organize anything more thoroughly. He compared the dignity of the operation to that of street urchins ringing doorbells and then running away. He asked a rhetorical question of the assembly. Was that an occupation worthy of fathers of families?

He reminded the house that Italians were always jealous of foreign vices and neglectful of their own virtues. 'Why should we feel ashamed or weak because we are a hospitable nation? Some of us wish we were in Russia. Some of us have been in Russia and are very glad to be here. I would rather be hungry in Italy,' he declared roundly at the end, 'than full of buckwheat in a paradise chosen for me!'

There was applause, not so much for the content as for the performance. A vote of some kind was taken, and after five minutes the train moved grudgingly out of the station.

I put on my dressing gown and went to congratulate the controller.

'Did you really mean all you said?' I asked him.

'No.' Oh, he was absolutely honest.

'My duty,' he said, 'is to get the train out of Italy. I am paid to do that. I may quarrel with my salary, but now is not the moment to do it, with a trainload of travellers.'

'And were you in Russia during the war?'

'No,' he replied, expressionless. 'But I didn't lie. I never said I had been. I just said some of us had been, which is true. Actually, I should very much like to go one day.'

'Where did you get the idea of buckwheat?'

'Oh, I'm not ignorant. I know what the other people eat. Throw out a phrase like that, and those who have been to Russia will never think to ask you whether you have been.'

'You ought to be in politics,' I said.

'Ah, *Dottore,* I'm not dishonest,' he replied. 'I just use my head sufficiently not to have to be. Politics would corrupt me.'

The American looked out into the corridor. 'Do you have any mineral water on ice?' he asked.

'Yes, sir,' replied the controller.

'Incidentally,' the American went on, 'I'd like to know your name.'

'Why, sir, have I done anything to displease you?' The controller was not in the least discountenanced.

'On the contrary,' said the American, blinking in an admiring fashion. 'I just saw you deal with a pretty nasty situation there. You sure kept your head. I don't understand the Italian language, of course, but I guess I've had enough experience of this kind of thing to appreciate what you did.'

'Thank you, sir,' replied the controller, 'but may I ask what you thought of doing with my name?'

'I'm lunching with the United States consul general in Milano next week when I get back from Geneva. I want to commend you to him.'

'To what purpose?'

'Well, I figured you'd appreciate it. Besides, we need every friend we can get. I know that and you know that.'

The poor man was a little lost. He had even said 'Milano' instead of 'Milan' as a gesture of solidarity. He believed deeply that most men were brothers. Desperately he sought to impose his fraternity on those he considered worthy of it.

'Well, let me give you my card,' he said. 'If you're in any kind of trouble, remember William C. Rosencrantz. I'm what's known as a trouble shooter with the—' And here he mentioned an agglomeration of initials which stood for one of the many overlapping agencies of the US government. The controller took the card, thanked him, and went to fetch the mineral water, which the American probably didn't want but had simply used as a sly conversational gambit.

'Yes, that was a fairly ugly situation,' said Mr Rosencrantz.

'Oh, the worst that would have happened is that the train wouldn't have gone on,' I said.

'Don't you believe it. It only needs a spark for a situation like that to ignite. Even been to Laos?'

'No.'

'Well, if you had, you wouldn't be so optimistic.'

I thought it perhaps too cruel to point out that we weren't in Laos, so in the interests of harmony I told him that he might be right. He took my concession very badly.

'I damn well know I'm right,' he snapped. 'I've seen altogether too much apathy in Europe.'

'Apathy about what?' I asked him sharply.

'The International Communist Conspiracy,' he barked back.

'Oh, that.' I relaxed and smiled. 'May I ask you how long you've been here?' I asked.

'Been where?'

I decided to take the initiative. 'We are in Italy at the moment, not in Laos.'

'I was in Laos six years,' he said.

'And here?'

'Two weeks next Tuesday.'

'Well, then, if we should have to spend several days aboard this train, I will listen with great respect to what you have to say about the Far East, but I will obviously be forced to take what you say about Italy with a pinch of salt.'

The controller returned with the mineral water just as the duchess opened her door. 'It's a disgrace!' she cried. 'The train moved out of the station just as I was on the point of taking my dog for his walk.'

'Normally we only stop in Florence for ten minutes,' replied the controller. 'Tonight you had over an hour to walk the dog.'

'Don't answer back,' said the duchess, malevolently. 'You mean we're already an hour late? It's a scandal! I only take the train because my dog's health isn't up to air travel.' She addressed the dog with a possessive love on the scale of Greek tragedy: 'Your ears don't support the altitude, do they?'

'Signora Duchessa, let the dog run up and down the corridor. If he performs any little duties, I will sweep them up.'

'And what if someone steps on her? Could the company ever refund a sentimental loss?'

'I will look after her. It's a her, is it?'

'See for yourself!'

'I can't without my glasses.'

The duchess smiled savagely and gave the dog some final instructions before surrendering it to the controller. The dog seemed neither to listen nor to notice the temporary change of ownership.

'Who is that old bitch?' asked Mr Rosencrantz when the duchess had retired.

'She's not a Communist, as you may imagine,' I replied, 'nor are you a Communist, as she may imagine.'

'She thinks I'm a Communist?'

'She doubtless thinks the whole of the United States is Communistic, and by her standards, she's right. The Bill of Rights is an appalling piece of emancipatory jurisdiction; the South was right; and there's very little to choose between Washington and Lenin. Neither of them believed in the divine right of kings, and that's enough to put them both in the camp of insurrection against the existing order.'

'That's ridiculous,' said Mr Rosencrantz, hotly. 'Why—'

'I'm only expressing the probable opinions of the Duchess of Calapiccola,' I interrupted. 'It's no use telling me that they are ridiculous. Tell her.'

'I don't speak Italian.'

'She doubtless speaks English better than either of us. She must have had a squadron of governesses when she was little.'

Mr Rosencrantz was so unhappy, I softened to him. 'How does it feel to find yourself suddenly a left-winger, along with Benjamin Franklin, Admiral Radford, and the Archbishop of Canterbury?'

The controller tried to put the dog down, but the motion of the train was too much for its legs and it rocked to and fro like a diminutive drunk. It proved to be even more difficult to pick up. The nun appeared and bent down with a look of self-effacing sweetness. The fact that the dog managed to bite her as it slid by her supplicating hands only served to sugar her expression still further.

The priest had been in the corridor all the time. 'You did well,' he told the controller sadly, 'but I do honestly feel those poor men deserve more money than they get.'

'I'm one of those poor men,' said the controller, 'so you won't expect me not to agree with you. No one is ever paid enough in this world, with the exception of those who are paid too much.'

The priest savoured the remark and nodded sadly. I translated the conversation for the benefit of Mr Rosencrantz, who frowned.

'Think the priest's in the conspiracy?' I whispered.

'There's an awful lot of well-meaning idealists who are fellow-travellers without knowing it,' he confided.

The dog managed to deliver itself of the thimbleful of water it had drunk during the day, and the controller returned it to the duchess, who was so well bred she neglected to thank him, but instead ordered a coffee, very hot and very strong, for eight-thirty, together with a half glass of lukewarm water, lukewarm, mark you, 45°C, to take some medicine in, and if the train should stop at a station, a copy of the morning paper and also a packet of Turkish cigarettes, and if the train didn't stop at a station, she would want to know the reason, and, incidentally, she had connexions.

The controller smiled when she had gone and explained to the suspicious Mr Rosencrantz that the Duchess of Calapiccola came from one of the oldest Roman families and that she owned most of the province of Basilicata.

'She seems a very ungracious lady to me,' observed Mr Rosencrantz, with understatement born of a desire to be conciliatory until such time as he knew precisely who was fellow-travelling with whom, and where, and, indeed, why.

'*We* don't own a province, sir,' said the controller. 'We can afford to be pleasant. Nobody ever wants anything from us.'

'Anticipating any more trouble?' asked Mr Rosencrantz, steering the conversation back on to familiar lines.

'In the north, they may be more difficult to convince.'

'On account of the industries?' Mr Rosencrantz flashed, sharp as a knife.

'Yes.'

'Does the same hold true of Laos?' I asked.

'Yes,' he responded earnestly, 'inasmuch as there isn't much industry. You see, it is a predominantly agrarian economy, based largely on—'

'Rice!' I flashed, sharp as a knife myself.

'Right!' cried Mr Rosencrantz. I had made a friend.

I slept well until I became aware that the train was no longer moving. There seemed something uncomfortably final about the general atmosphere of peace and quiet on this occasion. I looked out. We were in the confines of a large, un-utterably lugubrious station. There was an early mist of the most petrifying cheerlessness. One light was on in a signal box, and a man was reading. In the middle distance, a window was lit up. A woman with unkempt hair seemed to be setting a table, while a man in long winter underwear kept appearing and disappearing. As far as I could see, they weren't talking.

I washed, brushed my teeth, and dressed. Afterward I still felt as though I hadn't washed or brushed my teeth, or ever undressed. That's sleeping-cars.

Mr Rosencrantz was in the corridor. 'We've been here over an hour,' he said grimly, as though the situation were creeping perceptibly on to a diplomatic level.

'Where are we, Milan?'

'I guess so. Our boy's finding out what's going on.'

'Oh. Cigarette?'

'No, thanks just the same. I used to smoke over four packs a day. I gave it up when I had my appendectomy with complications – peritonitis – and I've never smoked since.'

I even preferred Laos to this topic, and so I returned to my compartment to await results.

After a quarter of an hour, the controller returned. 'It's going to be all right,' he said. 'The strike was only partially successful. Up here, they're all too tired to do much about it. There's nothing more exhausting than sitting up all night consciously avoiding work. One or two are still holding out, but I talked them into letting us leave.'

Soon we were under way again, and as the sun came out surprisingly and brilliantly over the still sweep of Lago Maggiore, impertinently hot for the time of year, picking out the folds in the flesh of the snow-capped mountains in pink and grey, I began to half forget my travelling companions in pleasant anticipation of my arrival in Geneva. Then, within five kilometres of the Swiss frontier, the train unexpectedly slowed down and finally came to a halt. I opened the window and leaned out. The lights were red. I saw that in the usual reshuffle of railway cars we had moved up next to the engine overnight, and we were now alongside the fifty yards of platform of what looked like a whistle stop. There was a station of sorts, but it seemed like a toy. There was a tiny buffet, but no sign of life.

The controller leapt on to the platform.

'Does the train usually stop here?' I asked him.

'I've been with the company twelve years,' he replied, 'and I've never stopped here before.' Then he called to the engine driver, with an oscillating gesture of a hand cupped towards the body, the Italian for 'What the hell's going on?'

'*Beh*, the lights are red,' cried the engine driver.

The controller placed his hands on his hips and just stood there for a moment, frustrated.

Then the stationmaster made an entrance. There was nothing consoling in the dramatic perfection of his timing. He threw open the glass door centre stage and advanced with the small, vigorous steps of a corpulent tenor sure of his reputation and therefore of his applause. His face was worn by conflict, his eyes unforgiving.

'What's going on?' asked the controller.

'There's a strike on. Didn't you know about it?' replied the stationmaster pugnaciously.

'You mean you are holding up the train in obedience to the strike order?'

'Certainly.'

'For how long?'

The stationmaster consulted an old gun-metal watch. 'Another eighteen hours and forty-six minutes.'

The controller smiled affectionately. 'They let us through in Florence and Milan,' he said.

'That's their failure.'

'You mean to say we've got all this way and you're going to stop us five kilometres from the frontier?'

'Certainly, strike orders are given to be obeyed.'

'Now look here—'

'There is no argument with me!' shouted the stationmaster. 'No argument!'

The controller looked up at the engine driver.

'It'll cost me my job if I disobey a signal,' the engine driver called.

The stationmaster nodded with grim satisfaction. 'In any case, I have pulled the switches, so that if you were rash enough to proceed, you'd find yourself on the siding.' And he pointed to a pair of buffers nestling under a moist rock.

Other controllers appeared, a guard, even the chef of the dining-car, having made their way through the train.

'What's the name of this station?' asked our controller.

'Mine di Trasquera,' replied the stationmaster. 'It's not marked. That is the fault of the state, not me.'

'But where's the village?'

'There is no village, just a cement factory and a chapel, to throw dust in the eyes of the workers.'

There were faces at every window now: the nun, an older nun with whom she had been travelling but who had retired early, the priest, the American, the duchess, even the dog – all were there, and many more.

'*Figlio mio,*' said the priest.

'Oh, it's you.' The stationmaster recognized him.

'Why do you pass such gratuitous comment on what has been a source of comfort for so many?'

'You know my point of view, Don Gioacchino. The church is a retrogressive element. Its force derives from the ignorance in which it keeps the working masses. You say our Lord built His church on Saint Peter. "On this rock, I will build my church." The rock is superstition. The rock is stupidity. The rock is witchcraft!'

Both nuns crossed themselves.

The priest smiled. 'Always in your arguments you betray a surprising knowledge of the Bible.'

'The great Stalin was brought up in a seminary. There's no better education for a leader of the people, I'll grant you that.'

'Thank you, at least you make me feel we're doing some useful work,' the priest replied quietly.

'I can do without your sarcasm, Don Gioacchino,' snapped the stationmaster.

'I can do without yours, and yet I accept it in good grace. Now, can we get a taxi into Iselle di Trasquera?'

'You can do what you like, but you can't use my phone.'

'We have Mother Mary with us. She has been poorly. We've just been up to Rome to see a specialist.'

'I'm sorry. We're on strike.'

'Oh, don't make any concession on my account,' said the older nun robustly, unable to conceal her annoyance.

The train officials tried to appeal to the stationmaster, but to no avail. He pleased himself too much in his role of a commissar to be swayed.

While this was going on, I turned to Mr Rosencrantz, whose spirit was once more in Laos. 'Well, how is it to be face to face with the real thing?' I asked him. 'Not a fellow-traveller, not a man pretending to be a solid citizen, but a self-avowed, proud, unrepentant Communist.'

'Is that what he is? A Communist in a key position, in a country allied to the United States by treaty?'

'A military alliance,' I corrected.

'That's true. That's worse. What's the name of this place?'

'Mine di Trasquera.'

'Would you spell that?'

I did so.

'And where is that?' he inquired.

'About five kilometres—'

'That's three miles.'

'—more or less from Iselle di Trasquera, which is on the Swiss frontier.'

'That'd be the border of Switzerland.'

'If you prefer it.'

Mr Rosencrantz took copious notes. 'Would you please ask him his name?'

I tried to attract the stationmaster's attention, but it wasn't easy, since he was engaged in an ideological discussion with the train officials. Eventually he came towards us. 'Yes?'

'This gentleman would like to know your name.'

'What for?'

'He's a high official of the American government.'

The stationmaster smiled maliciously. 'Cavalieri, Ferruccio, stationmaster, secretary of the Partito Comunista Italiano, Sezzione Iselle di Trasquera.'

'Would you spell that?' Mr Rosencrantz asked me again. I did so, laboriously. Mr Rosencrantz was more used to dictating than being dictated to.

'Imprisoned by the Fascists for a total of seven years.'

Comrade Cavalieri was greedy for a large and accurate file in the black book of the State Department.

'Major in the Paris Commune Partisan Shock Division,' he continued. 'Wounded three times, once seriously. Decorated with seven medals, one American, one promised but never delivered.'

The duchess could stand this appeasement no longer. 'I am the Duchess of Calapiccola,' she hissed.

'I'm very sorry to hear it,' replied the stationmaster, diverting his attention to her.

'My brother-in-law is Count Parri-Ponti, the administrator of the State Railways.'

'You ought to be ashamed of yourself.'

'I'll get you fired for this.'

'They've tried, they've tried, believe me. But stationmasters of my quality and experience don't grow on trees. I'd be in charge of a proper station by now if I weren't true to my convictions. Padua, Parma, Brescia, a station a man can be proud of. They leave me here, but they don't dare get rid of me. If I went, half the stationmasters in the north would leave in sympathy.'

'I'll have you evicted,' cried the furious duchess. 'I'm a very sick woman. I am registered in a clinic in Lausanne. I will die if I don't reach the clinic by this afternoon.'

'There is a very reputable funeral parlour in Iselle, run by Ronco, Guiseppe, a member of our cell.'

The duchess spat into the stationmaster's face. Regrettably, the stationmaster, having very little experience in the etiquette governing such cases, spat back, with greater power and accuracy. To its eternal disgrace, the dog refrained from barking.

The officials had made their way sadly back to their posts on the train. The priest and the two nuns had alighted and were standing on the platform with their belongings. I could hear the duchess breaking up the furniture next door. Mr Rosencrantz was taking a photograph of the station.

The battle was over. The stationmaster was in command of the field. The priest and the nuns stood there like prisoners of war, waiting to be told what to do. Even the controller, so used to success, sat in the corridor, his head in his hands. There were eighteen hours to wait. Eighteen hours of silence, with nothing to do but watch the hands creep over the clock face.

I looked up at the sky. Surely if there was an Italian God up in the Italian heaven, this was the moment to strike. Only five kilometres away was the realm of the Swiss God, dour, sensible, and accurate, who would probably allow the eighteen hours to elapse, for He is the God of the chronometer and timekeepers. The nuns were also looking skyward. Could it be that, from those tremendous heights, the frontiers seemed a little hazy? *O Dio, siamo Italiani!*

Then it happened. Quivering with excitement, the stationmaster's assistant emerged from his cubicle; a youth of eighteen, six feet four, with a squint and a stammer.

'Farther up the l-line—' he gasped.

'What? Speak up!' cried the stationmaster.

'A landslide near the tunnel—'

'A landslide?'

'Just around the bend where the s-s-signals are!'

'A landslide!' the stationmaster was thunderstruck.

In an evangelistic ecstasy, the youth addressed the train. 'If the train had been allowed to p-p-proceed, it would have been derailed. You'd all have been k-k-killed!'

The young nun fell on to her knees. '*Un miracolo!*' she shrieked.

The stationmaster stood there, grey as death, humiliated, stabbed in the back.

'Would you mind translating that?' asked Mr Rosencrantz.

We crossed the Simplon pass by motor coach and went on our various ways by Swiss trains.

Two days later, in Geneva, I happened to pick up a copy of an Italian paper. The headlines ran, 'Stationmaster's Presence of Mind Saves International Train from Disaster.' I read the article. It was in the form of an interview with Cavalieri, Ferruccio, stationmaster of Mine di Trasquera.

'Yes,' said the stationmaster to the interviewer, 'I've had thirty-six years in the service of the State Railways, interrupted, of course, by seven years in a Fascist prison. There's no getting away from it, experience counts in any profession. I knew that the coming of winter brings with it many hazards, especially in mountain regions. Only two days before, I had said to Finzi, Gianni, my assistant, "I wouldn't be surprised if one of these fine mornings we don't have a landslide near that tunnel – the one where the signals are." I don't know why, but when the express came in yesterday, I hesitated to let it go on. Oh, they tried to persuade me. They said it had been held up by some strike or other down south, advanced all sorts of reasons to get me to let it go, but I was adamant.'

'The Cardinal Archbishop of Milan has suggested it was Divine Providence which made you so stubborn,' the interviewer suggested.

'I am too humble a man to know the truth of that,' Cavalieri went on, 'but I will say that as I was debating with myself whether or not to change the signals, a voice within me kept saying, "No".'

'Just "No"?'

'No. "Thou shalt not let the train pass!" '

I marvelled at the extreme loyalty of the assistant to his chief until I caught sight of a photograph at the bottom of the front page. Both he and Cavalieri were being congratulated by Count Parri-Ponti, administrator of the State Railways, brother-in-law of the Duchess of Calapiccola, and both were beaming with pleasure. Medals would undoubtedly follow, the caption said, and promotion to a larger station.

The editorial of the paper carried the theme of the men's devotion to duty on to a level of mysticism and asked the burning question of the Italian conscience: 'How many such men are there in our land, hidden in remote places, only to be discovered by some quirk of fate for what they are, simple, trusting heroes, with the ability to recognize the voice of God when they hear it? It is time some of our politicians realized the simple truth which emerges with a crystal clarity from such a case as this. To be Italian is to believe. That is the strength of Ferruccio Cavalieri. This is our strength also.'

O slightly smiling God of Italy, you know, whereas abroad

money may corrupt, or power, or any of the galaxy of vices which man may choose for his temporal pleasure and eventual undoing, in your country it is not as simple as that. Alexander VI, the Borgia Pope, was not the best of spiritual leaders – some even say that he was a monster of evil – and yet, how much more unrestrainedly evil could he have been had he not been Pope! In his case, as in the case of Ferruccio Cavalieri, stationmaster of Mine di Trasquera, virtue corrupts. Never again can the poor fellow make a categorical decision in the hardness and clarity of his heart, never again can he address a meeting with the absolute conviction that he is right, never again can he assume the dogmatic air of the Soviet theorist. Why not? Because he is Italian, and because you, his God, are Italian too. Whatever he may do or say from now on, he will not be able to prevent his eye from straying upward in apprehension of your next move.

The Silken Dagger

The dust had not yet settled over Europe: there were corpses still unburied. Here and there, fanatics unwilling to surrender their dreams still resisted crazily, preferring, once it had to be, the chance bullet to the deliberate.

For Guiseppe Gargaglia it was too late for speculations of this nature. He had had his chance, and he had missed it. Captured ignominiously in the clothes of an old woman, he now sat in a cell with nothing but his thoughts for company. He would have preferred to be alone.

To make matters worse, his jailers were Italian, therefore compassionate. They made endless little gestures hoping that he would feel at home. One of them, Arnaldo, a fair-haired, pug-nosed youth from Reggis Emilia, even went so far as to ask him for his autograph. His autograph?

'Eh,' Arnaldo said with a shrug, 'you never know which way history will turn. Someday I may be able to give my son your signature and say that it was dedicated to him by Eccelenza Gargaglia, the Undersecretary of the Interior during the last days of the Fascist era.'

Gargaglia smiled a little grimly. The jailer's attitude was intimate and yet deferential, as if he realized that, although his charge was a prisoner divested of his liberties, the fall from grace had been from dizzy heights.

'All right,' Gargaglia growled with a trace of his habitual energy, 'give me a pen and paper.'

Arnaldo grinned. 'I have something more suitable than paper.' And he produced from his pocket a soiled clipping from an illustrated paper, showing Gargaglia at the peak of his achievements, snarling on a balcony, his nostrils puckered into folds of hatred and disdain, his mouth rising diabolically towards the corners of his eyes, while his hand reached powerfully into the air, tearing down some imagined enemy. By his side, the Duce stood in a pose of meditative appreciation, of heroic contentment.

'For God's sake! Where did you get that?'

'There are plenty of old magazines knocking around.'

A habitué of diplomacy could read the possibility of a hint in Arnaldo's evasiveness. Gargaglia glanced at him keenly. 'Are you a Fascist?' he asked quietly.

'No. Never have been. Naturally, we had to pretend.'

Exasperating, this young fellow. There was no knowing just how intelligent he was.

As Gargaglia wrote his name with a flourish: he took a certain satisfaction in sensing once again the liquid fanfare of his signature. 'What's the boy's name?' he asked.

'Benito.'

'After the Duce?'

'After his mother's father – a martyr to the cause.'

'The cause?'

'We are Communists,' said Arnaldo, by way of information.

Gargaglia's throat was dry. The last twenty-four hours had been fraught with confusion, both of spirit and of mind. He had not been seen in a good light, tottering down the street in the stolen rags of a harridan. He might have been a fiery orator, but he was no actor. His performance had lacked conviction; he had been foolish ever to attempt it. He still heard in his ears the laughter of the partisans as his clothes had been taken off and the sudden silent awe as they realized the magnitude of their capture.

Now he passed a weary hand over his sleepless eyes. 'If you hold convictions of that nature, why the hell did you ask for my autograph?' he asked.

'Oh, as I said, you never know,' replied Arnaldo pleasantly. 'Very few men can control history even for a little while. I may be a Communist, but I'm certainly not one of them. I've no talent; that's why I'm a jailer and not an officer, a man to make decisions, even small ones. But my son likes autographs. He's got several film stars already and one or two celebrities in other walks of life. Now, I love my son. He's young, but through no fault of mine he hasn't seen much of his youth yet. If he wants autographs, the least I can do is to get them for him, and they're cheaper than toys. I mean, I don't approve of Hitler, but if there was a chance to get his auto-graph, I'd leap at it, you understand. I don't know what they'll say about you in years to come. You may be considered a traitor or a man who did Italy a lot of good or else just forgotten. There's no telling with history. So I thought to myself, better be on the safe side, for Benito's sake. That's why I asked you for your autograph.'

'It's logical,' Gargaglia murmured, but he had not the energy to make what he said sound ironic.

There was a pause while Arnaldo folded the autographed picture carefully and put it away in his pocket. 'A cup of water?' he asked.

Gargaglia didn't really care for water, but he nodded economically, as he had done when in office. A nod which emphasized authority.

While Arnaldo was out of the room, Gargaglia remembered an operation he had had for the removal of his gall bladder. Recurrent jaundice had been the fault of Africa. He had pioneered in those grim wastes which put an enormous strain on the Italian economy in exchange for the mere title of Empire. His faulty bladder had taken on in his mind the character of a wound, gloriously achieved in the service of his country.

He remembered the hospital, the atmosphere of functional efficiency, fans whirling on the ceiling to whip the air into activity, the preoccupied cheerfulness of the doctors, with a kind glance to spare every now and then, the silent gliding of the nuns with their look of direct communication with heaven. It had given him courage to feel he was part of a factory for healing, and he had passed under the knife con-vinced that his own cooperation was vital if the thing was to pass off well.

'What is death,' he asked himself, 'but an operation from which a man does not recover?' The essential is to be casual, to collaborate with the men doing this duty job. In any execu-tion, the victim has his part to play. It is not so much a tragic event as a ritual, with its own prescribed rules and regulations, a kind of divine service. Nuns die to the world by prostrating themselves helplessly on the floor and are covered with a symbolic shroud before they enter into the jealous womb of Mother Church. The firing squad is no different. The prerequisite for the novice is a sense of occasion and resignation; at all times, resignation.

In the grand pavan of death, he must remember to refuse the handkerchief when offered. This refusal is the only permitted rebellion, which gives the ceremony its profane quality. Useless to protest innocence, useless even to cry out some platitudes about the nation. It only worries the firing squad, who are not there from choice and who have to go on living afterwards. It is good manners to listen to the consolations of the priest as though he were really a harbinger of comfort. Intolerable it would be for him if he thought for a moment that his warmly melancholy phrases were falling on deaf ears. That would be as socially ill-mannered as allowing your mind to drift while a well-meaning bore is telling you a story you have heard before.

Endlessly Gargaglia daydreamed, and endlessly it was the same daydream. He saw his own fine profile and distinguished head, a head curiously rendered more distinguished by its baldness. Unflinchingly he listened as the commander of the firing squad read out his sentence by the people's court. He even permitted himself a slight smile and one of his spare little nods. Perhaps the curl of his lips suggested in a remote and unprotesting way that his opinion of the people's court was low. At all events, the commander of the firing squad seemed momentarily stunned by such *sang-froid*. He saw the priest and heard the rapid muttering. There were so many sacred texts to rush through in such a short time. They tied him to the post. The handkerchief was held up. His black eyes hardened. 'No,' he said, loud and clear. Perhaps, on second thought, it would be better to say nothing, just to shake his head negatively. The film of his imagination ran backwards. The handkerchief was held up again. This time he shook his head. The commander seemed to take courage from this example and stared at him for a moment in silent admiration. The sword was raised. No, no, before this he must remember to thank the priest. He thanked the priest with great simplicity. The priest was amazed at such presence of mind and reinforced in his faith as he saw the magic of his words at work. The sword was raised again. The front row of soldiers dropped on to their knees. He looked above them at the opulent Italian sky and reflected almost happily on his honour. Somewhere he fancied he heard a shout, and then all went red behind his eyelids, as it will when you are trying to sleep in the midday sun. From red to black. The soldiers looked at each other and murmured, 'There was a brave man.'

He was just beginning the daydream again when Arnaldo reappeared with a cup of water. 'Sorry I've been so long,' he said, 'but there's a lot of excitement at headquarters. They've caught General Zaleschi and bank president Mora. Also Gozzi-Parella, the editor of the Fascist youth magazine.'

'What have they done with them?'

'I don't know. Nothing yet. Zaleschi and Mora were dressed as peasants – but as men.'

Gargaglia flinched. That observation was unnecessary. Still, you can't expect an ordinary soldier to have much taste.

'Gozzi-Parella just walked into headquarters,' Arnaldo went on, 'and said that it'd save everyone a great deal of trouble if he just gave himself up. There's no doubt about it, that fellow has guts, even if he has been corrupting our youth.'

'I suppose they'll shoot the lot of us,' said Gargaglia.

'Couldn't say,' replied Arnaldo. 'You'd have to ask someone with more authority. Up to yesterday, we were shooting without so much as a trial, but they seem to be hanging back today.'

'What happened to Colonel Gasparone?' asked Gargaglia, although he knew well.

'Oh, he came up before the tribunal – people's court, or whatever they call it – yesterday morning. The trial was very short; ten minutes, no more. Then they took him out and shot him.'

'How do they perform those little ceremonies?' This is what Gargaglia wanted to know.

'Oh.' Arnaldo was embarrassed. 'Are you sure you want to talk about it?'

'Of course,' Gargaglia snapped. It was easy to have bravura at this juncture. He thought he detected a glint of admiration in Arnaldo's eye, and it gave him pleasure.

'Well, they take the victim out, they bind his eyes—'

'There will be no need of that.'

'Then they sit him down in a chair, tie his hands behind his back, and shoot him.'

'A chair? It is facing the firing squad, of course.'

'Oh, no. The executions I've seen, they always shoot them in the back.'

Gargaglia paled. 'That's revolting,' he said.

'You may be able to change it in your case, if it comes to that. I mean, there's no harm in asking; they can only say no.'

'But, tell me, is there a priest in attendance?'

'Not in Colonel Gasparone's case. There was no time to find one. You've got to realize, we're not organized like a regular army. We're just partisans. Our justice is meted out according to the circumstances. I don't think we'd refuse you a priest if there was one available, but if there wasn't one available, we'd hardly stay the execution until they could find one.'

Gargaglia was no longer listening. Evidently, in the desire for revenge the opportunities for heroism, even for dignity, had been whittled away. They had changed the ritual, and it was almost like blasphemy, this denial of the ancient courtesies. Only cowards were shot in the back, and in their black hatred the changers of the rules knew that no gestures were possible when slumped in a vulgar kitchen chair, like some victim of a burglar. And no priest! No one with the intellect to appreciate the quality of one's silence!

Gargaglia took refuge in anger and stamped his foot.

'I told you we shouldn't have talked about it,' said Arnaldo. 'It doesn't make for good conversation at the best of times.'

'Silence!' shouted Gargaglia. 'If I'm accorded a last wish, it will be your silence.'

'You haven't drunk your water,' said Arnaldo softly. 'Didn't you want it?'

The cell door opened and Quattrospille entered. He was the local commander of the partisans, a chain-smoking intellectual with a perpetual frown and eyes that seemed to be looking into the distance.

Gargaglia gave in to a momentary panic when he saw him,

but then grasped at his annoyance for a platform. 'Well?' he barked, suggesting that if something desperate had to be done, it would be good to do it and get it over with.

Quattrospille lit a new cigarette from the stub of his old one and leaned against the chalky wall.

Gargaglia felt that the pause was an insult.

'What's the matter with you?' asked Quattrospille. 'You have no problems except to wait.'

'Wait, wait. For what?'

'Ah,' replied Quattrospille with a sigh, 'I wish I knew. If I had my way, I'd have shot you on sight, immediately when we had those women's clothes off you. It would have saved me a headache, and I'm sure you'd have been much happier that way.'

'Are you trying to be amusing?' Gargaglia asked with a gasp.

Quattrospille looked pained. His weariness had slowed down his reflexes. 'No. I'm saying what I feel. After all, these are tumultuous days, each one of which seems to last a week. We are destroying with one hand and trying painfully to begin rebuilding with the other. It's tough. The problems are so easy during battle; then, with the coming of peace, all the problems start again.'

Gargaglia cleared his throat. 'Did you come in here to tell me something, or are you just whiling away the time at the expense of my nerves?'

'Me?' replied Quattrospille. 'I'm putting my cards on the table. I'm telling you my problems, the problems of administration, because you yourself were once an administrator and might therefore be able to grasp them.'

'I always insisted on plain speaking.'

Quattrospille smiled, and as he smiled he yawned. 'Really?' he answered. 'Well, what could be plainer than my telling you that, if I had my way, you'd have been shot on sight?'

'But what are you telling me now?' cried Gargaglia. 'That you will have your own way and I will be shot, or that you won't have your way and I won't be shot?'

Quattrospille inhaled deeply and watched the smoke rise slowly into the room and spread in languorous contortions. 'The situation is not yet clear,' he said.

'Amateurs!' thought Gargaglia. 'When they're in power, nothing will function – trains, electric light, jurisdiction. Nothing.' But he allowed Quattrospille the luxury of further rumination.

'You see,' Quattrospille went on, 'for the first few days we were on our own. The criminals we captured we shot, and no questions asked. That enabled us to work fast and well. Now the main body of the Allied forces has arrived, not just soldiers but administrators, and not just Anglo-Americans but Italians as well. This inevitably complicates the issue. If I shoot you now, they will want to know why you were not handed over to the ponderous justice of some higher court. I could always say that you were killed while trying to escape, but then there's the risk that some ambitious idiot will testify the opposite and I'll be in the soup.' He glanced at Arnaldo, paused and lit another cigarette, although the one in his mouth was scarcely halfway smoked.

'I am not in a position to be interested in your problems,' said Gargaglia stiffly. 'I can only be interested in your decision. I would be grateful to know what it is.'

Quattrospille laughed softly and humourlessly. Then he asked Arnaldo to leave the cell. When they were alone he continued, 'You're quite wrong. I came here to seek your cooperation, to make you an offer, if you will. If I make it possible for you to escape, I could shoot you and therefore clear myself of any recrimination afterwards.'

'You're quite mad!' Gargaglia spluttered.

'Why? There is still a slender chance that our bullets might miss you; it's the kind of chance the English call "sporting". And before you jump to any hasty conclusions, think of the alternative. If you're not shot today, now, this very minute, you'll be handed over to higher authorities and be put on trial. You were a high Fascist official. They will blame you for quite a few crimes in Ethiopia as well as for your restrictive measures against the Jews, to say nothing of the deaths of numerous partisans and hostages. It will mean the firing squad in any case. Think, then, which is preferable – a clean shot now, while you are prepared for the worst, or a formal execution at a later date, after innumerable delays, when you have got used to hope.'

Gargaglia looked into Quattrospille's eyes and saw no humanity there, only interest.

'Arnaldo!' called Gargaglia.

'You will live to regret your decision,' said Quattrospille, 'but, then, most of your decisions have been stupid.'

'During the whole of the Fascist era,' Gargaglia stammered, his face flushed with anger and fear, 'I have never encountered such hatred.'

Quattrospille appeared surprised. 'I have been very charitable. One day you may realize the extent of my charity. There was no hatred in my offer, only understanding.'

Arnaldo came back and began beating Quattrospille's tunic. 'All white,' he said, 'from the wall,' and then he whispered some information into his chief's ear.

Quattrospille's eyes shut in exasperation. When he opened them again, he looked straight at Gargaglia. 'You have a visitor,' he said and left.

A visitor? Gargaglia trembled. In the language of melodrama employed by the partisans, this could mean almost anything. He cringed in the corner. It might mean no more than another prisoner to share the cell with, or it might mean the barrel of a sub-machine-gun through the bars.

The door of the cell creaked open and a man entered slowly, blinking as though unaccustomed to the light. He was fairly tall and obviously intended by nature to be corpulent, but at the moment he was thin and white, perhaps recovering from a lengthy illness. His neck was much smaller than his collar, and loose skin hung in folds from a firm jaw, shivering as he turned his head. The clothes he wore were sober to the point of constituting some kind of uniform. In his hand he clasped a hard-brimmed black hat and an ebony stick, on which he leaned.

'Signor Gargaglia? May I come in?' he wheezed in an asthmatic voice.

'Who is that?'

'Guido Manasse.'

Gargaglia felt an explosion of ice within him. He couldn't believe it, and he was afraid. Professor Manasse had been one of Italy's greatest forensic orators, a lawyer with a rhetorical style of such elemental power that no judge could trust his own judgement under its bombardment. He had nothing but a mind; his voice was unattractive and unresonant, his gestures stiff, and his two rows of teeth had never quite decided which should be in front of the other. Whenever he shut his mouth, it still appeared to be half open. But his mind was extraordinary, not only by virtue of its inventiveness but also because of its incredible discipline and selectivity. He remembered everything he was told and could filter the facts, grading them into relevancies and mere chaff while he was talking, and while he talked the words born of these simultaneous mental processes were always original, powerful, precise.

'Why have you come here?'

'Hmm. You seem to be comfortable here, your Excellency.'

Gargaglia found himself unable to move as Manasse walked slowly to the centre of the cell. 'Have you come here to mock me?'

'Not at all,' said Manasse pleasantly. 'You seem to forget that I have spent the last three years in cells, so that when I comment on the comfort of yours, I am not comparing it to a room but to a series of other cells. As you may know, I am quite a connoisseur.' He contemplated the disposition of the furniture for a moment. 'I see you have a stool and a box. May I sit down?'

'What's to prevent you?'

Manasse smiled, and his pale-blue eyes sparkled with an amusement which bore every mark of being genuine. 'You used to be such a good host in the old days,' he pleaded. 'Won't you please come out of your corner and make me feel at home here?'

Gargaglia didn't move.

'I am incapable of doing you any physical violence, even if I wanted to, since I have been gravely ill, and in any case, I have always abhorred the uglier side of life,' he went on. 'The doctors tell me I must rest as much as possible. It would be polite if, on purely medical grounds, you invited me to sit down.'

'Please sit down,' Gargaglia growled. He suspected irony in every phrase.

'Thank you. Now, since this is your cell, you must have a favourite between these two seats. It is immaterial to me, since I don't live here. Would you indicate where you would like me to sit?'

'I don't care.'

'That is probably because you haven't been here long enough. After a month or two, a man becomes very particular. Then, if you have nothing against it, I will select this one. It reminds me . . .' He sat on the box. 'Now, please join me in the centre of the cell. I am not questioning you for an exam. I am just visiting.'

'I should prefer to stand.'

Gargaglia saw that, at certain angles, Manasse's eyes parted company and gazed off in different directions, which gave him an all-seeing quality so useful in court. At other moments, his eyes were visible in miniature through the thick lenses of his rimless pince-nez, so that it seemed as though he had four eyes at his command.

'You are being very childish, if you don't mind me saying so. I never expected that a high functionary of the government would greet me in such a fit of juvenile sulks,' Manasse laughed.

Gargaglia sat, but to cover his embarrassment he asked, 'Are you here in an official capacity?'

'I could hardly be, since I am not an official.'

'But you won't wish me to believe that you made the journey for pleasure?'

Manasse laughed aloud. 'That's more like it,' he chuckled, 'the Gargaglia of old, the journalist with the vitriolic pen. We were at school together, remember?'

'Of course I remember,' Gargaglia replied curtly.

'Yes, I had a mop of red hair in those days. Look at it now – white, what there is of it, a few strands, but they still won't stay down when I comb them. I used to fall in love very easily then; that was before I learned to organize my thoughts and my emotions. The lovesick Jew, they used to call me. And I remember one rather charming occasion on which you became very angry on my behalf. I was always rather timid. You threatened to knock a boy down if he said it again – the lovesick Jew. Remember? Yes, life is full of little ironies.'

'Has your visit any bearing on my predicament?' demanded Gargaglia.

'Ah, Gargaglia the practical, the administrator, the man of iron! Another manifestation of a complex character.' Manasse patted the prisoner on the knee. 'Forgive me if I seem to tease you. It's my exuberance at seeing you again after so long, and, quite frankly, there were times in prison when I thought the opportunity to renew our acquaintance would never arise.'

'Enough of this,' Gargaglia said abruptly. 'You may have all the time in the world for banter of this nature; I have not. At any moment they may arrive to shoot me.'

'There is no hurry,' Manasse said. 'I have asked them to wait.'

'Then you *are* here on some official business. I demand to know what it is!'

'There is nothing official about my business,' Manasse replied patiently. 'It is just that, with the collapse of Fascism, my reputation has recovered. Suddenly everybody knows who I am. I asked the powers that be not to do anything about your case until I had finished my conversation with you. They agreed immediately. While I am here, you are safe.'

Gargaglia frowned. 'I don't know what you want with me,' he said, hesitantly, 'but it would be inhuman if your attitude towards me were not vindictive.'

'It would be inhuman? Why?' Manasse seemed to be amazed; then he suddenly saw the light. 'Ah, because it was you who instigated the repressive measures against the Jews. Yes, yes, yes, I never thought of that.' His tone abruptly changed to one eminently reasonable. 'How could you help that? Once it was important for us to cultivate the German alliance, in order, I presume, to hide the deficiencies in our armed forces; it was imperative for you to toe whatever line the Germans drew for you, wherever they drew it. If it helps you at all, I personally don't blame you for either the sudden wave of officially inspired anti-Semitism or for my own arrest. You must have had your reasons. I am inclined to believe the reasons for your actions in advance.'

Gargaglia tried to sound reasonable. 'Naturally, German pressure was considerable—'

'Considerable? I was sure it had been superhuman.'

'There was no such thing as pressure from the Germans which we could not resist. It would be wrong to assume that we took a single decision under duress. We were entirely responsible for each and every action performed in the name of the Italian government.'

Oh, Gargaglia was no fool. He saw the trap which was being laid for him, but he considered that a man of Manasse's temperament would appreciate apparent honesty more than any attempt at ingenuity.

'In other words, you are now telling me that the abrupt persecution of our Jewish population was an entirely Italian initiative?'

'Yes,' replied Gargaglia.

'But do you sincerely think that you would have had the idea of it without the example of Germany?'

'That is an academic question, professor.'

'Would Italy ever have entered the war without a signal from her big sister? – oh, half-sister, let us say.'

'That, too, is an academic question. The facts are that these events took place for definite reasons. It is useless to speculate on what inspired them or what might have been.'

'Useless, but so fascinating,' Manasse said, smiling. For a moment he studied Gargaglia, who pretended hastily to be lost in thought. Those four blue eyes, each pursuing its independent course, were too much to tolerate. Gargaglia felt himself outgunned.

'Tell me, then, since you wish to take everything on your own shoulders, what have you against the Jews?' Manasse crooned softly.

'The Jews? They are . . . different.'

'Different from what?'

Gargaglia betrayed his irritation with a brief gesture. 'You know perfectly well.'

'Well, I know perfectly well that we are different from each other. A shocking thought, isn't it? One which may never have occurred to you. When people talk about "the Jews", they tend to see an amorphous mass, a crowd, in their mind's eye, but never a crowd of individuals, a microcosm of the faults and virtues to be found in the entire human race.'

'The Jews were, and are, different from the Italians.'

Gargaglia's policy was one of disengagement, of monosyllabic replies where possible. Manasse held the initiative in this mysterious debate. Manasse alone knew where it was leading. Under these circumstances, Gargaglia held back, protecting his freedom of action as long as possible, conserving his reserves of energy and of logic.

'The Italians, too, are different from each other,' Manasse suggested. 'And even if you subscribe to the absurd dream that the race has altered not at all since the days of the Romans, you must remember that Rome herself had her Jews, and a damned nuisance they made of themselves with their hot-headedness and stubbornness and their waiting in the catacombs.' He laughed briefly and silently at the image he had created. 'Difference by itself is surely no cause for persecution. I would suggest that defencelessness is perhaps a more valid incentive. The Germans were different from the Italians, but the Italians never persecuted the Germans. They were in no position to. The Jews are much easier to persecute. Isn't that the real reason – facility? When you are angry with your superiors, you shout at your wife. Isn't that so? When frustrated, impotent, a nation always has the Jews to fall back on, as a man has his wife. Take a look at history, and you will see that in times of affluence and of national contentment, the Jews are usually left alone.'

'I personally have nothing against the Jews.'

'Aah—'

'Your assessment of the causes of persecution is extremely penetrating. There are exceptions, of course.'

'Of course. There are exceptions to most generalizations.'

'It would be an idiot who did not admit that the contribution of individual Jews to the advancement of humanity,' Gargaglia said, 'is out of all proportion to the size of the Jewish populations. Einstein, Spinoza, Ehrlich; one can enumerate quite easily a galaxy of people who have enriched thought, music, science. I am not an idiot; therefore I admit it. Still, there is a difference between individual Jews and Jews in the mass.'

'When Jews are in a mass, there are more of them,' said Manasse. 'The same is true of Italians. That must be one of the few rules to which there is no exception.'

The tone of gentle mockery inhibited Gargaglia, who faltered for a moment. 'It seemed to me at the time that a limited persecution was justified as an instrument of national policy.'

'At the time?' Manasse flashed. 'You no longer think so?'

'I – I may have been wrong.'

'As a politician or as a man?'

'As a politician.'

'And as a man?'

'As a man – I may have been wrong also.'

Manasse relaxed and scratched his almost invisible white moustache with his forefinger. 'Let us leave the subject of the Jews,' he said. 'I am a Jew, but I am not a Zionist, not a fanatic. Why? Because I am Italian, and you can't be both an Italian and a Zionist fanatic. I only spoke about the persecution of the Jews because I detest persecution, not because I love my own race with an unreasoning passion. The persecution of a horse by a farmer is, in its way, as revolting as the persecution of a minority by a majority. Evil is not something that should be judged by quantity but by quality.' Manasse looked at the floor. Suddenly he pointed to a crack in the tiles. 'Look,' he said, 'there is a spider. Kill it!'

'Why,' asked Gargaglia, 'are you afraid of it?'

'Not in the least. It is quite harmless.'

'Why should I kill it then?'

'Why should you not kill it?' Manasse asked. 'You are stronger than it is. It will not need much effort to step on it.'

'There is still no reason to kill it!' Gargaglia suddenly shouted.

'Find reasons. You're an intelligent man,' rasped Manasse. 'The spider lives in a rough world, a world without language, without communication, without debate, a world of the hunter and the hunted, an unsentimental world. Ask yourself: if you were the size of a spider and it were the size of a man, would it hesitate to kill you? No. Therefore, kill it!'

'No!'

Manasse relaxed. 'Why did we declare war?' he asked quietly. 'There was no reason to kill those men. The idea of killing a spider doesn't upset you, Gargaglia; it is only because I asked you to kill this particular one that you shrank at the idea. You saw it walking about harmlessly; you had time to think. From your high balconies, you saw the intact divisions of the Italian army stretched out before you, bayonets gleaming in a sun which seemed to be shining for you alone. You saw only the uniforms, not the men; and not seeing the men, you failed to see the women, the predestined widows, and the children, the orphans to be. You saw the golden wrappings but not the promise of misery they contained. You had no imagination, Gargaglia. With all your superficial intelligence, with all your brilliance, you were as irresponsible as a child left to play among the priceless treasures of a cathedral. Your guilt is enormous, incalculable, terrible.'

Violently, Gargaglia brought his foot down on the spider. 'Bravo!' Manasse clapped sarcastically. 'What courage! I had underestimated you. You are a man of fibre after all, a cabinet minister to the end!'

Gargaglia broke down in tears of humiliation.

'Why are you crying?' Manasse asked quietly. 'Are those tears for the latest widow of your creation?'

Gargaglia pounded his knees with his fists. His fury was that of a child, and yet the tears did not flow from his intellect.

Manasse became warm and tender. 'It's terrible waiting for the decisions of people you neither trust nor admire, isn't it? You've had only a few hours of it; I had three years. But I can tell you, the first hours are the worst. I don't know about you, but I was a coward. I kept on imagining how I'd behave if it came to the worst. I could never see myself keeping my eloquence in check. I was always sure I'd die spouting rhetoric, defending myself before a jury of rifles.' He paused. 'I'm sure it's worse when you're talented. A simple man can die with dignity, because in the last resort, it's all he's left with. Dignity is largely reticence, and what is more conducive to reticence than ignorance? With us, it's different. Don't you feel you still have so much to give, so much to do? Doesn't life, even lived to the natural end, seem awfully short to you?'

'Why are you torturing me?' Gargaglia screamed. 'Aren't you satisfied to see me like this?'

Manasse raised his eyebrows in surprise. 'Such a tantrum,' he said, 'and I came to bring you good news.'

The sobbing Gargaglia looked at his tormentor, and his breathing slowed down audibly. 'Good news?'

Manasse grinned charmingly. 'You're not going to be shot.'

'Not—'

'You're going to stand trial.'

Gargaglia managed a bitter laugh. 'I'm not going to be shot yet, in that case. Later.'

'You're not going to be shot at all.'

'How – how do you know?'

'Because I am going to defend you.'

'You?'

There was a long silence as Gargaglia studied the lawyer's face.

Suddenly Gargaglia leaped to his feet. 'So that's your revenge,' he cried. 'You'll defend me. You'll defend me in such a way that I'll be condemned before I ever set foot in that court. You'll use all your legal tricks to make it clear that you have no belief in my possible innocence. No, thank you. I stand a better chance defending myself. Thank you, though, for your generosity!'

Manasse waited patiently for the outburst to finish. Then he spoke with great sincerity to the creature who was now prowling the cell in his anger. 'I have enough pride in my own career to be unable to do as you suggest. I have made it a habit to win my cases. Do you think I, as a human animal, could bear it if my colleagues began to say, "Old Manasse is slipping"? Already I will be exposing myself to some disagreeable comment from my best friends by accepting this case. You think it is easy for a Jew to defend his persecutor? What possible motives will people be able to ascribe to my decision? They know I am different. I don't really mind if they think I am mad, but I can't face it if they think I am incompetent.'

Gargaglia stopped his pacing to listen.

'The truth is that justice has never interested me as much as tolerance. I have always defended, if you remember, never prosecuted. I am constitutionally unable to prosecute. For that a man needs a developed sense of justice; I am too emotional for that. I believe that the law in all countries is far too rude an instrument for the dispensation of justice. I hate the law for the cold, deaf, inhuman institution it is, all black and white, with hardly a provision for the infinite shades of grey which motivate human behaviour and which make good men perform evil actions and drive intelligent men to unbelievable stupidity. Because of this, I have often defended a man I knew to be a criminal and given him liberty with my gifts. As a lawyer I am bad but brilliant. I don't care, so long as I preserve what qualities I possess as a man living among men. That is what is important to me.'

There was stillness in the cell.

'If you want me to, I will get you off.'

'Why?' asked Gargaglia numbly.

Manasse smiled. 'There's hope for you yet,' he said. 'For a moment I was afraid you'd ask me how, not why.'

Manasse rose. 'I came here,' he went on, 'to see if you were vulnerable, if you were human, if you could suffer, and I'm satisfied. You cowered in a corner when I entered. You were afraid. That was a good sign. You tried to defend your actions and found it impossible. You have a conscience which is beginning to work again, slowly and painfully, like a child learning to walk. You cried, and it wasn't just out of exhaustion. You are redeemable, and, as such, you have reaffirmed a little of my faith in man. In these days, I need at least one reaffirmation every day, until I also begin slowly to take goodness for granted again.'

Manasse crossed to the door. 'Do you wish me to defend you?'

Gargaglia looked at the floor. 'Why do you bother?' he whispered.

'Why?' replied Manasse. His blue eyes were now cold, clear, and entirely unemotional. 'Because it is the most terrible vengeance I could conceive – to defend you successfully, free of charge.'

The cell was empty. Gargaglia saw his life stretching before him, out of sight, each day a cell as empty as the one he was in. He sank to his knees, not in order to pray but because the weight of his humiliation drove him there. He tried to weep again, but there were no tears left. At that moment, he would have obeyed any order, from anyone. The firing squad would have been an act of kindness; but, then, life is often more brutal than death, for it is rich in time, death rich only in silence.

The Loneliness of Billiwoonga

Europe occupies the same position in many European hearts as does a school, loved and hated at the same time. Its habits are irreplaceable, its secret, intimate pleasures cannot be recreated in wider pastures, and yet its stern rules seem to be built on firm foundations of bigotry, its actions obedient to an ancient stupidity. Every twenty years or so, at the blow of a bugle as casual as the chiming of a clock, it is *de rigueur* for the healthy men to go to the railway station and leave for the frontier amid a forest of sad white handkerchiefs and the blare of martial music from the crackling speakers. What frontier? Any frontier, for they shift like the tides; politicians call them historical, generals call them strategic, simple men call them a confounded nuisance.

Jiří Polovička was sick of it. He had been sick of it in 1939, he was sicker of it now. Born in 1904, of a Czech father and a Slovak mother, he had found himself a Hungarian citizen after the end of World War I, for no other reason than that his father had settled on the wrong side of a river. Eventually old Mr Polovička decided to move to his mother country, since minorities have their problems in Central Europe. Desiring to travel as far away from Hungary as the somewhat freakish geography of Czechoslovakia would allow, he opened a small grocer's shop in Teschen, a mining town on the Polish frontier. Life was relatively calm until the anxieties of the late thirties, when overnight the whole Polovička family became Polish. Since their entire capital was invested in the disputed town, it was economically impossible for them to emigrate again. Whatever patriots may say when unveiling statues, the threat of starvation is a more powerful argument than abstract sentiments of belonging. Before long, Hitler had made a nonsense of all the finer feelings in any case, and Jiří had not been in the Polish army for two days before he found himself a prisoner of war among people whose language he understood with difficulty, undergoing gratuitous hardships to the taste of the master race.

A spell of digging potatoes for a kindly Silesian farmer was interrupted with an offer to join a Bohemian-Moravian brigade, which was destined to fill the gaps on the eastern front when the time came. When this offer was refused with great politeness, the German government took it as a personal affront, and Jiři was sent on a visit to Ravensbruck, which was interrupted only after six months, when he was transferred to Auschwitz. The Gestapo made it clear that they considered his masquerade as a Pole a deliberate attempt to deceive them, by declaring that as a Czech he was now protected by the Reich and that his engagement in a foreign army had been nothing less than treason.

Luckily for him, they took several years to decide the exact extent of this treason, and so he survived, moving from one camp to another. It was the Russians who eventually liberated him, and he spent some more time in a camp, answering endless questions to the best of his exhausted ability. They found it difficult to decide whether he was a Pole, a Hungarian, or a Czech, and seemed to be sceptical about everything he told them. Eventually they relented, and he returned to a grey, unsettled Czechoslovakia late in 1946.

His father had disappeared without trace; so had his mother. The shop was no longer there. He was forty-two years of age and felt like an orphan, drained of emotion, hard, empty, without the energy for suicide. Self-pity would have been risible under the circumstances. The hibernation had been too long, the wound too deep, too clean. He wanted to walk, to use his legs, to breathe again consciously – in, out, in, out.

For a time he worked as night watchman of a sausage factory. He was used to solitude; in fact he felt lost without it. He was not used to freedom, however, and he boiled himself some atrocious coffee every night, and every night it seemed to him a kind of miracle that such a thing was possible: to desire coffee, and to make it. These were the nights of the slow thaw. Gradually he dared to think. In time, he even dared to doubt. It was like the slow, painful recovery from some accident, an accident of the spirit.

One day, when he was ready, he took stock. He believed he had a distant cousin in America. America – the *New World Symphony*, Dvorák – where Czechs could be Czechs under the Constitution. On second thought, he didn't care whether he was a Czech or not. He just wanted to exist, and perhaps even find a reason for not being a pessimist. He longed for a place totally without traditions, for escape from the hothouse of Central Europe.

A casual remark overheard at work gave him the idea of Australia. There was a map on the wall of the managing director's office, peppered with little flags showing the areas in which the sausages were selling well.

Bulgaria seemed to be consuming nothing but sausage if the map were to be believed. Hungary tended to make its own, but Greece and Turkey were surprisingly good markets. Down there to the right, tucked in a corner, was Australia, virgin land without a Czech sausage to its name, mysterious and far away from the nightmare. The centre of it seemed to have no town name for miles. This was the place for him. At night, he used to sit in the managing director's office and stare at this enormous island on the map, imagining the central space, unfulfilled, raw. Where there were no humans, there would be no inhumanity.

One day he knew instinctively that the moment for the great migration had come. It would have been unnatural if he had not developed a sense of impending disaster after his experiences, and now he realized there was no time to lose. Four days after he crossed the Austrian frontier, the Communists swept into power in Czechoslovakia, and once again slogans took the place of conversation.

From the International Refugee Organization in Vienna, Jiři discovered that workers were urgently needed on several hydroelectric power schemes in the highlands of New South Wales. Within two weeks he was on board the Italian steamer *Salvator Rosa*, heading towards Suez and freedom. The sea was calm and friendly and he stood on deck, a slightly ludicrous figure in his thick collarless shirt, staring at the golden water as though it were a fire, a background for fantasy. He was not dreaming at all, since he had nothing to dream about. He had no imagination about the unknown. Even in the office, gazing at the empty map, he had thought only of the emptiness, not of imaginary landscapes. Reality had been too ferocious for him ever to ignore it, even as an escape. The sun had never been so hot, and it induced an exquisite drowsiness, the voluptuous sense of well-being which dogs express when they find a particularly satisfactory undulation in the ground and blink half blindly, waiting for sleep to overwhelm them. Jiří was as happy as he had ever been. At the same time, he could never roll up his sleeves because of that number branded on his arm, a relic of the Nazi's administrative efficiency.

He did not talk to the other immigrants. There were Italians, Hungarians, Germans – you could never tell who was who. Safer to keep quiet. If he bumped into someone, he apologized inaudibly, or if a passenger held open one of the heavy doors for him, he muttered his thanks under his breath. The last thing he wanted was to become involved with some other Czech and wallow in all the bleak miseries, all the premature homesickness of weaker spirits leaving their habits behind them. He wanted to be alone.

In Aden he bought a silly black pillow, his first purchase in years. Stitched on it in colours alternately electric and bilious were a snowcapped peak, its reflection in some uncertain water, a minaret, and a pine tree on a slope. 'Souvenir of Aden.' He had begun to build a home.

Sydney was much larger than he had thought, and he was both disappointed and frightened. Loneliness gripped him as his eye took in the skyline and his ear the traffic, the mumble of industry. Still, he did not stay there long but was soon on his way to the town of Billiwoonga in a large modern coach. His new land was strange, with its reckless majesty, its great green sweep, flecked with light and shade as the pregnant clouds passed in an endless procession from horizon to horizon.

Although the landscape was inanimate, it seemed to be in continuous motion. Billiwoonga, proudly marked on the map in somewhat heavier type than some of the surrounding towns, turned out to be a casual agglomeration of houses in the modern suburban style, reminiscent of married officers' quarters on some remote air base. There was a Gothic church which might have wandered straight from a sad, misty section of London; a sparse little war memorial with one or two names on it remembered by the tiny bundles of flowers in its shadow; a row of shops; a long, low building boasting a wrought-iron arcade with tethering posts, proudly called the Royal Antipodes Hotel; and a very new construction in the contemporary bus station manner, where ex-servicemen could congregate, drink beer, play table tennis, and reminisce. Only the main street was tarred, and that only for a hundred yards or so beyond the town limits on either side.

The work on the hydroelectric scheme was tough, but the pay was good by any standards. He was perhaps a little old for some of its rigours, but the physical effort made him forget his troubles, and it was good to fall asleep out of sheer weariness. It was the weekends he dreaded. This was not like the ship; there was no chance of escaping comradeship here. There was not even a chance of avoiding other Czechs, and soon an unreasoning homesickness began to bewilder him, a longing for a country which had only vaguely been his home, and then under oppressive circumstances.

It was a clash of lonelinesses which brought him and Ida together. She was a blonde girl well into the years of established spinsterhood who served powerful tea out of not too clean cups in the Anzac Café, a wooden shed which was cheerful enough in a slightly desperate way, to emphasize the desolation outside. The blondeness of Ida was not of the kind that people are born with, and her skin was clogged with powder, which suggested a determined counterattack against the callousness of time and the brutality of nature. Her powerfully aquiline nose and the watery blue eyes set comically low gave her an air of some German princeling connected vaguely to international royalty at the turn of the nineteenth century. On the other hand, isolated from her head and stridently unmusical voice her body was full and generous, as Jiři noticed whenever the copious bosom shuddered over his table. He found it more and more difficult to concentrate on the slender menu.

She was not unmoved by his attentions. Often she would shoot a glance of studied negligence in the direction of this miserable little fellow with eyes the colour of dry stones, who was too shy to raise his voice in ordering his tea. His smile was pleasant though, and she liked his walk as he came in, the underslung, jaunty walk of a light man of unexpected strength. The back of his neck had never grown up. It was young and defenceless and undernourished.

After a while, the little smiles, the hesitations over the choice of food, the awkward jokes about his bad English became a habit, and before long they left the café together. He knew from experience when the place closed, and he consequently went for his supper later and later. One day they found themselves on the pavement side by side. It was dark, and she put her arm through his. After a few yards they kissed, both more astonished than passionate. They had both given up hope so long ago.

She lay beside him in her narrow bed, and all her being was alive, craving, warm. When he closed his eyes, he knew that the most beautiful woman in the world was his and that he was the most desirable of men. The illusion of perfection has many levels, and, being an illusion, it is obedient to the mind.

The romance did not last long. They were too old to spend much time dragging a ration of conventional poetry out of the moon's presence on a night too cold for kissing. It was too late in life for them to excite each other with the suggestive words of popular songs, those prefabricated bits of utility seduction, pumped out around the clock by radio, the people's Casanova. For them were the moments of pleasant indolence snatched around a fire, the crackle of a newspaper, the impact of teacup and saucer, the song of the kettle, the feeling that they had known each other a long time, since youth perhaps – security. Being a woman, however, and a big woman at that, Ida soon began to exercise those driving and sometimes sinister qualities which her sisters Messalina and Delilah and Lady Macbeth had put to effective use in more ample periods of history. Although both she and Jiří had so recently been forcibly content with mere survival, she took their new-found luck for granted much more quickly than he dared to and began to tell him that work on the hydroelectric scheme was beneath his dignity.

'But the money good,' he would remonstrate: 'sixty Owstralian pound a veek!'

'You're better than a mere labourer,' was her reply, always uttered with absurd yet dangerous passion. 'You got class. Look at those sensitive hands of yours. You goin' to spend your life in that crook tunnel now you've got me? Another Itie was blown to bits only last Friday, nice young fellow with a lovely singin' voice. Small wonder the money's good – the work's dangerous. No, Georgie, you've got responsibilities now, and it's time you was your own master.'

What did she mean? He gazed at his hands and saw nothing particularly sensitive there – ten spatulate fingers culminating in corrugated nails. He must remember to clean them. Without arguments, he could only repeat, 'Money good.'

'Listen,' she said softly, altering her feminine tactics with the grace of a locomotive, 'you know Aldo Zenoni. He started work in the tunnel like all the other new Australian boys. Then he began patching clothing torn at work. They'd all come to him. He'd do a dinkum job, you see. Then one day he got married to an Irish girl, local girl. She gave him the confidence he was lackin'. That's what wives are for. He left the tunnel and set up shop. Now he's got the Venezia dress and men's wear store in Billiwoonga, with a branch in Canberra selling sweaters to the embassies.'

'Yea, that's one case,' replied Jiři, miserably.

'One case? You seen them six-wheel trucks goin' around with that man's name on the door, that Polish man whose name nobody can pronounce? The biggest haulage contractor for miles. How did he start? In the tunnel. Kept his eyes open. Noticed there was a transport shortage. Started with one pre-war truck. Now he's got thirty, brand new. Or take the Germans. They stick together, like the Jews. Old Heidelberg Cordial factory, Otto's Delicatessen, K. K. Dry Cleaning, the new garage on the corner of Snowy River Street and Imperial Way, the one that handles the Volkswagen – they're all German owned, and the owners all came over to work on the tunnel. It's only no-hopers who go on working up in the mountains. 'Cause they make good money, but what they got to do with it? They come down here of a weekend with fifty, sixty, seventy quid in their pockets, and they go lookin' for women. There aren't any. Men outnumber women ten to one in Billiwoonga. You're lucky to have got me, you are. They get shickered, fight, and go back to the tunnel of a Monday dead broke. I tell you, Georgie, them alecks from the tunnels got a lot of money to spend. That's why the smarties in town open up shop. There's prosperity when you've got a lot of men loaded with money and nothin' to spend it on.'

There was no answer to this. It was true.

One day she added a curious note to her usual catalogue of temptations, saying, 'I'll have to get you in with the Germans; they're the hardest workers.'

Jiři had been in with the Germans before and had no desire to renew the experience, but when he talked, she no longer listened. She had a friend, a little younger than herself but quite as homely, a girl who had also braved the distant provinces in an unconscious search for men with less discriminating tastes. This person, whose name was Floss, had married one of the German colony of Billiwoonga, a Herr Willi Schumacher, now Mr Bill Shoemaker, an enterprising immigrant who had founded a radio repair shop, to which he had added a sporting goods shop and even a small factory manufacturing carbonated beverages.

It was not long before the ambitious Ida had talked the head off Floss and even succeeded in penetrating the wary defences of Bill Shoemaker. Her idea was a restaurant which would be run by Jiři and herself on a partnership basis with the Shoemakers.

'I don't like to stick my neck out in a business I don't know,' said Bill in his curious accent, half Australian, half North German.

'Did you know the radio repair business when you went into it?' asked Ida with her usual fire.

'I was knowing how to mend a radio.'

'Did you know about huntin' rifles and games of Scrabble and plastic dinghies?'

'Rifles, yes.'

'And did you know about fizzy lemonades and all those crook drinks you put out? Well, I do know about the caterin' business, and, as for Georgie, he worked in a sausage factory back in Czechoslavia where he came from. You've got a Syrian coffeehouse in Billiwoonga, a Yugo-thing one, an Itie one, and not one German one, although you're the biggest group of new Aussies in town. A disgrace, I call it!'

'What a woman!' cried Bill with a chuckle, while Floss looked at her friend with more than a trace of jealousy.

When Jiři and Ida were married, Bill was best man, and the reception afterwards was held in the newly-painted shell of the Rhinegold Restaurant. It was a day of elation, although Jiři felt, every time he looked at Bill, that he had seen him somewhere before. The memory was not unpleasant; on the contrary, Bill had a rather agreeable face, a long turned-up nose, twinkling blue eyes, hair with a tendency to curl, and a huge mouth, which was always eager to smile. He was ever ready with a proverb for a given situation, but he chose well from his fast compendium of platitudes, and this extreme quickness on the draw with the correct folksy comment gave his personality a twist of irony which removed him from the body of struggling mankind. It was as though he saw and studied the paradoxes of existence from a point of vantage, and that inspired confidence. Jiři admired such a man.

'I toast our new partners, George and Ida, or should I say, Ida and George Pollen?' said Bill, raising his glass of Australian champagne; and, holding up a hand to silence the enthusiastic clapping, he went on: 'I welcome the fact that Billiwoonga, the home for so many from us, will at last have a proper German–Czech–Central European restaurant of quality, where you can gather in an evening and enjoy Bratwurst, Königsberger Klopse, Kasseler Kippenspehr, and all the other dishes we remember and love from our home towns. We will give you quality with value, service with smiles, and I know I can trust you to give us your patronage. I now call upon Mr Victor Ludlow to propose the toast of the newly-weds.'

Mr Victor Ludlow, who had arrived in Sydney Witold Lumbomirski from Lwów, made an eloquent speech about the George Pollens, describing them as symbols of the new Australia, which was rising like a phoenix from the conflagration of European despair, and pictures were taken in profusion by Mr Bernie Peters, who was born in Bratislav Petrosevic in Zagreb. Ida found it intensely romantic to be treated as an immigrant, and late in the day she attempted a drunken Serbian folk dance to the accompaniment of an accordian, a fife, and two soup-spoons used as castanets. There were tears in many eyes as the party broke up. It had created a little intimacy, a little claustrophobia, in a land which so singularly lacked it.

Business was good. It could hardly be otherwise. The only problems were the weekend drunks and the licensing laws. Bill had been accorded a licence for beer and wines, but the sale of hard liquor in the Rhinegold was prohibited. Still, the lonely would force their way in on Saturdays and Sundays, begging for drinks in their various languages, and it was not always easy to refuse them. Not to break the law could be bad for business. Nobody, except the police, cares for a spoilsport. The Rhinegold could soon afford a three piece orchestra, which droned through the clink of cutlery as orchestras do the world over, making conversation impossible for those who have it and sparing the necessity for conversation in those without it.

As Monday was a slack day, Bill and George used to go hunting, like gentlemen in the Old World. It was on one of these jaunts that George told Bill of his feeling that they had met before.

'Funny you should say that,' Bill replied. 'I was having the same feeling. Were you spending much time in Sydney?'

'One day.'

'Ah, well, it couldn't have been there.'

There was a pause as they scanned the horizon for ducks.

'In Europe maybe?' George ventured.

'I doubt it. I didn't get about much. As soon as the war was over, I was packing my bags and come out here.'

'During the war—?'

'No. No, it couldn't be. Why, where were you to that time?'

'Me? Oh,' George sighed. 'You really want to know?'

'My motto is, ask no questions, you'll be told no lies.'

'I've nothing to hide,' said George. 'I was in Auschwitz, Ravensbruck, Belsen, Dachau, Mauthausen, and some others.'

'You're not Jewish, are you?' asked Bill, raising his rifle to his shoulder.

'No. Why?'

'Most of them poor bastards ended up in the camps, at least so they tell to me.'

'Oh, not only Jews.'

'No? Well, I only go by what I'm told. That whole time I could have done without. Like pigs they were all behaving, everyone – we, the Allies . . . I never think of it.'

'Where were you in that time?'

Bill brought down his rifle. 'Me? Where you think? In the army. Medical orderly. To Greece, they sent me. And North Africa. The flies was worse than the enemy. Then I was getting out.'

'How?'

'Ulcers.'

'You had ulcers?'

Bill smiled. 'No.'

George looked at his friend in intense admiration. Even then he had the makings of a great industrialist.

Bill said softly, 'You are not spending your time helping out a doctor without you learn something yourself.'

It was on a Friday that Ida announced she was pregnant. It was scarcely credible, and yet Dr Chalkburner, who as Dr Kalkbrunner, had been a leading specialist in Szeged, was categorical about it. Once again champagne was drunk, and George made a down payment on a small modern house. He also bought an American car, old but very large. His friend Bill gave him a magnificent hunting rifle when he heard the news. As George accepted the gift speechlessly, he racked his brains for all the kindnesses which he had ever known, trying to remember, trying to place his friend.

The Rhinegold expanded. It now had nearly thirty tables. As Ida's time drew near, extra help was hired. The standard dropped slightly, but people didn't notice. It had been established as the elegant meeting place in Billiwoonga.

Then, one morning when George was already at work, stock-taking, the phone rang. It was Dr Chalkburner, who told him that Ida had been rushed to the local hospital and that there was nothing to worry about. George called Bill immediately. Bill told him to close the restaurant and that he would meet him at the hospital.

'We can't afford close the restaurant just for this,' said George in the waiting room when Bill arrived. 'Is Saturday, best day of the week.'

'Listen, you're not becoming a father every day,' replied Bill. 'I remember when young John was being born I was near broke. I was only having the radio store then, and we wasn't make too good a start, but I shut the shop. As I was leaving to come to the hospital, a customer she arrived. I was turning her away.'

'All the same – Saturday.'

Bill laughed pleasantly. 'If the child is being born in the next few minutes, we can open the restaurant tonight. Don't worry about it. Here, I bring a bottle of schnapps, the real German schnapps. We need it.' As they drank, George was overcome by conflicting emotions, those of joy and an intense, inexplicable sorrow. He was frightened for his wife. Everything in the waiting room was so functional, so workaday; the weather was nondescript. It was hardly a fitting background for a great, a fearful event.

'What will you call it?' asked Bill.

George was grateful for his tact. Bill seemed to understand the anguish in his friend's heart, and his words were like steppingstones over an abyss.

'If it's a girl, Ida. If it's a boy, Malcolm.'

'Why Malcolm?' asked Bill with genuine surprise.

'I don't know. Is a good name. So far from the names we know. When I think on my life, I not understand how I ever came to this position – almost a father, married, with a car and house and a business. Them camps, they was end of the world—'

'Yes, yes,' interrupted Bill, almost harshly, 'but don't think of that now. In this Australia of ours, no one has a past, everyone has a future. I never don't want to see Europe again. I know the food's better, the workmanship is better. There's more amusement, there is no licensing laws, but I want a future for my kids which is different from what I was knowing. By the time they is my age, this shall be a place worth living in, and God only knows what Europe shall be like.'

'I ask to myself why we always is talk English to one other,' said George. 'We is both speak German better.'

Bill refused to go home for lunch, and as the afternoon wore on and the schnapps dwindled, the relationship between the two men became warmer than it had ever been.

'I will never know how thank you, Bill.'

'I need no thanks. You are a good worker, and a good worker is a good partner, and to have both together is good business. We have good wives. They're not beautiful, but beautiful wives means trouble. Wives should be good cooks, good housekeepers, good mothers, good in bed. That's all I am asking.'

'Everything good.'

'Everything good,' echoed Bill.

Just then the nurse came in and announced in a measured, air hostess voice that it was a boy. Malcolm Pollen had entered the world and, more particularly, Australia.

George would not hear of closing the restaurant, and at seven o'clock it was open for dinner and crowded. As the evening wore on, the usual drunks came in, begging for alcohol. Two in particular became obstreperous. One was German, the other a Czech. They banged the table and threatened to sing. They demanded that the three-piece orchestra play 'Lili Marlene'.

George tried to reason with one in Czech. It did no good. The Czech began to weep and said he was far from home. What did he want? Slivovitz – to remind him. Bill came up to the table. The German drunkenly began to run down Australia and demanded liquor. Anything they had.

'Better give them some slivovitz in a coffee cup to keep them quiet,' said Bill softly.

'When we serve them and they start break up the place, we not able call police. We no licence,' said George.

'We'll say they come in here drunk.'

'OK, if you say.'

A moment later, Bill glanced across at the drunks from behind the cash register. They were no longer drunk but were writing surreptitiously on bits of paper. He looked at the service hatch and saw the waiter approaching with two coffee cups on a tray. He rushed through the tables to intercept the waiter, and, just before the latter had reached the drunks, he pushed the tray on to the floor, shouting, 'You clumsy idiot, can't you look what you doing?'

George came up when he heard the noise and saw Bill apologizing to the drunks.

'Get hold of that cup on the floor,' said one drunk to the other, now cold sober.

Bill trod on the cups.

George knew at once that the drunks were detectives from the Twenty-one Division, a curious flying squad of *agents provocateurs* employed by the government of New South Wales in order to cajole restaurants into breaking the licensing laws. Acting drunk was one of their most successful strategies, and they were not above using agents of various nationalities in order to play upon the patriotism and homesickness and, worse, kindheartedness of the immigrant innkeeper.

George could well imagine the kind of German or Czech who would leave his own country simply in order to become a policeman elsewhere. To him that was hardly the point of voluntary exile, but he knew there were people in the world who felt lost outside a uniform or at least outside the strait-jacket of authority.

The German detective brusquely revealed his identity and demanded, in German, to examine the broken coffee cup. Bill went white with anger. He began shouting insults also in German. A great vein, like a tree, rose and throbbed on his temple. For a moment, his fury seemed to spill over into epilepsy. The two detectives shouted back, and a few diners rose to add the weight of their opinions to the brawl.

George had never heard Bill speak German before, let alone shout it. Medical orderly? He saw a room full of naked people, men and women some of transparent thinness, others bloated by hunger, and he smelled the odour of decomposition. The voice carried him back into the halflight, the white coats of the doctors, the parchment yellow of the naked flesh, the glint of glasses, the routine of the nightmare. Stout Dr Tichte, loading his hypodermic dispassionately, swabbing with cotton wool, holding out his pudgy hands for implements. 'Cough.' 'Cough.' 'Breathe.' 'Deeper.' 'Take him away.' 'Unusable.' A quiet, rational voice. And behind him, in brown, under a brown cap, shouting hysterically, a great vein, like a tree, throbbing on his temple, another man. '*Still stehen!*' '*Schweine!*' '*Schweine!*' '*Judische Rassenshänder!*'

As the shouting increased in volume, George tottered to the kitchen and vomited on the floor. Now he remembered his friend. When he got home, the house was empty. Ida was in the hospital, sleeping in her pain and contentment. He switched on the lights. It was too light. He switched them off. It was too dark. He opened the window. It was too cold. He opened another one and stared into the night. He was burning with fever. He must kill his partner, as a memorial to those who had died uselessly. First, he must torture him. He played out the scene in his head a hundred times, perfecting it, polishing it. He saw Bill scream, cringe, beg for mercy in a hundred different ways. There would be no mercy. He would shoot him with his own gun, his present. There's irony.

But why all these presents? Why had this savage been so kind to him? Could it be that he had developed some kind of conscience? Had Bill remembered him when they had first met in Australia? Out of the millions who had passed through his hands in Mauthausen? Hardly. Even if he were only a symbol of contrition, however, it could be that good and evil were not equated in that unhappy heart and that he, George Pollen, had become the means by which Bill was able to look men in the face again. Nonsense. Bill had existed comfortably and commercially in Billiwoonga for a long time without such help.

'In this Australia of ours, no man has a past, every man has a future.' How very convenient. It was made convenient by the Australians themselves. He remembered the rumours around the International Refugee Organization in Vienna. America was hard to get into, even Canada insisted on a thorough screening, but Australia would take those rejected by the other two. Who could tell what venomous seeds had been scattered in the wilderness?

The idea of murder gave him comfort, and he tried to sleep on the sofa. He dreamed, and his own shrieks awakened him. He looked at his watch. He had been asleep ten minutes.

A distant cock crowed, and a dog barked somewhere. He went out into the darkness and walked. He had no idea on which dirt road he was when dawn broke, but suddenly, after a few moments of slate-grey sadness, a vast, trumpeting sun burst over the black trees and a market-place of birds opened among the branches. The earth seemed to turn in her light sleep, and night died painlessly in a second.

It was hot almost at once in the sun, cold in the shadows. He stared at this curious land, at the weird boulders which had been scattered over the landscape during some prehistoric flatulence of the earth. The dying gum trees stood among the dead, white, unburied corpses, the aftermath of battle. Mauthausen again. The piles of bodies. He wanted to kick himself. That was self-pity, overdramatization. The trees had died not out of malice but out of neglect, which was almost worse. They had been allowed to die; permission for them to die had been granted. And those still alive were waiting.

He shuddered. Life was valuable, and everything mattered. Near his foot, a civilization of ants was building its empire, every bit as important as Australia, as Czechoslovakia: a microcosm, but none the less a world. The course of their labours took them over a large stone. They were building their hydroelectric scheme. He smiled slightly at the thought, then frowned as he realized that with one foot he could kill a squadron of them. He could do so easily, without remorse, since he could not communicate with them. A man cannot feel affection for an ant. Life is imperfect.

'*Still stehen!*' '*Schweine!*'

He was a father, for the first, doubtless the only, time in his life, a father in his late forties. It was a day of considerable importance, of joy. And yet here he was contemplating revenge. Oh, what to do? He held his head in his cupped hands and suddenly yawned. He was tired. When you are at a loss, nature takes over, irreverently, mockingly. He walked slowly back to town, his hands in his pockets.

If he broke the partnership, he would have to give up the house. By now he was probably too old for the tunnel. It would mean starting afresh, humbly. Was that fair for Ida or Malcolm? A new thought struck him. Could he have been mistaken about Bill? It was so long ago. He had heard so much shouting in his time. Voices resemble each other. They are bound to. Vocal chords have less range than faces, fewer possibilities for difference. In his heart, he knew there was no mistake.

He would give the rifle back. A rifle, of all things, as a gift! How could he without explanation? Explanation would break up the partnership. He would either have to destroy utterly or to leave everything as it was. Ants.

Ten minutes later he was at home. He looked at his house, something where there had been nothing. Through the window he saw the cushion lying on the sofa, still dented where his head had been, 'Souvenir of Aden'. He had started with that. He opened the front door. A pram stood in the entrance hall, new and gleaming. A price tag was still fixed to the axle. He heard a noise behind him. There, before the door, its tail wagging, its ears sharp, its eyes both generous and febrile, stood a red kelpie, one of the multitude of stray dogs which infested Billiwoonga, chasing cars in the main street.

Georgie found these dogs a nuisance.

'Don't go away,' he said, and fetched it a large meal from the kitchen.

At eleven o'clock he went to the restaurant, followed by the kelpie. Bill arrived shortly afterwards, haggard and furtive.

'It shall mean a thirty quid fine,' he said, 'and there may be a charge for assault. Never mind, if I was having it over again, I would use the same language on those bastards.'

'Those *schweine*,' said George in German.

'Ja, ja, *Schweine*. *Schweinehunde*,' replied Bill absently.

George continued to talk German. 'Like the Gestapo,' he said.

'*Genau. Die selbe Mentalität. Dass die Australische Regierung hier so etwas erlaubt!*'

'They exist everywhere,' said George, still in German, 'the police and others. It's not a question of uniform, it's a question of mentality. Creators and destroyers. Masters and slaves. An employee can be a master, an employer a slave, just as a policeman can be a human being and a man you'd never suspect can be a policeman. It's a question of mentality.'

'I suppose there's something in that,' murmured Bill, and then looked up suddenly with a hunted expression and asked, 'Why are we talking German?'

'Oh, I don't know. Force of habit, I suppose,' answered George.

'Force of habit?'

Bill blinked nervously, searching George's face. Suddenly Bill was pathetic, so strong was his desire to be liked. Every gesture was a bribe – the rifle, the schnapps – the payment of a debt on the instalment system.

'Force of habit. I'll be back soon. I'm going to the bank.'

'To the bank?'

George left Bill looking after him through the restaurant window, and after a short visit to the bank he bought a bunch of flowers and walked to the hospital, still followed by the dog.

PLAYS IN PAN

A SELECTION OF
POPULAR READING IN PAN

Fiction

☐	PASSPORT IN SUSPENSE	James Leasor	5/–
☐	SATURDAY NIGHT AND SUNDAY MORNING	Allan Sillitoe	3/6
☐	ROSEMARY'S BABY	Ira Levin	5/–
☐	CASINO ROYALE	Ian Fleming	4/–
☐	FOR YOUR EYES ONLY	„ „	4/–
☐	THE SPY WHO CAME IN FROM THE COLD	John le Carré	
☐	THE LOOKING-GLASS WAR	„	5/–
☐	PLAY DIRTY	Zeno	5/–
☐	THE WANDERING PRINCE	Jean Plaidy	5/–
☐	THE CAPTIVE QUEEN OF SCOTS	„ „	5/–
☐	THE SIXTH WIFE	„ „	5/–
☐	ST. THOMAS'S EVE	„ „	5/–
☐	A HEALTH UNTO HIS MAJESTY	„	5/–
☐	ROYAL ROAD TO FOTHERINGAY	„ „	5/–
☐	MURDER MOST ROYAL	„ „	5/–
☐	RETURN TO PEYTON PLACE	Grace Metalious	3/6
☐	NO ADAM IN EDEN	„ „	3/6
☐	THE SHOES OF THE FISHERMAN	Morris West	5/–
☐	NO HIGHWAY	Nevil Shute	5/–
☐	THE CHEQUER BOARD	„ „	5/–
☐	ROUND THE BEND	„ „	5/–
☐	IN THE WET	„ „	5/–
☐	A TOWN LIKE ALICE	„ „	5/–
☐	8th PAN BOOK OF HORROR STORIES	selected by Herbert van Thal	5/–
☐	9th PAN BOOK OF HORROR STORIES	selected by Herbert van Thal	5/–
☐	THE NYLON PIRATES	Nicholas Monsarrat	5/–
☐	MANDINGO	Kyle Onstott	5/–
☐	DRUM	„ „	6/–
☐	MASTER OF FALCONHURST	„	6/–
☐	FALCONHURST FANCY	Kyle Onstott and Lance Horner	6/–
☐	ONIONHEAD	Weldon Hill	5/–
☐	DEVIL'S CUB	Georgette Heyer	5/–
☐	FREDERICA	„ „	5/–

☐ BATH TANGLE	Georgette Heyer	5/—
☐ THE TOLL-GATE	,, ,,	5/—
☐ COTILLION	,, ,,	5/—
☐ THE QUIET GENTLEMAN	,, ,,	5/—
☐ BLACK SHEEP	,, ,,	5/—

Non-fiction

☐ **THE BATTLE OF BRITAIN (illus.)**
Leonard Mosley   5/—

☐ **GIPSY MOTH CIRCLES THE WORLD (illus.)**   Francis Chichester   6/—

☐ **QUEENS OF THE PHARAOHS (illus.)**
Leonard Cottrell   6/—·

☐ **RING OF BRIGHT WATER (illus.)**
Gavin Maxwell   5/—

☐ **THE HOUSE OF ELRIG (illus.)**
,, ,,   6/—

☐ **THE DAM BUSTERS (illus.)**
Paul Brickhill   5/—

☐ **THE INFIRM GLORY, VOL. I (illus.)**
Godfrey Winn   5/—

☐ **THE INFIRM GLORY, VOL. II (illus.)**
,, ,,   5/—

☐ **LIFE OF CHRIST**   Fulton J. Sheen   7/6

☐ **THE BIRD TABLE BOOK (illus.)**
Tony Soper   5/—

☐ **BEYOND BELIEF**   Emlyn Williams   7/6

Obtainable from all booksellers and newsagents. If you have any difficulty, please send purchase price plus 9d. postage to P.O. Box 11, Falmouth, Cornwall.

I enclose a cheque/postal order for selected titles ticked above plus 9d. per book to cover packing and postage.

NAME...

ADDRESS..

....